18504658

AUTHOR	CLASS
SOMERVILLE, P.	F
TITLE No	F
Hang glider.	

20. DEC. 1985	22. JUN 1989
19. NOV 1985	14. OCT. 1987
17. OCT. 1985	29. MAY 1987
27. SEP. 1985	20. NOV. 1986
	13. NOV. 1986
16. SEP. 1985	20. OCT. 1986
-3. SEP. 1985	19. SEP. 1986
	-5. SEP. 1986
30. JUL. 1985	26. JUN. 1986
-8. JUL. 1985	16. JUN. 1986
-1. JUL. 1985	16. MAY 1986
27. JUN 1985	-6. MAR. 1986
-8. JUN. 1985	18. FE
18. MAY 1985	28. JA
17 MAY 1985	11.
28. MAR. 1985	

WITHDRAWN FROM CIRCULATION
LANCASHIRE LIBRARY

SOLD

LAYTON
TEL. 33438
BLACK

HANG GLIDER

HANG GLIDER

by

PETER SOMERVILLE-LARGE

LONDON
VICTOR GOLLANCZ LTD
1985

First published in Great Britain 1985
by Victor Gollancz Ltd,
14 Henrietta Street, London WC2E 8QJ

British Library Cataloguing in Publication Data
Somerville-Large, Peter
Hang glider.
I. Title
823'.914[F]   PR6069.043
ISBN 0-575-03535-8

Typeset by Folio Photosetting, Bristol
and printed in Great Britain by
St Edmundsbury Press, Bury St Edmunds, Suffolk

The 1979 World Hang Gliding Championships at St Hilaire du Touvet were attended by Steve Moyes, the Popcorn Kid and the Frenchman with the flying Yorkshire terrier, but by no other character mentioned in this book. I should like to dedicate it to Tom Hudson, who took a very different Irish team to Grenoble, and to Robin Hall, my hang gliding partner, a geriatric like myself.

Chapter One

JUNE 1979. THE Hiace van with the red-wrapped, cigar-shaped bundle on its roof climbed a mountain road which had fir trees on either side. It passed a big reddish space where excavations were taking place for a new sporting complex. Bulldozers were gouging out ski runs through the trees upwards to where the Alpine meadows awaited their winter covering of lucrative snow. Further up, the road wound by a camping site, licensed, listed and signposted. Bright little tents were perched under a chalet farmhouse whose pastures nurtured a richer summer crop than herds of cows.

It had been difficult to find a place that was suitable for training, but away from curious eyes. At ordinary hang gliding sites where pilots assembled in their dozens questions would have been asked. The conspirators had been lucky to pick a place which was difficult for vehicles and therefore unattractive to the average flying enthusiast. But they had to compromise. Even here in early June there were bound to be holiday makers enjoying the mountain scenery. When the Hiace crossed a foaming torrent and entered a valley that ten years ago would have presented a scene of Ruskinesque solitude, the passengers could see a line of red and orange anoraks climbing a mountainside in single file. The climbers looked like soldier ants prepared to attack and devour anything in their path — the picturesque cattle of an alpage, perhaps. Such witnesses would have to be ignored.

The Hiace stopped below a wild place on the edge of the massif where rocks met the snow line near a glacial lake. Two men and a woman climbed out. The men carried down the hang glider from the roof rack and the pilot shouldered it, beginning his ascent immediately with scarcely an acknowledgement to his companions. The way up was long and hard — he had made the journey half a dozen times already. Today he climbed alone, bearing the heavy weight. That was part of the training. Both the others were needed below to record and observe. They got back into the van and drove on for ten kilometres to another valley, wide and U-shaped, along whose floor ran a stream, a sparkling thread in the sunlight.

The blue van drove off the track and the man and woman got out and began walking. After an hour they reached a meadow. The time was a few minutes before noon. If one of the hikers further up the valley — for even here they were not alone — looked down through a good pair of binoculars, he could have studied the man's tall figure dressed in jeans, with a matching blue denim top and a pair of American loafers on his feet. Hardly climbing clothes. His features wore a permanently tired expression, and as he smiled in response to a comment by the girl, the gloom did not lift. The pouched eyes, sallow skin and tremor of a black moustache contributed to the sad clown image.

The girl's appearance, too, was misleading. She was in her late twenties, a short, dark woman. Although she wore no makeup, her doe eyes gave the impression that they had been touched with some blackener. She had a sultry air that suggested musk or patchouli, and the heavy sexuality displayed by certain Indian film actresses. Her blue jeans could not disguise this aura of the bedroom — or perhaps the harem — nor could the pale blue parka and matching sweater with the machined Fair Isle pattern across the yoke. She was not the sort of woman you would take for a terrorist. It was the fault of press and television that the general impression of women terrorists was that they were handsome athletes dressed permanently in khaki fatigues.

The man carried a walkie talkie and they both had rucksacks. When they eventually sat down on the grass they were sweating from their long walk in the sun. She took out some chocolate and Seven-Up. When they had finished drinking she put back the tins in the rucksack while he adjusted the walkie talkie, trying to make contact. He spoke into the microphone in Arabic. It took him nearly five minutes to raise a reply. Ah! He talked briefly and listened. He told her:

"He has reached the take-off site. He is preparing to rig."

"One of us should be with him."

They had plenty of time to arrange the target. They marked out a rough rectangle about the size of a swimming pool in area. They had brought white towels, and a roll of white cotton which they spread out on the grass. In the beginning she had wanted to daub boulders with paint, but the men objected, since paint was evidence. Bad enough the bits of cloth. They were unremarkable for the moment, because the mountaineers visible earlier had moved out of view. But yesterday and the day before other hikers had been in the valley.

The last of the spring flowers showed in the rough grass, narcissi gone to tasselled seed, giving way to orchids and daisies. The mountains shimmered in the strong sun and the sky above was bright blue. The man made contact again.

"He's ready."

"We've wasted enough time."

Further delays were punctuated by the staccato conversation that comes naturally through walkie talkies.

"I don't like it," she said.

He ignored her, listening for the pilot who was his brother. Previously he had accompanied him to the take-off. Every day she had waited here below. She had watched the pilot coming into view, circling, hovering and aiming at the target. Landing seemed to be the problem. He managed to land in the centre about half the time. But for his task he had to be absolutely precise. Otherwise there seemed to be no difficulties. When he was in the air he appeared to be flying with as much assurance as the bird drifting lazily above the valley in the sun. But today, probably because he had taken off alone, she felt afraid for him. Her hesitation was intuitive and had nothing to do with the strip of cloud they could see now, a lazy tentacle that curled across the ridge above them.

More white clouds were puffed very rapidly by a wind they could scarcely feel where they stood. It annoyed her companion that she should have some justification for her whining fears. He hated intuition, feminine logic, sixth senses. Could she feel static in the air in a way men did not? He smiled sadly, but a clap of thunder above them brought him increasing unease.

All the time the clouds thickened, and in less than five minutes

3

the sky over the valley was covered over. A sweep of wind shook the flowers at their feet. Where the pilot waited the wind would have become savage. He would not have taken off. He knew all about the horrors of high-mountain wave lift. Turbulence could be as destructive as a hurricane, a rampaging monster, a King Kong well able to smash gliders to pieces. Or in a wild caprice it could take a machine up so high into the atmosphere that the pilot passed out.

The man below tried to make contact after the first sound of thunder. "Acknowledge . . . acknowledge . . ." No answer, only a wild crackling that did not quite coincide with the rhythm of the second thunderclap. "Acknowledge . . . de-rig and take cover . . . take cover . . ."

"He must have done so . . ."

They both jumped at a nearer crack of thunder accompanied by a black ball of cloud that puffed up like a cobra ready to strike.

"The weather forecast . . ." she said needlessly.

"Mentioned electrical disturbances and possible storms. But for later in the evening. Not for now. Not for now."

"You fool . . ."

He shrugged. "We have to take some risk. We have so little time. Every day is of importance." He went back to listening and calling. "Atlas, Atlas. Over. Atlas, Atlas. Over." Why did his brother, ten kilometres away and more, not acknowledge? Could the static electricity produced by the thunder have interfered with transmission? The metal king post of a rigged hang glider would be a perfect conductor for the fierce electric discharge. The man below felt another twinge of apprehension — not fear, not yet. It was just possible the pilot might be flying already. On previous occasions he had been up there with him and it had been his task to keep up the ritualized chatter with the girl on the ground all those miles away. But today his brother was by himself. For the first time the conflict of take-off was a lonely challenge in which he had not involved his helpers.

In fact the pilot was airborne when that first crack of thunder had shaken the waiting people below. He had taken off in sunshine from a point 3,000 metres up, far out of sight of his brother and his wife in the meadow.

4

After the Hiace had dropped him he made the steep, exhausting climb with the glider straddled over his shoulder. He had to carry around 30 kilos of sail and tungenized metal, not including the harness and extras like his helmet and gloves and a little thermos of coffee that he would abandon in the snow.

The point of take-off was high above the snowline. Thankfully he lowered the hang glider to the ground and drank in the sun. No clouds were visible; they waited in ambush. To his left the ground dropped away sharply until it was bitten off in a cliff. To the right he could gaze down along the route by which he had travelled up, the lower ridge and the main escarpment of the mountain. His flight of a little over eight kilometres to the marked field would simulate the distance he would have to fly when the time came for his mission. In three days, when the moon was high, if conditions were favourable, he would fly the same route again — by night.

In the thin air it took him the best part of an hour to rig the large blue and white Atlas, folding out the wings, pushing in the king post, screwing in the rigging wires and slipping the gold anodized frame batons into the fabric. Then the checking had to be done. That also took time. No abrasions on the leading edges, check the bracing wire attachment at the rear of the keel tube and the heart bolt, see the flight deck with its vario and altimeter screwed into place. Everything fitting, everything right.

His brother had suggested that he switch to a more sophisticated glider, one of the new American breeds with aerodynamic innovations devised by computers. But he had always preferred a French glider. He had flown when the sport was new, during that first holiday in the south of France five years ago. Later he flew in the snows all over the Alps. Those carefree years in France and Italy at various lavish resorts had allowed him to get to know about flying in mountain conditions. Acting the playboy before becoming a revolutionary had its advantages.

He had been with the Atlas for over a year. He was familiar with its glide angle and its good minimum sink performance that was so essential for the flight that he planned. Most important, he liked its stability.

He was a small man, shorter than his brother. He wore a black

5

flying suit, the bottoms tucked into his boots. The elbows and knees were padded in the American fashion — perhaps the Americans wore padding in imitation of their football players. Under the suit next to his skin was an old cashmere pullover, thin, yet so warm. In his dissipated youth he had stolen it from a shop in London's Piccadilly where he had been a typical rich foreigner, his pockets full of money.

His lined leather gloves were as thick as was compatible with mobility. He strapped the compass to his wrist and checked stirrups and the harness to which was attached a small emerald green bag containing his MK shute. He was the sort of pilot that put little faith in his parachute, rather as the dare-devil motorist is contemptuous of his safety belt. However, he carried it like a charm. On his back was slung a rucksack weighted with slivers of lead similar to those used by handicap jockeys. They indicated the approximate weight of the arms he would be carrying on the mission. He talked into the small transmitter and exchanged a lighthearted though ponderous series of comments with his brother — neither was the sort who joked and wisecracked. Then he switched off, ignoring his brother's "over!" signals.

Before he flew he went down on hands and knees in prayer.

All ready. His comrades standing by the target were far away out of sight, waiting and watching the empty sky. He thought of the flight with a grin of anticipation. It was the seventh day he had been training here and so far there had been no real problems. The take-offs had been smooth and the eight-kilometre flights merely pieces of travel. Some of the landings near the target zone had not gone well, but he was confident that his performance would improve to the extent when it was totally reliable. He had to reach the exact target and give himself a failure rate of less than ten metres at the end of the long journey. He had to get it right. He did not like to admit to himself that he could never be a hundred per cent certain. He knew, in his heart, that when the time came there would be a strong element of chance in his success, and that the slightest shift of wind direction at the wrong moment would lead him to failure — disaster.

He looked forward to weeks of night training. He had never

6

done much night flying. It was generally considered a frivolous danger. But he considered that there was little to it. In fact, given reasonable visibility, in some ways it was easier than flying by day. Weather conditions at night, particularly in the mountains, were generally more stable. He recalled once again that particular flight by moonlight that had lead him to train with the help of his brother, his friends and his wife. To train for his country, for martyrdom and for a seat in Paradise. (In all those wasted years as a playboy he had never quite lost faith in Islam. It possessed him with new fervour when the revolution came.)

He checked his watch. He must go. In these mountains most days you had to stop flying in the afternoon when the wind became the slave of the sun. Often it died away altogether, at other times it changed to something unpredictable. There was no point in testing the Atlas against down draughts and sudden changes in wind direction.

His arms held the A-frame of the *cerf volant*. (He had learned to fly in France, and the gliding terms he used were French.) The blue-and-white-striped wings fluttered on the rocky platform where the rigged Atlas waited to go. His altimeter showed that he was just over 4,000 metres above sea level. He took a small run and was in the air.

"*Décollé!*"

The audio vario began pinging away like a dentist's drill. It was almost a straight plummet at first, as if he had jumped off without his wings. He had that distant ridge to cross, but there was plenty of lift. The vario changed note as it wandered from four down to a steady two up. With the bar to his waist he ascended like a supercharged lift while the world below was stationary. Below him were wrinkles and clefts of Alpine topography, and far ahead he could just make out the fold of the valley where his friends stood watching for the speck in the sky which would look black at the distance they viewed it. Any bird in the sky looked black from the ground. Up here he was above the birds. All was beneath him. He liked the thought of the two, the man and the woman, waiting for him. His attendants.

He flew some more, travelling a little over 3,000 metres before passing over the ridge. He had little manoeuvring to do. It's no use

7

working your ass off looking for thermals. (An American had given him that advice at Kossen. Strange, when he thought of the perfidy of the U.S., how many Americans he had met and liked.) The ridge seemed knife-sharp, a thrust of bare rock against the sky. The *cerf volant* felt good. He looked ahead towards the valley where the white rectangle of the target would be marked out on the long grass. From now it would be sink, burning off excess altitude until he reached the target and made the spot landing.

The high-pitched whine of the vario told him that he was rising fast. He had not seen the first wisp of cloud, and the black thunderheads that rose suddenly out of nothing into the clear sky were a total surprise. He felt an absurd resentment, a feeling of invasion of privacy which was enforced by the threatening bellow of the first thunderclap. The aluminium alloy frame of the glider began to be buffeted. The right wing dipped violently and he shifted his weight to regain control. The *cerf volant* seemed to have a life of its own. As he struggled with it the vario was giving a disturbing ten up and two down. Mountain turbulence. That was bad. He realized suddenly that it was worse than anything he had experienced before. He needed all his strength and concentration to hold back the bar and move his weight against the thrust of the thermal.

The machine lurched and pitched, jogging up and down with a violent movement that turned his stomach. He felt seasick. The groaning protest of the rigging made the same sound as wind blowing the steel mast and wires of a yacht. The desire to vomit was a dangerous distraction. He must control it, concentrate on flying out of the inner core of the thermal, out of its corkscrewing strength before ... before what? In less than three minutes he had progressed from a smooth sunlight glide to this. He remembered stories he had heard about other pilots. Stabs of fear combined with the waves of nausea that shook his body.

The hang glider had risen to the cloud base and thin cirrus clouds streamed around him. The world below vanished fairly rapidly. Already he knew he wouldn't see it again. A massive tug at the wings sent him into the heart of the steamy vapour. "Cloud suck," he thought, desperately fighting to keep the glider level. He was choking, and felt the pain in his arms as they strained at the

8

bar. His legs and neck ached and his skin tingled in the heavily ionized air. He felt cold. He blacked out to another crash of thunder just as he was attempting the one-step system of deploying his shute. He never knew if he succeeded. He had no time to call on God.

The storm passed quickly.

Down in the meadow the man kept trying to make contact with his brother, speaking into the loudspeaker with none of the formalities of radio communication. He merely called out his name over and over again. It was the woman who first saw the speck of the hang glider high in the sky drifting into view.

They watched the smudge gradually enlarge, and suddenly they could see something was wrong. The angle was unusual. Looking through binoculars they made out the broken collapsed wing, and high above it the white shute waving gaily.

"He managed to deploy." They knew the thermal could have taken him up thousands of metres and smashed the glider into pieces.

They were silent as they passed the binoculars to each other, studying the broken delta wing shape and the pilot in his prone harness swinging about. It was impossible to tell whether any of the movements they saw came from his body. He did not take his feet out of the stirrup.

The girl lit a cigarette. Down here on the valley floor there was no wind and the curl of smoke wafted upwards in the still air.

"The turbulence must have broken the leading edge. Strange how only one wing broke."

"The damage may have happened after he threw out the shute."

The hang glider, still a thousand metres up, was falling in their direction. Now the man could see the asymmetric broken wing, quite straight and the prone black line beneath which was the pilot's body. Through the binoculars the woman could see the colours of the Terylene and identify the black flying suit and blue helmet. Like the broken wing, the head was lopsided. It seemed to be looking at them.

"His arms!" she cried out suddenly. They were not holding the bar, but stretched downward towards the ground.

The man seized the binoculars and watched his brother wafting down. He focused on the body yawing to and fro, suspended under the crooked wings. It seemed unsupported by them, flying on its own. He put down the glasses and watched with naked eye the black figure coming nearer, arms pointing downward, feet wedged in the stirrup.

The woman shrieked, "He is not going to hit the target area!" He made no attempt to stifle her laughter and sobs.

She stopped abruptly and watched the parachute making its gentle and silent descent. They could see the break in the wing was almost halfway along its length where the leading edge had snapped. The binoculars revealed frayed wing cloth.

The pilot's head continued to hang down loosely. As the hang glider skimmed the last few feet his brother had a last hope that he had blacked out from the effect of opening the shute. How strong had the turbulence been? The maximum a man could stand was about plus 3.G.

Amazingly, the woman was almost wrong, and after drifting all that distance the Atlas landed about 50 metres from the target. The blue and white wings folded over the pilot and concealed him. Beside him the parachute crumpled in the windless air.

They ran towards the figure caught under the sails, supported by the harness with its carbiner buckle so that it did not touch the ground.

"Cut him out, cut him out!"

The man only had a penknife, and time was wasted while he unhooked the buckle and sliced frantically at the webbing. He cut away the parachute, slicing through the straps that held the transmitter and the bag full of lead. Together they dragged the pilot away from the harness and laid him on the grass. His dark eyes were open. His brother wrenched off his helmet, revealing black hair drenched with sweat.

"Kiss of life?"

"Cardiac action." He unzipped the flying suit and smelled urine. The dead pilot — for all their frantic activity they knew he was dead — looked up at the sky. He was a small man, and lying there he resembled a dead boy. His brother continued trying to believe that he could be brought back to life. He remembered an accident he had seen only a few weeks before at Lachènes. A gust of wind had thrown a hang glider in the air and the pilot had come down without a parachute — not from any great height, but high enough. When he reached the ground a smear of blood dribbled out of that man's nose and he had not been breathing. The speed with which cardiac action was applied saved his life.

"Quick. . . ." Four pumps for cardiac stimulation. One blow for ventilation.

Four pumps, one blow. Later the girl took over. They tried the kiss of life. For over half an hour they worried at the body, before they gave up and sat back silent, panting with exertion. The man closed his brother's eyes.

What had killed him? The turbulence that had thrown the glider about like a leaf? Cold? Sheer fright? His neck and arms were swollen, a difficult fact to spot because of his brawny physique. They noticed a thin red line behind his ear that continued under the flying suit. They took off the elbow and knee pads, the top half of his suit and looked under the cashmere pullover. He had a number of similar lesions on his back. Could he have got them from hitting the metal keel or some other part of the A-frame? Were they burns? Those black clouds and the thunder cracks would have been accompanied by lightning, although they had seen none from where they had stood. Had a massive charge of forked lightning struck him as he staggered about in the clouds? But wouldn't he have been burnt to a cinder? Was his neck broken?

The nagging desire for unnecessary knowledge left them as abruptly as it had been inspired.

The sun moved behind a peak and the valley was shadowed. They did nothing until people began to assemble.

"You are like vultures gathering," the woman told the fifth lot of arrivals, a middle-aged Swiss who showed signs of hysteria, and his silent wife who had been looking for wild flowers. She left the withering bunch she had gathered beside the twisted glider.

The inquisitive strangers made sounds of disapproval. For

them, like so many others throughout the world, hang gliding was *imprudent, téméraire, idiot*. So many foolish young men had died unnecessarily.

The strangers took over, arranged for the ambulance, the officious gendarmerie and a bored newspaper reporter. There had been a number of fatal hang gliding accidents in the area already that summer.

Later at night, at her insistence, the brother took the man's wife back to the hotel where she had stayed with her dead husband. It was at Villeneuve, south of Grenoble, a suburb built in the last decade in an area accommodating the expanding population of the city. The hotel was bright, clean and comfortable. The bedroom was filled with reminders — smart clothes for a small man, diagrams, maps, squared paper covered with neat handwriting, odd pieces of velcro, spare varios and the hang gliding magazines he used to carry around like holy books — all recalled the dead pilot. His brother brought a bottle of cognac up with him. In the bed in that hot room she welcomed him instead of the man who died and sought comfort in passion. When they talked afterwards they tried not to see the accident as a useless waste of life. They talked of the motives for revenge, the months of planning. The idea had always been so full of risk. It had meant death for husband and brother, the price of a glorious revenge. For the man who had perished that day revenge had been a powerful driving force as pure and strong as the exhilaration of flight combined with the idea of death from the sky.

The brother was weeping again. "He was not a madman, but a true revolutionary. And the plan must be forgotten." Forget the hours of spring and summer spent flying at Montaud near St Quentin sur Isère, at St Hilaire du Touvet, at Chamrousse with its thousand-metre downhill flight and tricky landing field beside the bulk of De Moucherotte. Think of other ways for the assassin to find his mark.

Chapter Two

AUGUST 1979: THE Volkswagen minibus inched its way through the Paris traffic. Even though one car in three seemed to be supporting bicycles, canoes, hang gliders, surfboards and similar paraphernalia belonging to French sporting freaks, the vehicle from Ireland attracted attention. The orange and yellow stripes along the sides clashed with the tomato shades of the Dublin number plates and the scarlet jacket of the Super Scorpion whose noble length stretched along the roof. Amid the stripes the words LACKEN LIFT — LEARN TO FLY were painted in dark purple beside the silhouette of a hang gliding pilot. The rear side windows had stickers advertising Pim's Cola and Griffin's Men's Outfitters. These firms were sponsoring the Irish team for the World Hang Gliding Championships at Grenoble. Henry Brennan, the team captain, planned to give the people who handed out the cash a further boost in advertising. When he flew in the championships, teams from 30 competing nations, together with the citizens of Grenoble and several hundred thousand television viewers would learn about Pim's because the name was emblazoned on the wings of his glider.

Paul had a less reverent attitude towards sponsorship. He had thought of stencilling I SHOT J.R. on the wings of his Scorp — it was the height of the Dallas foolishness. He had contented himself with putting a sticker of his own composition in the middle of the rear window of the van beside the little Irish flag. HANG GLIDERS DO IT IN THE MISSIONARY POSITION.

He drove forward into a tunnel which took twenty minutes to negotiate. Maura sat beside him, map in lap.

"The fumes . . . they can't be good for anyone. Don't they have any sort of regulations? Is every large vehicle in France a juggernaut?"

"The one in front isn't."

"What's that inside?"

"Pigs."

"You're right. That's what the stench is."

The pigs mingled in an olfactory cocktail with petrol fumes and smells of vomit and disinfectant inside the minibus. Tony had been sick four times since they disembarked at Le Havre. The discarded clothes were in a polythene sack and the back seat was awash with TCP, but the stink was still there. If he was sick twice more he'd have to complete the journey in pyjamas.

"Where do you think the others are by now?"

"Miles ahead."

Once again Paul regretted they had been unable to leave Tony behind with his mother-in-law. But the old bitch (his relationship with her was conventionally hostile) had chosen that week to go on a pilgrimage to Knock. That meant she couldn't look after the child and they were stuck with a restless four-year-old. Pleasure in the journey was confined to the periods when he slept. When that happened they hardly spoke in case he woke. He woke nearly every time they drove through a town of any size. He woke every time they had to stop at traffic lights, since the rhythm of the car acted as a narcotic. At best there would be the fretful "Are we there?". Mostly there was whining, something like a Gregorian chant.

Through the tunnel. A glimpse of the Eiffel Tower, the gleam of the Sacré Coeur and miles of traffic snarl-ups and high-rise flats. Another hour before they reached the outskirts of the city. They stopped and bought an ice-cream to assuage the little voice behind. Maura also bought grapes, cheese and salami which they ate as they moved. Thirty miles on they stopped again and Tony drank some Pim's Cola, of which they had an unlimited supply. Then he was sick while the terrible traffic roared past. Paul had to turn off the autoroute into a road lined with poplars so that Maura could do yet another clean up, changing the yelling child and scrubbing with a J-cloth.

The heat got worse after they climbed in again and drove on. Tony settled and slept and so did Maura. Paul drove among the wild French careering south for the August holiday, auto-matically casting his eye over the heated countryside and the rolling fields of corn and maize for the sort of places that might induce thermals which would send hang gliders spiralling upwards into the sky.

The rest of the day was bad, the evening meal where they were overcharged, the search for a night's accommodation. In every town they met the word *complet* and came to loathe it. Everywhere was *complet*, big hotels and smaller guest houses. In the end they had to sleep at a lay-by on the autoroute. There were other cars, other weary travellers. Having slept much of the day Tony was suddenly wide awake and lively. In the midst of his discomfort Paul felt panic. He ought to be in good shape, even as sub for the team. The way he felt now he might as well throw himself straight off a cliff without any wings at all.

They began driving early in the morning and stopped at the first restaurant they came to, a Routier special that looked as if it had been made out of Lego. It had a decent clean lavatory where some of the ravages of the night could be repaired. They ate a miserable French breakfast and pressed on. The mountains appeared. After hundreds of flat, vaguely undulating miles, hopeless for hang gliding, they were suddenly visible, cut into the summer sky.

The minibus had to slow down for traffic. Tony woke. He hadn't been sick today, not once.

"Are we there yet?"

"We will be when we get to those mountains."

"Will you fly off them, Dada?"

"I will."

About three o'clock they reached Grenoble, a far bigger and more impressive town than Paul had imagined. He followed the car in front across the main bridge into the Place de la Bastille. Some ruins hugged the side of a precipitous rock and nearby the perspex bulbs of the *téléphérique* attracted tourists. They had an hour before he was due to rendezvous with the other guys at a place called the Alpine Congress Centre. There was time for a quick snack, pleasant and not too dear. Maura sipped Perrier water. Typical of the austerity of her nature that she took to mineral water as if it was champagne.

Paul said, "The get-together will be boring enough."

"I can imagine."

"Why don't you and Tony go off?"

"Go off where?"

"Go and explore. Take the minibus."

"I really hate that thing. Every time I drive it I feel like the air hostess in the disaster movie who has to take over when the pilot is incapacitated."

"Okay, then go to that park. Any park. There's five at least. Go shopping. Buy something for your mother." He riffled through the tourist guide. "Museums. Stendhal lived here."

"Who was he?"

"There's a grand-looking museum with old cars."

"Thanks. All I need to do with Tony is to look at old cars."

"What about a park then?"

"In this heat?" But reluctantly she agreed that a little stroll outside might be preferable to handling Tony and his temper tantrums in the middle of an assembly of hang gliders. He dropped her off at the Jardin de Ville beside the river. There were swings and roundabouts for kids; she could sit in the shade of an acacia and then follow in a taxi.

With the aid of the xeroxed map Henny had issued before they left Dublin Paul located the Alpes Congrès, a big modern glass building on the Avenue d'Innsbruck at the outskirts of Grenoble. Outside were stuck posters showing a hang glider superimposed on a globe. *Championnat du Monde de Vol Libre*. Cars and vans from all over Europe were assembled in the main courtyard. A minibus decorated with a large bearded head wearing helmet and horns announced VIKING TEAM from Oslo. Some Germans had painted their van in rainbow colours, the word HANGOFLEITER tripping in and out of the spectrum. Slogans abounded. HANG GLIDERS STAY UP LONGER. LE VOL LIBRE — C'EST LA VIE LIBRE. HAVE YOU HUGGED YOUR HANG GLIDER TODAY? Owens Valley stickers on cars with English number plates meant that in spite of the recession plenty of people could afford to go and fly in California. Other Icarus symbols proclaimed obsession just as much as the long hang gliders clustered like logs on roof racks. Paul parked the minibus, so distinctive when it drove along the autoroutes, so much one of a crowd here.

Inside, bad-tempered French officials were shepherding

people from 24 countries. There were plenty of men with shoulder-length hair in shorts and T-shirts, decorated with pictures of hang gliders. About a third of those present wore scratchy little beards, while a smaller percentage kept their locks in place with hairbands like Bjorn Borg. Paul noticed a few women with rather too much muscle for his taste. Some were actually on the national teams, but most were just hardy girlfriends. Ten Japanese and another little Oriental who stuck with the Americans and turned out to be from South Korea. Swedes, Swiss, Yanks, Poles, Brazilians and Germans. No black men. Nasal accents from Australia. A guy from Fiji. You could deduce something about geography and social custom from examining the competitors. You could pick out the types at once, the individualists, the self-proclaimed heroes and the quiet braggarts who told you of their achievements in a couple of sentences.

Watching the members of the French team, which consisted of ten little Napoleons determined to win their own competition, Paul wished he himself could be more excited about the idea of competing. He was only spare man, and considering his form in the training sessions it was not very likely he would be picked for the team. However, at least he should get a chance of experiencing a bit of Alpine lift.

He listened to voices around him.

"... ridge-soaring ..."

"... weak thermal ..."

"... turbulence ..."

"... glide angle ..."

"... pitch, stability and control ..."

"... speed figure eight ... duration ... spot ..."

He checked with the other members of the Irish team. Sean Duffy and Johnny Hayes had arrived late last night and actually managed a flight that morning.

"Whoopee! Wait until you see what take-off is like up in them there hills!"

He talked with other pilots, fitting in his own bit of jargon-ridden boasting. He got a bit of crack from circulating, learning new gossip about familiar subjects and gathering information about flying systems in the Alps. He met a Pole who seemed to have made his hang glider out of bed sheets and coat hangers, and learned the Polish word for hang glider — *lotnia*. He listened to an American who was reminiscing about the individualists flying in California in the early days of the sport. The guys who wore no helmets or shoes, or who'd taken a spot of acid and launched at night without wearing a harness.

He met a couple of Australians who pointed out Steve Moyes, and he gazed in awe at that stalwart Aussie pioneer of hang gliding. Of course, the sport had got off to a good start when Melvin Rogallo, an American who worked for NASA, and his wife invented the Rogallo wing which revolutionized flying and introduced the model-T Ford of the sky. A few years later the Australian paragliders, Moyes and Bennet, paid their celebrated visit to California and encountered the Rogallos, a moment in flying history that saw the fusion of two concepts of moving through the air. That was in 1971 in the dark ages, long before Paul had ever seen a hang glider.

Flying in those days had been pretty terrible. The hang gliders had been rudimentary — downers with no lift in them. You lugged them up the hill and flew them down like paper darts, usually ending up on a heap of stones. Very little research had been done on lift. Now at the end of the decade things had changed with great rapidity. For the price of a colour television set almost anyone could fly, and when he had finished for the day he could store his glider in the garage. And the concept of competition had developed.

". . . cored out in a boomer . . ."

". . . kite bucked like a wild horse . . ."

". . . fifteen to twenty knots . . ."

". . . went on circling in this blob . . ."

". . . topped out a mile downwind . . ."

". . . did a one-eighty and flew back into wind . . ."

". . . vario went berserk . . ."

Listening to a group of English flyers, pleased with themselves, talking about their chances of winning, he didn't notice Maura when she came in. He saw Tony first, racing up and down, sliding on the parquet floor. Then there was Maura, glaring. He would like to disown her. Hell, couldn't she show just a little interest in the proceedings? He didn't want her to be glamorous, or what was the French word? *Sportive*? Or did that mean sexy? Just to be part of the scene.

"The heat's killing."

"You could have come earlier. These official functions take time."

She met a few people grimly, greeted Henny, Sean and Orla and glared at the other women.

"I think we should get on. Tony's had a long day."

He followed her out reluctantly, self-conscious, although that was hardly fair. But his domestic image was a contrast to the freedom boasted about by the band of brothers he had just left. They walked downstairs and through the glass and marble hall. Outside the heat struck like a fist. Getting into the minibus was foul.

More maps to be consulted. They were aiming at a resort called St Hilaire du Touvet, 25 kilometres beyond Grenoble. He would be staying at St Hilaire. Maura and Tony would be dumped elsewhere. He had warned her before they left Ireland. Far away, where they would not interfere with training. She had said she didn't mind.

He moved cautiously through the traffic looking for the Chambéry road. God, these French drivers! He nearly collided with a Peugeot full of wild-looking men with black moustaches who shouted and waved arms.

"Algerians," Maura said. "The park was packed solid with them."

The route to St Hilaire du Touvet was along the same river Isère that flowed through Grenoble. As they drove they could examine the great chain of mountains on the far side of the river that divided France from Italy and Switzerland. Snow, cool snow, draped on barren mountain peaks contrasted with the heat down here liked Baked Alaska. He saw the cliff face before the Massif de la Chartreuse. Somewhere on the summit of that escarpment the championships would be held. A perpendicular line of rock rose sheer from the valley floor to a green wedge of meadow that looked as if it could be Conan Doyle's lost valley. Scattered behind that again were more massifs, more jumbles of cliffs and pyramids of glossy white rock rising up to the sky.

Near Saint Nasaire an arrow pointed up a twisted road. The minibus followed behind a Volkswagen with Austrian number plates and three hang gliders on top. Behind them again a queue of cars crept up the corkscrew road towards their destination. Paul's exit must have precipitated the break-up of the proceedings at the Alpes Congrès.

It was cooler and greener and they had left the tyranny of the main road. Banners proclaimed the world championship. Tony screamed happily as they passed through the long tunnel that emerged near the first village of St Pancrasse. What a name! Was he the same guy they named the station after in London?

Beyond was St Hilaire du Touvet set in the green plateau covered with small wooden tourist houses that aped more robust chalets. Paul had been booked into one of these with other members of the team. A Granada with Irish plates was already parked outside. Two hang gliders lay on the grass. Inside were cabins with bunk beds and a large sitting room leading to a wooden balcony. Joe Boland and Pascal Regan were sitting there drinking beer.

"Henny's the fourth in here. He'll be along." A man's life, a soldiery routine. Comrades in arms.

Maura and Tony had to be disposed of. There was a stylized relief map on the wall full of pictures of mountains. He pointed. "You'll be here. Theys."

"I didn't realize it was so far away."

They left his gear, including the Scorp and drove across the river to the far side of the valley.

"It's like going into quarantine."

However, she liked Theys which was pretty and rustic without the mushroom spread of tourist bungalows. The pension was in the main square. Her room overlooked a fountain, a small church and houses with sloping roofs and geranium-filled balconies. Nearby, on the Isère, or in the Isère, they couldn't make out, was a swimming pool. Ann Brennan, Henny's wife, a tough woman with five children she had managed to leave at home, would be staying in the same place. Company.

He left Maura the minibus and she would drive it tomorrow morning. She realized she'd be well and truly stuck without it. She'd come to St Hilaire about noon when some practice hang gliding would be in progress.

"Don't get hurt." She always said that whenever he went flying.

He got a lift back to St Hilaire with a couple of hang gliding Spaniards. The little cabin was ablaze with light, and inside the table was covered with bottles — beer, wine and a litre-sized bottle of duty-free Paddy. A couple of the other lads on the team came in, and they had a regular party, with Henny fussing like a mother hen, talking about getting down to business and practice tomorrow, and no one was taking a blind bit of notice.

Morning brought a blue cloudless sky above the blanched white cliffs and the crest of hills silhouetted above the strip of green fields. The Dent de Crolles and the Rocher du Midi loomed alarmingly.

A world championship, even a small one, had brought momentum to the three villages on the plateau. The grim little statue of St Hilaire, imprisoned in a glass box under a stone cross, looked on. From his vantage point he had seen the changes of the last 50 years. First there had been the consumptives. Between the wars Somerset Maugham-type patients languished in wicker *chaises longues* in St Hilaire's huge gabled sanatorium which rivalled in size and eccentric shape certain lunatic asylums in Ireland. Then came the skiers. Thousands flocked here during the winter months, and the hills where the saint had sought peace and sanctuary were scarred with *pistes* and lifts.

If winter laid the area open to the mob, for a long time summer was relatively quiet. This was not a popular mountain-climbing area, and mountaineers preferred to trudge around Chamonix or clamber on the Matterhorn. But a few years before, someone had discovered that here was a good place for hang gliding. It was as if a little oil well had been found beside a gold mine. The dour Dauphinois suddenly realized that *le bon Dieu* had provided them with a new source of income.

This year the best hang gliders in the world had come among them, together with an endless number of officials and the sort of

21

entourage necessary for a *Championnat du Monde*. A special contingent of gendarmes had been drafted in, while soldiers waited to carry the furled gliders back from the landing ground up to the launching site in their military lorries. Spectators would flock out from Grenoble. Restaurant owners and shopkeepers in three villages would benefit.

The Irish lads woke with hangovers. Even Henny.

"You getting up?"

"For Christ's sake, it's only six o'clock."

"Tea?" Pascal had brought a giant polythene sack of tea bags and a tin of freeze-dried milk. Four pairs of hairy legs swung off bunks, four drowsy faces gazed out.

"There's no fucking wind."

"Thermals. And plenty of turbulence, you bet. The rules are different here."

They had discussed the competition and tactics until a late hour, consulting the book of rules for the competition with the aid of Henny's pocket dictionary. *Les épreuves* — that must be tasks. There was a picture of a target which helped them work out that *précision d'atterrissage* meant spot landing. *Le cross-country*, that was easy, while *le mini cross-country* must mean going a distance along a given route.

Paul had never gone in for competitions. He had no wish to indulge in target spotting and the like. The concept of "tasks" ranging from cross-country flights to spot landing had revolted him. He might as well have joined the boy scouts. He had the reputation for being a loner. Strange how the sight of other pilots had irritated him. He hated to arrive at a site and find other guys flying there already. (And yet he'd liked teaching with Lacken Lift.)

Then Henny had picked him for the team after Gordon had been killed and someone was needed to take his place. Henny came out to Mount Leinster and watched him perform semi-radical manoeuvres — high bank stalls, slipping and full-bore dives. He felt flattered even to be going as an extra man.

They dressed and were out in the windless heat by eight o'clock. They drove in Henny's Volvo down to the village to the take-off field. Henny beeped his way through the mêlée of cars and vans, soldiers in green fatigues, sweating pilots and girls. Some girls wore bikinis. Paul stared at a blonde in a T-shirt with SEA. SEX, SOAR written on it.

They unloaded the gliders and waited for the rest of the team. By the time they arrived, the ridge of grass overlooking the valley appeared to be settled by ants and butterflies. Communication was polyglot.

"Dynamite flying!"

"*Ça va, mon vieux!*"

"A piece of piss!"

Pilots unwrapped their machines. New Atlases stood up on end, their wings unfolding like bats. Paul recognized an American Fledgling with fixed wings, and more French kites, Gryphons and Sabres. Sigmas galore. He was glad to see a good few super Scorps like his own. There was one taking off now. Paul had flown briefly in the Alps the year before, but it still gave him a shock to see those take-offs in absolutely windless conditions. You didn't want to worry about that drooping windsock.

There was the steep descent like a slide into a swimming pool. Then nothing but a drop down a precipice. A pilot had to run down that thing and take to the air as if he was jumping out of a plane with a parachute. First the dreadful sink, and then the secret force of the dizzy thermals that caught each glider and lifted it high into the sky. More and more joined the scramble, and a swarm of them were doing 360s, twisting and turning before suddenly dropping and going steerage further down.

All around were sounds of zips as covers were peeled off. He undressed the Scorp and set her up. Tested batons, sails, rigging, harness. He put on his helmet. Screwed on the flight deck with its vario and altimeter.

At a wave from Henny he joined the line up. A lot of time passed before it began to break. Three paces ahead of him a pilot, a German with an Atlas, stalled. It could happen to anyone. A good clean run, but with no wind he had pushed out too soon. The result was a badly twisted A-frame and a broken leading edge. He was lucky there was no damage to the person.

Paul was nervous all right, but that was the way to be. Nerves were the stuff that created adrenalin. In front of him Pascal crossed himself, not an easy accomplishment considering he was holding on to the bar of an A-frame. Good man, he was airborne. Now it was Paul's turn.

"*Quand tu veux!*" shouted the official at the head of the *piste*. He had been shouting the same thing all morning, the signal for launch. Run like hell, and don't push her out. Paul felt as if he was deliberately killing himself. He was behaving like a lemming, following the crowd to oblivion. He ran down in the heat, seeing the dead windsock out of a corner of his eye. And then the miracle. Not a miracle according to the laws of dynamics, but the transformation from the inert, troubled, two-legged, worried creatures tied to the earth by gravity. Suddenly the ground had slipped from under his feet.

"*Décollé!*"

He was like a bit of steam rising out of a kettle. The wings of the Scorp were catching a thermal. From his prone position he looked down on the village with its church spire and the funicular station. Then in what seemed a moment he was thousands of feet high above the valley, still ascending with the bleep of the vario two to four up. There were several good cores before he started to sink at around 5,000 feet. I had better make for the landing. He was beginning to be buffeted. Far below he could see the valley with its clusters of red roof tops, the river and the tiers of mountains beyond.

Losing height was easy. He swooped down towards the fields of maize and lines of cars and burned off the last few hundred feet until he was aiming for the landing area. He dodged around the target, landing well off its yellow centre. He'd like another go at that. He thought it was merely a matter of getting his eye in. Yellow or orange is the colour, they've figured, that stands out best in this blue-green-brown world. Even tennis balls are yellow now.

A band decked out in sweltering blue uniforms was playing a Viennese waltz on silver trumpets. Maura and Tony came up, Maura carrying the picnic basket.

"Been here long?"

"About an hour."

"Let's find some shade."

24

They did what many other people were doing and sat under the striped wings of the Scorp while she dealt out the food.

Was it the plastic containers that made the rations she had brought look so ordinary compared to what people all around them were eating? As she distributed the ham and bananas from the Tupperware, Paul found himself gazing ravenously at other picnickers' chicken, salami, salad, melons, peaches, pâtés, pizzas and chocolate-filled pancakes. A family just beside them was picking out goodies from a vast hamper, the size you would associate with nineteenth-century pheasant shoots. Delicious things kept emerging from the *buvettes* and refreshment tent. Tony nagged and whined until Paul went over and bought him a hot dog served by a bikini-clad girl.

Soon the brat was moaning some more.

"Why doesn't he go and make friends with kids like the ones over there?"

"How can he, poor little fellow, when he doesn't speak a word of French?"

Now he began yelling for a Coke, a proper one, not just Pim's. He wanted a real one out of a tin. He didn't care if it cost a lot. He didn't care that Mammy had brought plenty of extra bottles of Pim's. He wanted a Coke. Like the boys there, they had Cokes out of a tin. So did those men over there, they all had Coke. Paul looked across at the group of dark young men, mostly with dark eyes and hairline moustaches. Foreigners — Arabs of some sort, by the look of them. Probably Algerians like Maura saw yesterday. Unlikely they'd have Coke. Didn't Arabs drink Pepsi because of the Jewish connection?

"How do you know they've got Cokes? They're too far away to see."

"I saw earlier, Dada, I saw, I saw. Please, Please!" Even the silver band was playing the Coke song about perfect harmony.

Reluctantly Paul got up and walked into the boiling sun with the little boy towards the refreshment tent. Fifteen minutes of waiting around in the heat before Tony got his way did not improve the Dada's temper. When at last they were ready to run the gauntlet of sunshine back towards Maura, he was seething with irritability.

"Hello, Paul."

He looked round, startled. He could not concentrate in the glare. A girl talking to him. She had taken off her dark glasses with the mirror reflections to help him recognize her.

"Hi . . ."

"I'm Leila . . . you remember?"

"Of course," he said insincerely. Then it came back in a rush. Hell, I knew her. Then followed: Hell, I fucked her.

Chapter Three

HE COULD HAVE done without a meeting like this. Why should she want to renew acquaintance? My God, was she making something out of those moments of lust in the heather? Remembering the pleasures of her body didn't make it easier to conduct a polite conversation in the sun with Tony dancing around him and in the distance Maura peering through the glare.

It must be a year since he saw this one. Leila. A year exactly. He stood there remembering how this time last August he had been a partner in a hang gliding school in West Wicklow. Gordon had started it up, Gordon who was dead now, and had asked him to join him. Intermediate and advanced courses. Beginners mostly, from all over Ireland. They had people coming down from the north.

Gordon had supplied the premises and most of the capital to buy the gliders and the rest of the gear. Paul hadn't been anything like 50 per cent involved. He just didn't have the money. With a wife, a child and a mortgage there was no way he could consider giving up his job in the building firm. Not yet. It is every addicted hang gliding pilot's dream to be able to earn a living by flying hang gliders. Might as well try and earn a living by playing computer games.

Paul came out at the weekends and taught novices in tethered gliders and double harnesses. They had worked out this course which combined techniques. The beginner got his tethered flights which were the method of teaching flying approved by the British Hang Gliders' Association. Then as soon as weather permitted he went up in the Cyclone to which a double harness was fitted. This first flight was supposed to be nothing more than a joy ride, what the pedantic called air experience. It gave the sensations of free flight and was exhilarating for anyone who felt the primitive urge to move through the sky.

He remembered taking this Arab girl up in the double harness for the first time.

The business hadn't been established very long, but things were beginning to go well. The summer was good, with plenty of hot weather creating thermals and plenty of people interested in novice flying. Paul had his holidays at the beginning of August while Maura and Tony went down as usual to stay with her mother at Courtmacsherry. He moved to Gordon's house for the duration and every morning he drove into Dublin with the minibus to pick up the pupils.

He had seen her first waiting for the minibus at the pick-up point in Rathgar with the other six novices, all men. She was dressed in Glora Vanderbilt jeans and matching denim jacket. She carried her white helmet in her hand carefully as if it was an egg she was afraid of breaking. She was small and busty. Big eyes — hidden now behind the mirror glasses.

He learned she had this boyfriend, some rich darkie who was doing medicine at the College of Surgeons in Dublin. This guy had never been near Lacken Lift. He didn't have to, he could hang glide with the best. He told Gordon he had the Delta gold badge from the FAI which put him into international class. And his girl didn't know the first thing about hang gliding. The lover was keen to get her airborne so that she could be an accessory flying near him like an ornamental bird. He appreciated that you should never teach your loved one to fly any more than you teach her to drive. So he made her sign with Lacken Lift.

Paul shouted at her right away. She wore heavy earrings hooked to her lobes by things like coat hangers and he roared at her to take them off.

The boyfriend was away flying in the Alps.

"Ever been up before, Leila?" Paul had asked. It was a sport for first-name relationships, although she looked haughty, shaking her head.

"We'll go up in the two-seater. Later you can take an active part in the control of the glider."

She stood imperiously waiting for the glider to be rigged. The others were put to work erecting the control frame, seeing to the king post and brace and strapping up the bracing wires. With

28

novices rigging, the pre-flight inspection always took hours because explanations and demonstrations went slowly, slowly. She stood and watched. Once or twice he tested her, getting her to identify the heart bolt and walk along beside the leading edges checking for tears or worn seams.

She was trembling a little as he helped her buckle on her harness and saw her helmet was fastened. Then they were off into the warm summer sky seated side by side above the Wicklow hills. Blessington Lake shimmered in the distance. Dual flight is a clumsy affair. He didn't talk much during the five-minute flights, just shouted a thing or two, and then they were landing in the heather and she was laughing with relief.

At the end of the afternoon, when he had given time to the other novices, she said she'd go up again. They flew in the silky evening air. The erotic urge was sudden, very sudden. It was a crazy feeling. A fat little woman in her denims. Her face was a bit gaunt, the nose slightly curved, the big black eyes beneath heavy brows always slightly frowning. It was the face of a good-looking vulture. Legs hung down from the harness below the A-frame, tapering into neat black suede boots unsuitable for Wicklow bogs.

When they landed they kept busy dismantling the hang glider before Gordon came down with the van to collect them. That took a few minutes. They were fairly silent. Paul should have been lecturing her about flight experience, about evening wind patterns.

Half an hour later they were all in the Blessington Arms for a raucous pub session. Hang gliding pilots are generally an aggressive, boastful lot. Nothing they like better than the après glide experience, sitting over their pints exchanging accounts of flights, accidents and near accidents. At times you'd think they'd just landed in Spitfires after fighting Jerry.

Novice flyers talk even more than the rest — something to do with the relief of having got through the day safely. And Gordon, who had the gift of the gab, was giving out, going on about his experiences in Australia and California. This girl, Leila, didn't say a word, but sat sipping soft drinks. A couple of times Paul caught her eye.

29

Next day was sunny and the wind forecast was for fifteen, sixteen knots. He had her phone number from the list Gordon supplied him with. He knew Gordon would be out at Lacken with a crowd. He would give Lacken a miss that day.

When he phoned her she agreed to a flight without hesitation. He picked her up in his own car and they drove out to the Big Sugarloaf. After she helped him haul the kite up the slope, they rigged the double harness. No one there. The short flights in the sun. And afterwards in the heather with the hang glider like a moth beside them. Impulse on her part as well. Taking off the helmet and the black hair falling out in a shower. Stripping. Pressing the big mouth with the faintly uneven teeth. The scent of her heavy French perfume, so different from Maura's astringent cologne. So out of keeping with the wild mountainside. Stripping off the neat blue clothes and getting to the delights underneath. Fucking among the frockens. Something more than just a quick screw on the hillside in the sunshine. It was outside his experience altogether, caressing the smooth sallow skin and prolonging the ultimate exhilaration of union. It had a feeling parallel with some of the great soaring flights he had achieved. Something extraordinary, an experience for the gods. It was crazy, it was beautiful.

Afterwards he planned to blow £30 on a meal at Lamb Doyles and then take her back to his house. Maura wasn't there. Poor Maura. But Leila wouldn't have it. She put on her clothes and acted mulish. She made him drive her back to her flat. He drove in a fury. They were lovers for a few moments, but she made it clear they were not friends. He was really angry. When he saw her again at the weekend she was with the swarthy boyfriend. She didn't take any notice of Paul at all. She didn't come out on the slopes again.

In the ensuing year he thought of her from time to time especially while he was watching news on television and they showed what took place in her country. It was odd how he would conjure up her image as he watched scenes of men with machine guns, crowds chanting, women wrapped in black cloaks, shaking their fists, car bombs exploding, buildings in rubble. Cheerful reminders of his afternoon's bliss.

And now, what the hell. She'd gone off without a by-your-leave, teamed up with loverboy and then left Ireland. He'd been a right fool. And now she was all smiles. She was peering at Tony. Not a child lover. She regarded him as if he was a snake.

"Is this your little boy?"

"That's right. He and his mother are over for the championships. A holiday. I'm flying on the Irish team."

It appeared she was with the dark-eyed Pepsi swillers. They were Almutis, her fellow countrymen. She lived in Grenoble. Well, well, small world. How's Hassan, he asked, amazingly remembering the name of the rich boyfriend. How was he to know that the guy had gone and got himself killed in a hang gliding accident? Only a few weeks ago, seemingly.

And your friend Gordon? How was she to know that he, too, had died flying off Mount Leinster at much the same time? A great big happy coincidence. They were silent for a moment, contemplating their dismal bond.

What was she doing here at St Hilaire, he asked, and that wasn't the right thing to say because it implied she was cold-blooded to be out and about in this festive atmosphere so soon after the lover had swapped a hang glider's wings for angels' wings. No more cold-blooded than Paul coming out to France so soon after Gordon's death.

He remembered Gordon's funeral in the little Church of Ireland cemetery in West Wicklow. It was appropriate, they all said, with the mountains all around and an eighteen-knot wind blowing the clergyman's surplice around his legs. The mourners — mostly fliers — made a forlorn little group. No man is an island.

Gordon was an experienced pilot. It is always disconcerting when the good people are killed. The nonks, the fools, the boys with the homemade gliders, the men who can't put their feet into the stirrup when they are learning to fly prone, the stallers, the over-confident and the careless could be said to invite their accidents. But a proportion of fliers die because of bad luck. Gordon was among them.

The team came out to St Hilaire a couple of weeks later. There was no hesitation about taking part in the world championships.

"It's what Gordon would have wanted," they all said. People always said something like that when there was an undignified haste to resume frivolous activities after someone died.

Leila was shivering. Her man had died in the Alps. Death . . . she shook her head and the images in the mirror lenses shifted a little.

Tony was pulling at his arm. Well, I must fly. Ha, ha.

"Who was that?" Maura asked.

"It's a small world. I gave that girl a few flying lessons at Lacken." Luckily he was already red-faced because of the sun.

"You could have introduced me."

"Nothing to stop you walking over."

"Did you teach many women in Lacken Lift?"

"A few. That one just lost her boyfriend. Killed in an accident."

"Like Gordon?" She was silent as she sipped lukewarm Pim's in a paper cup.

He knew she'd never come to terms with the dangers of the sport. Maura had taken a long time to worry. At first her reservations about hang gliding had concerned neglect and expense. But she hadn't been afraid for him.

Two things had put her wise to her chances of becoming a widow some weekend. One was the opinion of her cousin who was a pilot in Aer Lingus. During a dreadful Christmas session down in West Cork, out of boredom Paul had been induced to boast about his experiences. This character, so respectable, so admired by the mother-in-law, had shouted: "My God! Nothing on this earth would induce me to take up a damn fool hobby like that! It's an unacceptable risk!"

The second thing was the hang gliding magazines that Paul brought home. They seemed innocuous with their pictures of happy pilots up in the air under kits of ever newer and more aerodynamic design. Or on the ground receiving silver cups for skills in flying them. They featured first-person accounts of pioneering flights down mountains in the Alps or in Africa across lakes, rivers and seas. But occasionally — quite often, Paul had to admit — the magazines contained material that suggested the sport had its perils.

"Nineteen seventy-seven has been a bad year for fatal accidents and nasty non-fatals...." He read the reports conscientiously. You could learn much from the mistakes of others. He read about avoidable accidents, about the way the windspeed varies according to height, and followed the controversy about deployment systems and parachuting malfunctions.

Then Maura took to looking over the bleak obsequies.

"Listen to this one. 'The pilot took off in turbulent wind conditions. The glider stalled and impacted.' What exactly does that mean?"

"It means that an irresistible force met an immovable object. The ground. They use the same word about a wisdom tooth meeting another tooth."

" 'The pilot was dead of multiple injuries....' Oh, that's terrible! Here's another. 'This experienced pilot failed to maintain adequate airspeed.' "

"He made a mess of things. See how it says 'accident attributed to pilot error'?"

"Nearly all of them say that. He died anyway. I suppose you would never make that kind of mistake."

"Jesus, hang gliding is no more dangerous than riding a motor bike."

"Yes it is."

In the early days she came out and watched him, acting as hand maiden, holding helmets, altimeters, nose wires and wind gauges. Then she disappeared from the hillside, defeated by a combination of cold, boredom and finally fear as she watched her husband plunge into space. To give her credit, she persisted long enough to acquire a bit of knowledge about 360s, top landings, A-frames and B-bars. When she washed the dishes she'd look out of the kitchen window and assess wind strength and direction by watching washing on the line or smoke gushing out of suburban chimneys. She sat in the living room full of house plants with variegated leaves that looked like acne, and waited for his return. Or for bad news. The moment when she would be called upon to play the Home they Brought her Warrior Dead role. Her fears had been justified to a large extent by Gordon's death.

Still, she'd been pleased to come out here. He watched her sitting on the grass in the sun looking at an Atlas dodge around the target like a fly around a light bulb. He hoped she was enjoying herself.

"It's okay. At least, touch wood, I've got you intact. And it's nice being in France. But this . . ." She waved her hand. "Well, it's hardly a spectator sport."

He had to acknowledge that the bustling humanity around the landing area consisted very largely of people who were directly involved with flying. The organizers had some difficulty co-ordinating public enthusiasm. The take-off area just below St Hilaire and the landing ground near the river were two distinct places and it was not easy for those watching to link them with eye and mind.

The take-off was before a small crowd which might or might not be half-expecting something bad to happen as the men with wings slid off one by one into space. Following a few minutes circulating to gain height the pilot vanished from view. Only those who flew hang gliders themselves understood the choice and frustrations of flying different courses, catching or losing thermals and fighting with sink.

Like eventing with horses, competitive hang gliding was a sport that penalized the spectator. How could he appreciate the skills involved in compulsory figures performed out of sight? He was not going to be viewing the figure of eight around a pylon and variations of a slalom on the sky involving 360s. The chances were that all he would see would be the pilot heading for home, trying to control the inexorable descent of the glider as he made for the landing ground, avoiding the nearby field of ten-foot-high maize.

Worldwide there had only been three or four previous hang gliding championships. The organizers didn't know what to expect, teeming masses or empty grandstands. The competitors, selfish to a man, were not worried about whether or not the landing area was deserted. For them any non-flying activity centred around the two buffet *buvettes* that sold drinks and snacks. That was because of the heat — you simply had to replace lost liquid. Paul worked out that if you weren't drinking Pim's, it cost ten francs an hour in soft drinks and beers just to stay cool.

By the second day he had plenty of time to make this calculation because he was just standing around. Although his practice flight that first morning wasn't bad — he figured he'd flown better than several of the other guys — Henny told him he would continue to be reserve and not on the team. That meant he got no flying and he was on his own much of the time without even Maura to keep him company. After that first morning she decided to desert the flying area and concentrate her time taking Tony here and there.

By the middle of the week it appeared the two of them were enjoying themselves. She'd drive up in the evening and report on the way they had spent the day. She took Tony to various playgrounds — the French had beautiful playgrounds, so different from those at home. They went swimming — it was great, if expensive, with the special little pool for Tony to paddle in. She was getting used to the minibus. She drove right into Grenoble to do some shopping. She took Tony to the leisure park to enjoy the delights of the *Train du Far-West*, the *Mississippi Bâteau*, the Pony Ranch and the Water Carnival. Nine pounds, it worked out for a day's entertainment, but it was worth it. She couldn't be expected to stick around the site all the time.

That was precisely what Paul was doing. He became adept at stationing himself by the landing ground watching the gliders appear and assessing the performance of the triangular specks overhead.

He learnt something by noting the set figures and the 540-degree turns on the two parallel axes. He might be burned up with envy, but he found time to listen to competitors' experiences — how they did in duration, set duration and cross-country. Weather conditions were not favourable for cross-country because the thermal activity just did not allow for anything very adventurous. Flying tended to be confined to rock faces and the ridge, since there was little usable lift over the valley. For much of the time cross-country meant going down the ridge and back. The tasks favoured lift and drag ratio and sink; they were all downers, racing to the pylons and then achieving a spot target at the landing field. They did not benefit the Irish team.

At other times Paul would be at the take-off. Things began early each morning, and by eight o'clock the road leading to the landing field was clogged by vehicles with gliders on roof racks.

The activity was furious, gliders and pilots getting rigged and togged up in harness, announcements in French and English. "I a remind you that Class Five will commence with Pool One. . . ."

The system of pools was devised as a fair way of coping with the capricious nature of the weather conditions. Names were taken at random and computerized. Officials in yellow trousers studied a weather map. Other minor functionaries held two flags, one red, one white. The teams kept to themselves, huddled with their managers who held walkie talkies to their ears. Lantern-jawed Australians in green track suits, Americans in blue with writing on their chests: USA WORLD HANG GLIDING TEAM, neat little Frenchmen were all confident they would go well. The Irish lads were less assured.

Paul was grounded while others flew off one by one, circled and vanished towards the landing field. His job was to help the boys rig, check the forecasts and watch them disappear. He was like a dresser to actors. None of them were on form. He watched Johnny and Martin Macken claw down the side of the ridge, vainly making for the marking pylon, and he felt angrily that he could do better.

On the third day of the actual competition they awoke in thick mist. The whole valley below was blotted out by cloud. Teams gathered near the take-off area shivering in flight gear and track suits. It was not until eleven o'clock that the mist cleared to thin wisps of vapour and as these slowly vanished the pools began lining up. Paul rigged the Scorp more as a gesture of hope than anything. Then he gave a hand to rigging Gerry Lynch's Emu.

Henny came over from where he had been talking to officials. Paul waited instructions for some lousy job like driving down to the landing stage to describe landings and results through the walkie talkie.

"You rigged?" Henny asked. "Will you do wind dummy?"

"Sure." An errand boy begging for a flight. This job was to go and search out thermals — what they called bloomers — that came off the ricks and fields with monotonous regularity. Hardly today though, with the morning mist. He launched in what seemed an abysmal period of sink. Still, the heat was fierce

36

already and you never knew when and where thermals would reappear. Behind him the pools waited expectantly as he took off and circled above the high escarpments. Looking down he could see the little towns and far down the valley the gleam of a swimming pool. Was Maura stretched beside it? The only thermal he could find was weak and the sink was unending. He made the best of things and flew out and high from the ridge, banked and did a 360. He sailed along the ridge, doing another turn before heading down to the landing ground, feeling idiotically exhilarated.

Above him the pools took note of his progress, both by observing his flight and listening to his report over various managers' walkie talkies. The pilots began to do their tasks which were tempered by the sluggish air currents. In the Irish team Martin crashed on take-off and his Cyclone was a write-off.

Paul's pleasure at his own little flight soon wore off. He felt that as reserve one of his few privileges was being able to avoid dismal post mortems. He couldn't even manage that, but had to sit and listen to Henny nagging at Martin and complaining about the team's overall performance. Martin would be fortunate to end up in the first couple of hundred for the individual.

It seemed like a lifetime since Paul had imagined that there would be long solitary hours of flying when the teams weren't competing. Now he was expected to do his duty to his country.

"You can take my Scorp, if you like," he said dutifully.

Martin shook his head. "I've had enough. I'm off form. Can't get used to this Alpine flying. No way will I fly a strange kite."

After another hour's argument Henny said to Paul: "You can have a go."

No one on the team was thrilled. However well he flew he couldn't take Martin's place officially and put the team on the map. Having missed two days he could not accrue anything like enough points to make a dent in the individual. It was stupid to be excited. But when he saw Maura that evening he couldn't contain his enthusiasm. She must wait at the landing stage and see him come in. She seemed pleased enough, saying it would be great for Tony to see his Daddy flying for Ireland.

Next day he rigged at the take-off and waited in the pool with the rest of his group. He found two top Americans were flying against him. Perhaps he would do better than the German girl, although he knew she'd had a relatively good flight the day before.

Below beside the landing area Martin waited with the walkie talkie far out of sight. Up here Henny gave advice, checked and rechecked.

Paul watched a guy ahead of him flying an Emu launch himself and swoop downward, dragged by the helpless sink. Everyone watched and a lot of people swore. It was his bad luck that his chance should come in such conditions. Some pilots refused to fly when they saw sink like that, although refusal meant disqualification. Martin had been scared by the notion of suicidal plunge, which was why he had cried off and Paul was in his place. The first two pilots in front of him, the American whose name he didn't know, and the German girl, ran, pushed out, vainly scraped the edge of the cliff face and vanished. They had to resign themselves to a direct swoop down to the valley floor. They might as well have had parachutes on their backs as hang gliders. Then came the turn of the second American, Hank Matheson, a great flyer who seldom made a mistake. He did better. Trust him to find lift on a day like today, crafty bastard, although his flight was nothing to boast about.

Now it was Paul's turn. The official was waving him on with the white flag, his "*Quand tu veux!*" a hoarse, automatic refrain. A moment to concentrate, ignore the faces and cameras, hold her steady and rush down.

In spite of Matheson's performance that indicated something was about, Paul didn't expect anything in the way of lift. When he hit it, the force took him by surprise. His vario was bleeping, and looking down to where it was mounted on the control frame, he noticed a three up. He turned into the thermal which received him like a warm river. Instead of the feared turbulence, the kind of stuff that made struts creak and groan, the going was uncannily smooth. The altimeter needle was spinning, notching up height.

Luck was with him. *Vive le vol libre!* Wherever the thermal came from — probably from the face of the cliff — it was benefiting him while other pilots were going down like stones. Even Matheson's little hop had taken him down fast enough. Paul was going up. Below him the landscape shrunk and took on map contours. The broad arm of river dwindled to a skein, the gliders to coloured dots. He was on a level with the white mountains on the other side of the valley. Here was the whole Alpine panorama. It distracted him. He was still flying on min sink, and without wasting more time he turned for the two most distant pylons. You could chase how many you wanted to tackle.

The more pylons, the better the score. Five was maximum. They made some sort of formula added to or divided by the flight time to get a score. Each pylon rounded had a different value. In spite of the sink rate he would make for the farthest. He would have to fly six kilometres from take-off, finding lift along the way, twirling around the other designated pylons and then clawing back to the landing field.

Speed was demanded, and he appeared to be going fast enough. He did a 90-degree turn around the fourth pylon. Then, at the fifth, he banked as easily as a sailing ship going about and made for home. Here it was coming, the target area spread all over the ground, visible from a mile away. The ideal was to land squarely in the central orange blob on his feet without letting any part of the machine touch the ground. Birds did it, bees did it . . . how quickly the ground reached up, the vineyards, the strips of yellow wheat and the wide square of green which was maize. He didn't want to land there in the popcorn. But the Scorp was handling as if it was part of him.

A turn downwind, and there were the two stands, all the people, the limp windsock and the tents. He pushed out the bar and gained a little height. Christ, if he wasn't careful he could hit the judges' tent quite easily. Now things were happening fast. The green field, people watching, a sudden sound of waltz music from a loudspeaker. Hold it 30 feet up, 20. There was the circle and a glider hurrying away. A pilot from another pool. How had he done? Not as well as Paul. Ten feet away now, and then legs down from the harness. Hanging up corpse-like, losing height fast.

39

Then the first outer circle, the second and third, a strong flareout and he was standing on the bullseye.

Some applause drifted across from the stands. After he had scuttled out of the target area he began noticing people. The Aussie pilots who shared the nextdoor *gite* at the top of the hill. The Englishmen who struggled so earnestly to be top. The insufferable French. The soldier who arrived to take his glider up on the military lorry. Those Almutis again, and Leila waving towards the rainbow colours of his Scorp. Here was Martin, and with him Ann Brennan.

"Good man," Martin was saying. "You'll get maximum points. Pity you're not in line for the individual."

Paul felt really pleased and more so when Ann held up the walkie talkie and Henny's voice came over. "Congratulations, Paul." Crackle, crackle. "Good work. The best yet." Henny was an old fool, but the praise was good. It was worth it, worth coming to France and he wouldn't exchange that flight for anything.

"Where's Maura?"

"She went back," Ann said. "Tony was a bit fretful. I think sunburn's the problem. At any rate, Maura thought it would be best to take him back to Theys."

When he'd told her about being on the team she had seemed pleased enough. And then she hadn't even waited the few minutes for his flight. By now he knew well enough that this wasn't her scene, but even she must have recognized the importance of the last quarter of an hour.

It was funny how let down he felt. He would go back to St Hilaire and get a cheer from Henny and receive more congratulations. He wouldn't wait around here lingering in this hot stage with a white-topped background of mountains.

He saw the bus that took competitors up to St Hilaire and felt a revulsion from sitting among hearties all talking competition. He could go back by *funiculaire*. He wasn't wearing a shirt, the day was so hot, but he had his pass in his shorts, together with a few francs. The idea had been to treat Maura and Tony at the *buvettes* after his flight. To hell with that.

He strode off down the dusty lane leading from the landing field which was flanked by six-foot-high maize. In the distance he could see descending specks. Other *delta planeurs* were using another field as a landing ground. . . *Dégueulez, mes amis*, and good luck to you. . . *Dégueuler*, the word they used for sink, meant literally to vomit.

At the main road a gendarme directed traffic. Sightseers craned out of car windows to spot the coloured dots over their heads. He came to the small *caisse* outside the *funiculaire* and showed his pass with its mug shot. (The New Zealand boys had a caper and produced mug shots of their behinds. Ho, ho!)

He walked up to the main building with its pitched Alpine roof and French flag, red, white and blue. He sat on a hard bench with other passengers looking at the *plan de situation* and a framed piece of cable that had presumably snapped off at some time or another. Or was it there on display to prove how strong cables for the funicular were? He couldn't read what it said. He glanced around at his fellow travellers — a couple of locals and several competitors. In winter their place would be taken by skiers. There was a girl . . . oh, God, not her again. Sexy, in spite of the beaky face. He ought to know. Did she have a crush on him? All week when he had been acting the spectator he had noticed her and her friends. He had greeted her the odd time, saying Hi, that was all. Forget about Lacken and the slopes of the Sugarloaf.

Chapter Four

THE FUNICULAR ARRIVED. He picked up his flight deck and helmet and made his way towards the three yellow, old-fashioned compartments pretending not to see her. He followed behind a couple of Japanese. This was his first time in the funicular. He'd read in a blurb that the gradient was the steepest in Europe. So that meant that when the girl took the seat opposite she was almost vertically above his head. A bell rang and the driver slid the doors shut. She was smiling at him.

"A great day for the Irish," she said.

"Huh?"

"I was watching your flight. So were my friends. That was a fine precision landing you made."

Maybe he had helped put Ireland on the map. It might take less explaining in future around these parts to get the message of Irish nationality across. You had to mention Belfast, bang, bang! Ireland was a member of the EEC and yet the amount of people in Europe who knew nothing about it was legion. More knew about Iceland. It was different, he conceded, if you got hold of a Gaelic music freak.

The funicular gave a jerk and with another ring of the bell pulled forward and began to move up steeply. Green trees, brown forest, paths and rocks and if you looked back, a wide view of the Isère valley. Beside him a Japanese switched on his vario and the bleep-punctuated conversation.

"Your country got a team competing?"

She laughed sourly. "My poor country has no time for frivolities."

"But your friend ... your old friend ... the one who died ..."

"My husband."

"Oh? Well, Gordon said he was terrific. Great flier. One of the best."

"Gordon?"

"My friend . . . who got killed too."

"Of course." They were quiet. Big sad coincidence. People like Maura would say it wasn't coincidence at all, that whenever two or three hang gliders gathered together they would have friends or associates who had been pilots and were now dead, or at best in wheel chairs. Not true at all — in Ireland, for instance, there had been less than half a dozen fatal accidents. Pity one of them had to be Gordon.

The funicular stopped on the double track just before entering the tunnel. Its companion, coming the other way, had precedence. They waited for it to descend, bringing down another three carriages with tourists on their way to the landing field.

"It is strange meeting again," she said.

"You are interested in hang gliding. This is a get-together of all the talent. Which includes me."

"It is something like destiny."

Oh, come on . . . that was rich. Crude thoughts came into his mind. A bit soon after the death of the loved one. Would he have had her that time on the Sugarloaf if he had known she was married? Maybe she wasn't married then. It seemed she wanted more, at any rate. She must be chasing him. The element of coincidence in their meeting was reinforced by his presence on this funicular, since in the ordinary way he would have taken the lorry. But had she followed him? They were in the tunnel now, and speech was almost impossible. The only clear sound was made by the vario the Jap was handling. Japs were mad keen on hang gliding. They gave it the earnest attention they gave to everything they undertook. They flew doggedly, although they were not yet in world class. Perhaps they never would be. Wrong temperament.

The train arrived at the small red-roofed station below St Hilaire.

"How about a drink?" he found himself saying. He should be chasing up Henny. She was walking beside him. He must be mad. Tiny little thing, bird-sized. She came scarcely up to his shoulder. Head down. Remembering Ireland. Couldn't see if she was blushing.

43

They walked through the village glazed by the sun. Past the small church and post office and the war memorial. *Le Commune de St Hilaire du Touvet et ses enfants morts pour la patrie.* A café with chairs outside in shade. One of the few places around unconnected with hang gliding.

In the distance they could hear the sound of loudspeakers.

"Sure?" She only wanted a *citron pressé*. He ordered a cold beer for himself. Six francs. Nearly another pound gone. He moved his chair into sunshine and let the sun beat on his chest. He was prepared for an exchange of sexual banter. But you could not say she was flirtatious. All she could talk about was hang gliding. They discussed his Scorp and its performance. Again she congratulated him on his landing. She had seen it from near the judges' tent.

"You can always land like that?"

"No." Even Paul could not pretend. But he droned on a bit about his good co-ordination and the difficulties in flaring out so that your feet touched the exact spot in the target zone.

"I've got to like precision landing and competitive flying. You could call me an all-rounder."

"Do you mind if I take notes? For my friend?"

"Your friend?" He felt absurdly disappointed.

"He writes for an Arabic magazine." She said a name which sounded like she was clearing her throat. "He has been writing articles about brave sports. The ones that require courage. Climbing, motor racing."

"Is that a fact?"

She hesitated. "My husband was his brother."

"About hang gliding . . . your friend could ask plenty of guys around here who are better than me."

But he was handy. She took some detailed notes, pumping him about his experience over the years. He talked freely. Told her how he had got interested in cross-country.

"I learned to fly on a Cloudbase. Good beginner's kite. Then I bought a Super Scorpion. English kite. It changed my whole concept of flying. Like riding a racehorse after a carthorse. I was one of the first in Ireland to get interested in cross-country. When I started most pilots were still at the stage of gaining confidence

44

about top landings. Cross-country was at a rudimentary stage."

He told her how he began from the Sugarloaf — blush — casting around, hooking thermals that had him gliding off in the direction of the Dublin suburbs. That soon palled. He became obsessed with pioneering new sites. He began with flights at Achill Island. Then he toured the country to throw himself off high spots in Sligo, Clare, West Cork and other places where cliffs and mountain ridges were high and far from any roads.

He learned the mysteries of thermal-soaring when the sun warmed the ground which in turn warmed the air above and sent a glider swooping upwards. He learned the combination of ridge-soaring and using thermals which enabled him to move considerable distances.

He heard himself boasting about his string of good flights, like the one in West Cork that carried him from Mount Gabriel towards Roaring Water Bay, and the fantastic ridge-soaring he achieved down the Maamturks and the Slieve Miskish.

He told her about his trips to Crossmaglen. It had been easy the first time, flying in the north of Ireland. He had ignored paramilitaries and British army alike. Saracens roared down the narrow northern roads without taking a blind bit of notice of the van with the southern number, and the hang glider on top. He had a successful flight — there is great lift and take-off among the hills of Armagh.

He went up again a few weeks later. He was ridge-soaring quietly by himself when he was buzzed by an angry helicopter.

"I never had such a scare in my life. When I got down some RIC men came rushing up in a Land Rover and started firing questions at me. It turned out that the Secretary of State was visiting some army units around there and they were afraid I'd thought up an unusual way of assassinating him."

He laughed at the memory and she joined in. She wasn't great on humour. "Another beer? No, you are my guest." A waiter came over. "Perhaps a little cognac?"

"Beer will be fine." He should be getting home to Henny. But there wouldn't be another flight for him today if the usual weather pattern in these mountains continued its leisurely course. It was as if nature took a siesta each day. He glanced at his watch.

45

Twelve. Perhaps he should give Maura a ring.

This girl Leila was asking him about Lacken Lift.

"Now that Mr Waters is dead will you continue to run the school?"

"No. It has to be wound up. I haven't the money to keep it going. I couldn't give up my job and do the hang gliding bit full time."

"You are sorry? Naturally about the death of your friend. But also because you have to close the school?"

He shrugged. "Of course I'm sorry. I'm like every hang gliding pilot. They all have this dream of making a living from it. But hang gliding is a luxury sport — something that doesn't turn out to be a great money-spinner during a recession. And I have a wife and child."

He checked the time again. "I'd best be off . . ."

"Myself also. I'll be going down by *funiculaire*." She was making no attempt to disguise the fact that she had been following him.

He walked with her towards the station. She was still nattering about hang gliding. They passed the gendarmerie where four gendarmes in navy trousers and light-blue shirts laced with white revolver straps sat outside in the sun.

She said suddenly: "Remember flying double harness?"

It was he who blushed. "Yes, I remember."

She put her hand on his arm.

"Paul. You know what would be good. To take a flight once again. In double harness. Just for the memory of that time in Ireland."

He was confused by the *double entendre*, lost in a haze of sexual imagery. Then he remembered you could hire a glider up here which had a dual flight harness. Nothing to do with the competition. Quite a lot of the pilots took their girlfriends up just for the crack.

"Maybe tomorrow." The wind was dying. He had to get to Henny. Phone Maura. A flight in the double harness could cost a hell of a lot.

But she wanted now. The take-off was just over there. Please Paul, for old memories. He was a fool to be so easily persuaded. What the hell. She wouldn't let him pay.

Soon they were partners at the ramp which was almost perpendicular in its lead down into space. Two of them running very hard, her arm around his shoulders. He had never flown this way with Maura. He pushed out the frame when flying speed was achieved. Then that lovely woosh! and they were airborne.

Flying conditions were lousy. "Look at the wind socket. It's against us. We're flying in a miserable tail wind."

She said nothing, sitting beside him, her legs out, feet up like a child on a swing. Her small size made up to some extent for the ungainliness of the flight. Dual harness was always a bit of a mess, and they moved with as much grace as if they were in a box kite.

They swooped down slowly towards the landing ground, the other one, well away from the competition area. The actual flying was lousy, but he found he had been enjoying himself. Little groups of spectators were standing around as they came in. Very different from that other landing in Wicklow. There were her pals. Almutis. Funny how they were here and not where the competitors were landing. She said a quick goodbye and went over to them without offering to introduce him. Curious way of passing a succession of hot days, watching hang gliders come down. Especially when one of them had died like that.

Still, here he was himself only a month after Gordon's death. He had a sudden vision of how Gordon's Cyclone had folded as if it had been shot and plummeted down 600 feet like a bluebottle sprayed with fly killer. Icarus flew too near the sun. This was more or less what Gordon did, although he didn't mean to defy the gods, only to travel on a fast updraft. The Cyclone hit turbulence, a faster gust of wind like a mini-hurricane that caused it to break up.

Paul shook off the gloomy memory, so discordant with the bright holiday atmosphere imparted by the colourful gliders all around him. He said goodbye to Leila and her friends and hitched a lift back up in an army lorry. Henny was in a temper because Paul hadn't shown up until then. How was he to know that he had not been selected to fly in another pool that day? As it happened he hadn't. But that was not the point . . . no sense of responsibility.

47

He drifted off and found Maura and Tony at last. They had been so far out of his mind that he had forgotten his anger towards her. He stayed with them the rest of the day, and even had a swim. He didn't nag her about not being there to see him that morning. He felt good about his two flights. Strangely, he thought less about his outstanding performance that morning than the clumsy descent he had made with Leila.

Maura got Madame at the *pension* to babysit and Paul took her to a small restaurant in St Hilaire. The meal, less expensive than he feared, wasn't bad. You felt you had your money's worth, even if the soft little steak was no bigger than a doughnut and the cheese platter smelt of dirty feet.

Maura was wearing a summer dress she had made herself. The peacock blue was a bit bright, but it made a contrast to her frizzy mass of red hair. Men either love or hate foxy hair like that. Plenty of heads turned and looked at her, which made Paul feel good. They drank a bottle of red wine and ended up with cognac and cherry brandy. The evening ended early. Madame would be impatient. You couldn't trust Tony not to act up. Paul toyed with the idea of going back with her, but it wouldn't be much fun. The two of them sharing the bedroom with the child — quiet Tony! — and you couldn't guarantee she'd be all that relaxed. And Henny would make a fuss if the boys on the team didn't return to bachelor quarters.

In the end he gave her a kiss and she drove off happy enough. He wandered back to the *gite* where a roaring party was going on. Maura loved parties and she had missed them all. They had taken place most nights. Maybe she wouldn't care to be mingling with these overgrown schoolboys swilling beer and getting into fights.

This evening's celebrants were the neighbouring Australians who welcomed Paul like a lost brother. He chattered and caught up with news. A West German was now ahead in the individual and the feeling was that neither the fancied French nor the English had a chance of beating him. But the French would win the team championship. There wasn't much chance that the English would sneak up on them.

"Cocky bastards, those Brits."

"Funny thing . . . you wouldn't normally think of the British as patriotic."

"Quite the opposite, always running down the country, you hear them at it all the time. Then all of a sudden they'll come out all red, white and blue."

"Like my mother-in-law's begonias. Dead all winter, and then in no time there's a display of loud colours."

"They ought to wear begonias instead of poppies on Remembrance Sunday."

An American in a Fledgling had catapulted over the cliff without being hurt. The crazy Pole had been disqualified at last. This character's home-made glider, steered with a giant rudder, consistently overflew its target. It had been one of the big jokes of the competition, like the Yorkshire terrier belonging to a Parisian hairdresser that flew in a special harness wearing red goggles. The Polish Albatross was so unmanageable that nearly every flight ended up in the maize. Today he had gone too far and crashed into the first-aid tent.

There were other Poles beside the Popcorn Kid at the competition. Was their presence an indication of the independence of Polish thinking?

"No other Eastern bloc country has sent a team."

"Wait a minute, how about the Yugoslavs?"

"They hardly count as Eastern bloc. They are individualists too, if you like."

Paul said: "There's plenty of Russian hang glider pilots. I've read there are something like three thousand."

"They're officially discouraged," said one of the Englishmen. "If the Soviet state sanctioned hang gliding and gave it government support, Russians would be here competing and most likely winning."

"So these three thousand Russians are doing their own thing and leaping off mountains in the Urals and Caucasus?"

"Just like the Poles, all matchbox gliders and mackintosh wings."

Paul took more wine. He'd always thought Aussies were beer drinkers. "Typical of the conservative socialist mentality to disapprove."

49

"You're right, sport. Hang gliding requires too much of what's unorthodox. Commies have no imagination."

"Here's to imagination. Hurry with the corkscrew, Stan." Paul was beginning to enjoy the usual preparation for a day's competition.

Someone clapped him on his sunburnt back. Ken? Barrie? Stan? No, this one must be Simon. The story went that down under Simon was considered a pooftah name and this guy had taken up hang gliding to improve his macho image.

"Saw you flying today. Great stuff. If it was wartime I'd hire you as a carrier pigeon." He was standing half-naked, a beer can in his hand.

"Fosters. Brought a supply over from London. Sorry, can't offer you any."

"I'll stick with the wine, thanks."

It turned out that this Simon had known Gordon in New South Wales.

"Too bad him going like that. It happens to lots of the good guys. He was among the first. You should have seen the hang glider he built himself. Years ago. Seventy-one? Seventy-two? ... thereabouts. Compared to it Popcorn Pete's outfit is like a Sigma."

They drank some more. "You're a good man, Paul. ... Can't stand Poms but Micks are fine. ..."

They went outside. An Alpine breeze had got up.

"How about a flight?"

"You sh ... should wait half an hour to get used to the darkness."

"Darkness? This isn't dark."

"Night vision ... chemical changes ... rods and cones ..."

"Fuck rods and cones ... wear a pair of red goggles ..."

"Haven't got red goggles ..."

Just the two of them went hang gliding.

Paul returned to the *gite* and took a torch out of the front of Henny's Volvo. He went and selected a glider as if it was a log of wood out of the pile belonging to the Irish team. He lugged it over to the launching site about three quarters of a mile away. Never felt the weight. He rigged it by torch. A Cherokee ... must belong to Joe. He should check it, not treat it as if he was putting up a tent. Where was that Simon? He had disappeared. Lousy Aussie. Paul wasn't going to fly on his own. Not in a lousy Cherokee. Disappeared completely. Then he heard a voice cut over the valley.

> "Twas a cold winter's night,
> There was snow on the ground,
> O'Leary was closing the bar . . ."

Darkish. Stars, though. Simon was able to see okay. Paul was able to see okay. Quite okay. He ran down the shute whose outlines he could dimly make out. "Whee!" Lift. Of course there was lift. It was the first time he had ever flown in the Alps without being apprehensive.

He could hear the disembodied voice ringing out in the dark air. Like an owl singing.

> "Her mother never told her
> The things that a young girl should know . . ."

He could sing too. Better than any Aussie bastard.

> "My name is O'Hanlon
> I'm just turned sixteen . . ."

They were doing a simple descent. They needed no navigation lights. They wouldn't be bumping into each other. Paul concentrated more on singing than on flying.

> "I gave up my boyhood
> To drill and to train . . ."

And the other fellow was roaring out as well.

> "Remember your sisters and mothers, boys . . ."

Paul drowned him out.

> "Six countries are under
> John Bull's tyranny . . ."

It took all the verses of "The Patriot Game" to help him land somewhere down in the valley in the darkness. He came in as smooth as a duck on a pond. Trouble was he came in right in the middle of the maize. A stir and a wrestle and then he was up to the eyes in unharvested agricultural produce.

He shouted, "*Les agriculteurs entretiennent la nature! Respectez leur travail!*" He was quoting from the handout passed around by the official committee. How the hell could you respect any farmer's labour if it so happened you were messing up your landing?

The Cherokee was the worse for wear. A couple of broken leading edges. He himself was fine. Nothing wrong at all. Face a bit scratched. No sign of Simon.

Trampling through the maize carrying the dismembered Cherokee wasn't easy. It took him a long time. He ended up just beside the target area where he had landed during the day. Amazing how many people could gather in the middle of the night to await his appearance — a gendarme, no doubt an *agriculteur* or two, officious Frenchmen all shouting at him.

He couldn't remember much. French tirades ringing in his ears. When he shaved he noticed his face was scratched. It was nearly noon as he sauntered out of the *gite*. They must have left him to sleep off the fumes of last night. He walked down to the take-off site where the first thing he saw was Henny striding towards him accompanied by two members of the committee and an interpreter.

Everyone was excited. Paul had listened to much of this stuff last night without understanding it. He might think that disgraceful episode was inoffensive. *Au contraire*. Rules. He had broken rules. He had put people's lives at risk. He had wantonly destroyed property. Flying at night among electric pylons was, of course, *absoluement interdit*. And of course he must know that this was so, it was right here in the rule book. And the dictates of common sense must tell him in his ear that he had disgraced his country. The officials shouted, the interpreter interpreted, crisp and low, and Henny echoed. Then, when everyone had sprayed Paul with saliva, Henny dismissed the Frenchmen. "*Bien . . . assez . . . je lui parle . . .*" Had he picked up any other French during the week? The officials and the interpreter retreated.

Henny took him by the arm. "You've got us into a load of trouble. You'll have to accept disqualification."

"You might have stood up for me better."

"I've been arguing for over half an hour, for Christ's sake. They didn't like it. They're not prepared to forgive or forget."

"You could have told them I was the best guy on the team."

"Listen, Paul, stop thinking that one flight you made was unique. A lucky thermal and one spot-on landing doesn't make you world champ. It's your own fault. Won't take advice, let alone orders. You've always been too much of an individualist. That's why I hesitated to pick you in the first place."

"All right. I get the message. Hope the team puts up a better performance than I did." Forget about the one flight that gave a little lustre to Ireland's reputation.

"I'm really sorry, Paul. And that's God's truth." And that was his only word of regret before he stomped off to do his hen and ducklings act with the rest of the team.

Paul stood round the take-off stage watching the launches. For the first time in the competition conditions were perfect, with the right wind for instant lift. He felt angry. He'd like to kick Henny off the limestone precipice.

As he watched, people came up and he received sympathy like a deposed monarch. Simon had a word, looking sheepish.

"Did you get the boot as well?" Paul asked him.

"They never found me out. My buddies came down and picked me out of the hay. Lucky I landed close to the road."

Why hadn't he pals like that? "Did you hurt yourself?"

"Ankles a bit sore. Nothing to stop me flying. The Lord helps fools and drunkards like us, eh sport?"

"He's helped you a hell of a lot more than He's helped me!"

Later Simon took off in a pool that included a couple of the best — an Englishman and a Frenchman set to be winners. By contrast Simon's performance was poor. He didn't take advantage of the lift, and last seen, trotting out of sight on some task involving zig-zagging round a given point, didn't look as if he was going to do much for the Australian team.

Paul knew he could have flown better. But he had flown his last flight at St Hilaire du Touvet. The last carefree quarter of an hour. No more dropping towards the maize. No more flights like yesterday.

He'd go elsewhere. Henny didn't rule. He could get great hang gliding at other sites — Chamrose, De Moucherotte. . . . He could go further afield . . . Chamonix, Chambéry, with its view over the lake to Aix les Bains. Half a day's drive away. He had been hearing about these places all week. Good thermals grew from them like mushrooms. Or he could go a little further, to Mont Lachènes. You could see the Mediterranean sprawl from there. Maura could go down with Tony to the sea and take part in the great bake while Paul went flying. . . .

The snag to any plan about floating above French mountains was money. Exchange and expenses. Everything was crazily expensive and there wasn't much left out of the budget. He supposed he could stay on across the valley. If he wanted to fly it would mean day trips in the minibus. Expense was terrible. The minibus cried out thirsty! thirsty! most of the time. Even with the concessionary coupons moving was costing. And the system of autoroutes with their plastic buckets into which you threw francs — what a racket!

He had promised Maura a day in Paris. Maura was enjoying herself here. She was not going to be pleased when she heard.

Absently he received commiserations from an Englishman and then watched him launch confidently into a thermal that would help him in a magnificent task. Where was Maura? No doubt off to the swimming pool with Tony.

Here was Leila approaching him again. To hell with the woman. Naughty Leila, the hang gliding groupie. There were plenty like her among the continental teams, young women who were not all sweethearts and wives. Like the motor racing circuit, girls going after sexy dare devils. The difference was that everyone associated with hang gliding was a little less glamorous, a little more scruffy.

He could do without Leila's condolences. Had someone shouted the news from a white-topped mountain?

But he found himself seeking her sympathy. "Flung off the team. Indiscipline." He told her about the unfairness.

"Is this your first experience of flying by night?"

"Oh no, I've done it plenty of times back home."

"How do you see in the darkness?"

54

"There's no real problem if you know what to do. You have to wait around for half an hour before you set off. You wait for the cells at the back of the eye to adjust to the dark."

She seemed to know something about them. Rods and cones. Cones clustering near the centre of the eye to pick up colour. Rods at the edge of the eye picking up black and white images. They were the lads responsible for night vision — what there is of it. You could pep them up with vitamin pills. You look a little to one side at night as the rods pick images out of the darkness. You have to be careful that a glare of light like headlights from a passing car didn't destroy in a moment an hour's adjustment to night vision.

"You waited last night for the chemical changes that occur to the sight?"

He grinned. "Not exactly."

"You just flew off into the darkness."

"There were a couple of stars." Curious how it reminded him of the very first night flight he had ever taken. Must have been a couple of years back. He had been pissed then, just like yesterday. He had been with a couple of guys on Mount Leinster. They had been flying all day and retired to the Angler's Rest at Bunclody in the County Wexford. The pub closed and they found themselves in the cold night air.

"Grand moon."

"Visibility like daylight ..."

They had read a ventimeter by torchlight.

"South-west, steady, twelve or thirteen ... that would make it about eighteen knots up there. How about it?"

Some reckoned it was time to go home but four of them had rushed to their cars and driven back to Mount Leinster. Like last night with Simon. Same feeling. The rounds they'd downed gave an edge to their madness. Very solemnly they had drawn lots with batons for the men who wouldn't fly but would go down and collect the others after they had finished their flight. (It was Johnny Hayes and he had seemed relieved.) Then the other three rigged their kits by car headlights. No proper inspection. Like last night. He remembered how they had run off the slope, not exactly into darkness, but into something very different from daylight, a

55

faint odd light that made every angle a bit wrong. He recalled those few minutes of silence under a clear moon which shone down on frost-whitened fields. Then the series of chaotic bottom landings in the deceptive moonlight. They had been lucky to escape without so much as a twisted ankle.

After that he had taken to night flying. He did it properly, of course. Sober. Waited half an hour. Took off into the night sky. Moving through darkness afforded a special excitement. Something to do with the mystery and the silence, or perhaps it was merely that the air at night was smoother, with less turbulence, and the wind did not gust to the same degree as it did by day. Then there was that eerie element of danger. He flew from places he was familiar with by daylight, making sure each time that he was not plunging towards electric pylons.

Trying to explain the exhilaration to Leila he became eloquent. She listened as he described how frost, snow and moonlight were his allies. (He didn't tell her how he crept out of the marriage bed those winter nights to drive out to the mountains.) Winter flying in the cold, in danger, induced a good feeling when the surge of adrenalin obscured the chill and tiredness.

"Do you take any of the standard precautions? Flare paths? Illumination by car headlights?"

Surprising how much she knew about hang gliding. He had to admit he did not, nor did he carry glider lighting, the five candels you are supposed to show in all directions if you are flying by night.

"In France or Switzerland you would be arrested."

"I probably would be in Ireland if anyone saw me." Some of his landings had been fairly hairy. Without friends to light up a mini-landing strip he had blundered into a bog, once a river and once a rock, nearly breaking himself up.

Questions, questions. She went on. Nosey bitch. You will be returning to Ireland? Spying on him all week. He was fed up. He made to move off. "I have to go . . . sorry . . . have a hell of a lot of things to deal with."

"A moment, Paul." She was handing him a card. None of these people seemed able to move about without dealing out little pieces of cardboard. He had collected nearly a dozen from

French and German pilots who were trying to make a living from the usual individual hang gliding activities, like building their own gliders or starting their own schools, God help them.

The card she gave him seemed similar to the rest, representing one more little outfit trying to take advantage of a pastime that was growing in popularity. A silhouette of a hang glider. *Alouette et Cie. Manufacture de Cerfs Volants.* Growing opportunities for business. Three and a half thousand pilots in France to be catered for. Eighty thousand throughout the world. All set to flying heavier-than-air fixed-wing gliders capable of being carried, foot-launched and landed by the energy and use of the pilot's legs. Paul knew the official definition of a hang glider approved at the International Hang Gliding Commission in June 1975.

"My brother-in-law runs this firm."

"Does he fly?" They didn't look like fliers, the group of picnickers he associated with her.

"Oh yes. Not, of course, to anything like your standard."

The men who actually made money out of hang gliding were few and far between. It was nearly every pilot's dream. It had been his own ambition, sadly knocked by the demise of Lacken Lift. A few managed to struggle along just for the love of flying. Or just possibly they were beginners. Francis Melvin Rogallo hadn't been known as a flyer, merely as an engineer associated with NASA.

"We are bringing out a new type of hang glider." Like everyone else — every week someone produced a glider which put up a better performance. Third generation they called kites like his Super Scorp. Give a few more years and a few more experiments with aerodynamics and by 1984 hang gliders would really fly like birds. They would be fifth generation by then, with pushed-out wing space that could perform like a bird on low wind, say eight or nine knots. But such hang gliders would not emanate from a little set-up like Alouette et Cie.

"We have the prototype." They all thought of themselves as mini-Rogallos. "We are looking for good pilots to try it out. Would you be interested?"

She's crazy. Why pick on him when France was full of pilots

burning for that sort of work? Very likely she was making a pass at him again. He must not feel flattered.

"Faisal has been canvassing pilots all week. He would like to consider you. He was impressed by your performance."

"Is that a fact?"

"I have written on the card. Here ... this is a restaurant in Grenoble — in the old town, near the river. You'll find it without trouble. If you are interested I will be there this evening with my brother-in-law. We could discuss possibilities."

"Don't expect me ... I've too much on my mind."

She went off leaving him examining the card. What to make of that? It sent him into an instant daydream. He imagined leaving Correy and Sheridan and coming to work in Europe. The job at home wasn't bad. It supported his little family at a time of economic recession. It gave him time to fly at weekends and on summer evenings. He shouldn't want more. More flights, each an individual unrepeatable experience. A good or bad trip, literally. He remembered how when he first bought the Scorpion he thought of it as Lucy — Lucy in the sky with diamonds.

An outfit something like Lacken Lift flying forever in the Alps. Above snow mountains. He wouldn't go back to Ireland. He'd heard EEC regulations would allow him to work in France. Maura would settle down here somehow. Tony would go to a French school, become bilingual. Was there any possibility in it? He didn't think Maura would care for the idea.

Where the hell was she?

The sun was stifling when he made his way back to the *gite*. Joe was inside. He had acquired some beer and handed Paul a bottle in silence.

"Sorry," Paul said. He meant sorry about the Cherokee.

"Okay. We've got it fairly well patched up." Joe had spent the morning running round looking for spares. He had missed a flight, and Paul felt bad, since he was so obviously doing the decent. But there was no doubt he felt sore. The silences grew longer and longer as they sipped the beer. In the end Paul lay down on his bunk and closed his eyes. His head ached, his ankle was sore and his face was scratched. He thought a bit about Alouette et Cie.

He woke to the depression a siesta can bring on a hot afternoon. Joe was asleep in the adjoining bunk, snoring gently, the way he had kept people awake over the past week.

Tea. Boil water in a saucepan and add a teabag. Mix in a heaped spoon of Marvel. He heard the noise of a vehicle driving up and peered out to see the minibus. He must owe money on it to the hire purchase people.

Maura was in a fury; Tony trailed after her snivelling from his cold. Too much paddling in the swimming pool. When Maura launched into a row, Joe woke and listened to the argument, so that they went outside to continue fighting like a couple of cats rolling out of a barn. The shame of it. She had heard all about it of course. Ann had told her what had happened. Everyone knew about it and sniggered. The ruined holiday. He tried to quieten her down.

"We can stay on for a few days." He would hang around until the championships were over and everyone went home. Just for her. They could even stop the day in Paris like they had planned. While they were here they could do things together with Tony. They might spend another day at the safari park. Or go in a *boule* from Grenoble, one of those lifts like giant Christmas tree balls, and get wafted up the mountain. Or a day's window shopping.

He was trying to be reasonable, but she got angrier. Once again she came second best to hang gliding. She slammed into the minibus, picking up a yelling Tony. Nothing had been decided about today, tomorrow, any time, as she drove off.

To hell with her. The holiday accompanying the hang gliding championships had been a grand idea. It was meant in part of assuage some of the guilt he felt about his obsession with hang gliding. She had been keen. They hadn't had a bad time up until now, had they? She had to realize that he had to concentrate on competition. And then all the stuff about golfers' widows being one thing, hang gliders' widows another. He had done his best to arrange for her to have a good time. Last night had been unfortunate, but she might have shown a little understanding.

Had she gone back to the *pension*? Would he chase her up? The thought of another party in one of these little chalets nauseated him. It would be an early night for the Brits in any case and tomorrow some sort of celebration after the final decisions had been made.

He had the choice of facing another evening with the boys or getting hold of Maura, begging pardon and taking her out for another sweet little meal.

He went over to the bar and obtained a couple of *jetons* to ring the *pension*. Madame answered. She did not speak English, but his French was up to understanding that *Madame Mooney n'était pas ici*. He bought himself a beer. He'd ring again in ten minutes. The time was nearly six. Most likely she was giving Tony chicken and chips some place.

The Aussies sat at a table on the balcony and greeted him with back slaps.

"We're going to Grenoble for a spot of fun. Like to come?"

They were off in half an hour. He went back to the *gite*, thankful to find it empty. He showered and shaved and then splashed his face with Henny's Tabac. He borrowed Joe's jacket supplied by Griffins. He felt in the front pocket and found a 50-franc note. He'd pay it back sometime. After a little hesitation he searched in his shorts. In the right-hand pocket he found the crumpled card that Leila had given him.

He rang the *pension* once more. Still Madame Mooney had not returned.

Chapter Five

THE VAN WITH the sticker showing the Southern Cross roared down the road beside the Isère. Inside Paul tried to disguise his irritation. They were nice enough lads, but noisy. He could visualize the evening's programme beginning with them all entering some smartish restaurant and doing imitations of frogs — hop, hop, croak, croak — in order to get frogs' legs served to them.

When they parked in the centre of Grenoble near the Rue Stalingrad and disembarked with a passable imitation of commandos landing on a beach, Paul edged away. In a minute he found himself alone as distant Aussie voices boomed in the distance. There would be a problem getting back to St Hilaire.

He consulted Leila's card, struggling to figure out where the Rue de l'Arte could be. It didn't help that he had no map. Or that he had assumed the address she had given him would be located in an area more slick than the maze of back streets where he found himself wandering.

The Rue de l'Arte turned out to be an alley between two lines of old four-storeyed houses covered with peeling plaster and paint. He passed a row of little shops which included a sex shop called La Boutique de O. Two men were studying the display in the small window. There was a seedy restaurant a few doors up. Could it be the place? Chez Mamoud. He consulted the card. Ethnic. That figured. Really grubby-looking with a bead curtain. Not the sort of place the Aussies would be seeking out. They would be bouncing into something that looked obviously French. Hand-written incomprehensible menu in the window, copper saucepans on the walls. One thing Paul really hated was red check table cloths.

Nothing like that here. For a start there were no customers. A small dark man with a drooping moustache came out from behind a little bar. Uncertainly Paul held out Leila's card which made the man clap his hands to summon a pregnant girl with bright Titian hair. She sauntered out of a kitchen at the back of the bar and wiped the surface of a table. A bow and a slanted hand indicated that Paul was to sit; a Pernod in a thick fluted glass on a white saucer, that he was to wait.

"Madame Faroon arrive bientôt . . ."

Paul sipped the fiery peppermint, staring at framed pieces of Arabic writing and a photograph showing the dead Algerian leader, President Boumedienne. The man went over to a large glittering object which appeared to be an old-fashioned jukebox with knobs and records. There was a difference, a modern development in the large glass screen on top. When a record was put on, it lit up and showed two ladies in glittering evening dresses shaking their hips. The music was loud and wailing.

He listened and watched the undulating action on the screen. Another tune, a different pair of dancers. Customers began coming in and the pregnant redhead went round taking chairs off tables. The customers all seemed to be Arab apart from one black man. Paul was given another Pernod.

When Leila entered she greeted two old moustached men with napkins tucked into their chins, and then came over to where he was sitting. Apologies. What must you think of me, etcetera.

"That's okay . . . it was hardly a firm date."

"However, I was expecting you to come."

"I nearly didn't." There was no sign of any sort of business associate with her.

"Your wife is not with you?"

"No . . . it's difficult with Tony."

She ordered wine, a couple of bottles labelled Abbas Rahmin. Food was brought in by the redhead, mutton stew on top of sago.

"Couscous." He thought wistfully of the celebrating Aussies. He managed to get the muck down with the help of little dishes of searingly hot chutney. The wine could barely be tasted. He was gulping it like water.

Talk was not easy, since they had to pitch their voices against the music. She had a way of being distracted by the action pictures, watching them as she poked her fork into her food. At the same time she would announce each title as it came along.

"Chalim .. Yal Ghuddar ... This one is very beautiful, listen ... Va Rabbi sidi ..."

He couldn't tell one set of wails from another.

"Arab?" he shouted. "Your country Arabic?"

She lectured. "Almut is largely Arab in composition. But it has a large Farsi minority and other minorities too. There are Tajiks, Kurds ..."

"But mainly Arabic ... this restaurant ... the nearest thing to home?"

She smiled.

"What brought you and your pals to France?"

"My husband and his brother came here to Grenoble ten years ago as students. Almut has many cultural ties with France. The two nations have been closely associated for nearly a century. At one time after the First World War France ruled Almut as a mandate like Syria. Almutis talk French rather than English as a foreign language."

"You were here before the revolution?" He remembered there had been a great fuss for weeks at the changeover. They had a very tough crowd in charge now. Was she one of the new lot? She seemed — sort of aristocratic. "You a friend of the old boy? The Sheikh who went into exile?"

She got annoyed. "You insult me."

"Okay. I'm sorry." He knew a bit about the old fellow. He'd read articles in the English tabloids. My Week with the Sheikh. Diamonds and the Sheikh. A Girl's Best Friend. There had been plenty of headlines like that. Girls from all over. Jewels plastered all over his wives. Three of them were like his palaces, glittering and ugly.

"That fourth wife of his is pretty. The Miss World Finalist."

"She is a whore."

"Oh." He remembered some more. "He was a cruel guy, isn't that right?" The newspapers had been on about his behaviour. Reports in Amnesty. Torture. Secret police. Nothing out of the ordinary, but the usual nasty combination of the old and new. Medieval punishment hotted up with electricity.

63

"Was it true about the beheadings?"

"Don't speak about them please."

"You in exile? Can't go back?"

"No."

If that was the way she wanted it. "I thought you had a friend for me to meet."

"He will be along soon."

She got another bottle of wine which slipped down easily. Wine was civilized when it accompanied food, even food like this. He was brought a couple of figs on a plate. Then brandy appeared, accompanied by muddy coffee in glasses. Contrary to his habit he smoked the two Gauloises she offered him. Maura wouldn't like this place, that was for sure — with its lurking suggestion of lust and cockroaches.

What was he doing here anyway? Lured by the usual will-o'-the-wisp. The idea of making a living out of hang gliding, of flying up and down the Alps, of spending the winter taking ski lifts up to high places and hovering over the snow. And being paid for it. He knew at heart there wasn't a hope in hell, really, that anything would come out of the little card she had given him. And yet he came along tamely. You'd think the violent end of Lacken Lift would have spelt out the truth to him — that there was no way he could turn his obsession for hang gliding into a money spinner.

But. ... This girl Leila and her pals — they thought he was great. He had flown well, they'd seen. Maybe he would fly in France, in Switzerland, in Italy, in Austria. Maybe he'd manage to live where he could fly most days.

"Hang gliding's a non-starter in Ireland. ... There's less than a hundred people doing it. In England they have something like eight hundred ... nine hundred. Figure doesn't go up very fast ... guys give it up. Many more here."

"But you would consider yourself among the best?"

"Course I would. Lack of opportunity. ... It's no wonder the Brits do better in competition. ... If I had the chance I would have beaten all those fucking Brits, excuse my French. Not fair. ..."

"Another glass? Tell me again ... about flying at night."

"Night flying? I know all there is to know about night flying.

Listen, not many guys have flown something like eight, ten miles the way I've flown. Not once mind you. Plenty of times. Plenty of times off Mount Leinster on a westerly. Eh? No . . . you have to be sober to do something like that. Last night? It was a little different. More like a dare. Harmless. And then the fuss those French made."

Dual harness? Of course . . . well she knew all about flying dual harness. He grinned and she grinned.

"Where's your friend? When's he going to show up? Offer me a job. The best hang gliding pilot he could get . . ."

She left him for a few moments. Must telephone. Must find out what has delayed him. Excuse me. The brandy bottle was still on the table. The other diners appeared to have disappeared apart from the two old men lingering in the corner out of earshot. By the time Leila came back the redhead was piling chairs back on the tables. The music seemed less intrusive. First it was turned down, and then when some record or other had wailed to a sobbing conclusion, the machine was allowed to rest.

Memory blurred. He could recall the man with the drooping moustache seeing them out. Out of the restaurant? No . . . out of the dining room. Upstairs. An old-fashioned bedroom with a lumpy double bed and wooden bedhead and a dingy light. The room was as hot as hell. He felt a twinge of disappointment that he hadn't met her chum who built hang gliders. He thought of Maura, but only for a second or two.

He concentrated on the matter in hand.

Her plump little body was as white as a grub — only the hawkish face was sunburnt. Her hair spread on the pillow was frizzy and crimped. Not like Maura's. He was thinking of Maura again. Maura was a redhead, a real one, not like the waitress downstairs, reddened with henna. This one was different. She was wearing a great strong scent and she had a way of instructing him like a school mistress. In a way it was useful. Maura had a lot to learn. He had a lot to learn himself.

"Hang gliders do it in the missionary position," he told her.

She set out to prove otherwise with a concentration that was almost grim. Hot slippery hours passed, the sheets wrinkled and damp, their wrestling marked at intervals with the scent of

65

Gauloises, a sip of Courvoisier. He had carried the bottle up himself. She turned off the light again. A night flight in the dark. It was dark so long that the rods at the back of his eyes got used to the blackness and he could make out the white body and the black hair. Much later he lit his digital watch and read 2.27. He sat up on the bed which creaked and reached for the little pearl-shaded side light. The destroyed bed with the walnut ends and the lady in the midst of it burst into view.

"Hello, I must get back."

She lay there without a stitch on. He didn't feel tenderness. Would he see her again? He didn't feel guilt either.

"That was great, really," he told her, slipping on his socks. Something he had missed out on all his life.

"Stay," she said from the bed. "Show me again how hang gliders do it. Prone — naturally."

He should get back. Twenty-five miles from Grenoble to St Hilaire. It would have to be a taxi. It would take all his money and Joe's as well. Could he even get a taxi this time of night?

He took off his socks again and stayed. After they had played in the bed one more time, a good long time, he went off to sleep. And then when he woke it was light.

"Hell." Reached for the clothes again.

She wasn't sentimental either. Gymnastic. "Paul," she said from where she sat back against that terrible French bolster which was like having another body in the bed. "Paul, we never discussed business."

"Business?"

"You remember I asked you to come into Grenoble to discuss a job?"

"Is that a fact?" He grinned lewdly, pulling on his shirt.

Now she was dressing too. "My friend will be free to see you now."

"At this hour?" The digital numbers had jerked along to 7.21.

"I phoned."

"When?"

"While you were asleep."

Had he slept that soundly? Tired, of course. Brandy. Exercise.

Had she gone out stark naked to phone? She was dressing now. Had she dressed, then undressed?

"What's going on?"

"You must come down and meet my friend."

"The one who makes hang gliders? Alouette and Company?"

"Yes."

"I can't. It's impossible. Sorry Leila, I must get back to my wife." The lies he would have to tell.

"This is important. It concerns your wife too."

"What do you mean, it concerns my wife?" Had he been set up for blackmail? A camera in the bedroom . . . like that James Bond film? To get money from him? Or have him work for the Russians — otherwise they'd tell Maura. They had him wrong, though. He'd confess to Maura. If the worst came to the worst. He'd tell her all about the carry-on last night. She wouldn't be thrilled. In the end, though, she'd be understanding. She had always been understanding about hang gliding. She was a great girl.

Like a fool he didn't feel worried. Not even guilty. Last night had been something different.

Maybe there was still something in the guy offering him a job.

"I need a shave." Leila didn't answer. He put on Joe's jacket, found a little comb in the pocket and ran it through his hair. In the long mirror stuck on the imitation walnut wardrobe his unshaven face looked vengeful. Her appearance was haggard too, and they made up a couple who had spent a long weary night together.

Dark little hall, twisting stairs. He'd really like to give Maura a ring. Tell lies. Last night he could have stayed with Simon and his friends.

The redhead was there on hands and knees washing the red-tiled floor with a grey rag she dipped in an orange bucket. Leila led him through the tables burdened with upturned chairs to a room on the side. A dingy office was furnished with olive-coloured tin filing cabinets.

Paul noticed the chairs with narrow black tapering legs like knitting needles. Moulded plastic seats. A swivel chair behind the desk in the middle was more comfortable. The man seated on it was boss. The three others behind him were cronies, yes men. Too many for the space, small and hot, in spite of the open window which looked out on to somewhere dark like a yard.

The men were alike, like sheep or Chinese. Once again Paul had an impression of dark eyes and neat black moustaches. They resembled the people he had seen accompanying Leila at the championships and were presumably the same crowd.

The boss was the only one she introduced him to.

"My brother-in-law, Dr Faisal Rahman."

The boss got up and shook hands. He was slightly older than the others, gloomy looking with a turned-down mouth. There were bags under his eyes. He was a little tubby. Small, like Leila, like Paul.

A nod. A question addressed to Leila in a language Paul took to be Arabic. A reply from her and a long exchange.

"Doesn't he speak English?"

"He speaks French."

She knew very well Paul's French vocabulary did not exceed a couple of dozen words.

They continued to talk. There was acrimony.

"What's it about?"

"He says he wishes you to do something for him ... for us. ..."

"What?"

"He says will you first listen."

There was a small tape recorder on the desk in front of him, similar to the one that Gordon had used for lectures at Lacken Lift during wet and windy weather. The brother-in-law ... his name ... Faisal, that was it ... switched on.

Maura's voice came over sharpish. The electronic refinement that eliminated its warmth emphasized the Cork accent. She sounded frightened.

"Paul ... we're all right. Nothing to worry about ... Paul ... we're all right ... See what it is they want ... Shh ... hh ..." She must be trying to soothe the snivelling sounds in the background of Daddy, Daddy. Tony never sounded like that. All the rage and temper tantrums and pain he had expressed in his life were nothing like that. Paul pictured the familiar obstinate pouting little face with its look of Arthur Scargill and tried to match it with this half whine, half scream. Then Maura speaking again with a note of panic. Paul, do whatever seems best . . . whatever they say . . . please Paul. It was funny how there was that bit of reproach in her scared voice. Talk to them, Paul.

Faisal lifted his finger and stabbed the forward button. Squeak, then play. Sobs. Christ. The two of them. Not sounds he had ever heard before. Not sounds he could recognize. And then the sobbing suspended for a moment. Find out what they want.

The tape was switched off. There was a long silence broken by Leila shouting. She sounded really angry. He might not understand the words but he knew the gist of what she was saying. You laid it on too thick. Then she talked to him.

"You must not worry too much about them, Paul." Don't call me that. "Those sounds . . . it's not so bad . . . they are fine, believe me . . . your wife and son. . . ." He'd like to hammer her head against the wall. He'd like to push her face in.

"What have you done to them?"

"They have been taken into custody."

"What do you mean?"

"Supposing a friend of yours . . . were to ring the *pension* . . . they would not be there. They are with us."

"How?"

"Last night while you were away. . . ." Don't smirk, you bitch. "Some time after midnight your wife received a telephone call. She was told that you were in trouble at a party near St Hilaire. There was a fight . . . you were shouting at people . . . making a nuisance . . ."

It was a story that Maura would believe instantly.

"Of course it would be better if she came and took you home. She said at first why couldn't one of your hang gliding friends take care of you? The caller mentioned the police. Your wife was given instructions. She had to drive towards the Isère road and turn off at a country place. There was a lane that was a cul de sac. The van was stopped . . ."

"What about Tony?"

"Tony?"

"The boy. He would have been sleeping."

"We did not plan for her to bring the child then. We would have picked him up this morning with a story about you being sick or injured. Your wife unable to leave your side. Something like that. But it appears that last night as a good mother Madame Mooney did not wish to leave her child alone."

Tony had a cold. He must have woken, any damn thing woke him. And Maura wouldn't have left him with that useless rapacious woman who ran the *pension*. The old bitch would have been annoyed, she would have been woken by the telephone. Paul hated French women. A French landlady in a tourist centre was like a spider crossed with a crocodile. Maura wouldn't have left Tony behind. She would have carried him down to the van wrapped in a rug.

"Where are they?"

"They are safe. You heard them."

"Where?"

"They are in good hands. They will remain in protection while you help us."

"Help?"

"Of course you will be helping with something that will be explained to you. Do not worry. They will be safe. And when you have helped us they will be released."

Kidnapping was something Paul associated with Italians. Although, if you thought about it, there were few countries around where some innocent had not turned into a bloody bundle in the boot of a car. Maura was a woman, but sex was no guarantee of life for the kidnapped. How about that poor English lady and her friend in Italy whom they said had been left for the wolves? That had been for money. He had no money.

"What do you want? I haven't any money."

"We do not want your money. We need your expertise."

"Expertise?"

She said with a note of patience in her voice: "We wish for your help in a task that requires hang gliding. If you do not help us perhaps your wife and boy will not be so safe."

He let the pretty accented voice continue. American, learned at some rich private school. Maybe the one where the headmistress shot the dietician. He hated the voice. He wanted to stifle it. "You will naturally be rewarded. We would deposit fifty thousand

70

pounds in your Irish Bank. Pounds sterling, of course, not your devalued Irish money. Or, if you prefer, in a Swiss bank account." She spoke to the brother-in-law. He pointed the tape recorder at Paul as if it was a weapon. He made the tape retract with a whine and Maura's frantic voice came on again. One of the moustached fools standing at the window gave a smile.

Paul felt tired and nearly tearful.

"What do you want?"

Faisal spoke to Leila for a long time while he thought about Maura. It was a bit late for the surge of tenderness and guilt that shook him.

After a while Leila said, "We require you to do some night flying."

"Night flying?" They were all watching him. The room was stuffy. "By hang glider?"

"Of course."

"To a target?"

"Certainly. It would be a distance of about eight kilometres. Five miles."

"Cannot be done. At least it can't be done predictably. The whole flight would be a downer. No thermals to help you rise."

"Naturally that has been calculated. The hang glider would fly downward from a height."

"In the Alps?"

"Yes."

"It'd be very tricky. With night flying you can't forecast anything. Where to?"

"We will tell you in due course."

"I mean what sort of target to land on?"

"A helicopter pad."

That would be about the same area as the target in the competition during the world championship. "Much too chancey. Given daylight and perfect conditions you might get somewhere near. Even then you couldn't guarantee a spot-on landing."

"We know there is an element of chance." She paused. "You would be flying double harness."

"That's impossible," he said instantly.

71

Faisal interrupted urgently.

"It is risky, but we have worked out that given the proper conditions the task is feasible."

"You're mad."

She persisted. "You would have to take a passenger."

"Who?"

"Him."

There was a pause while Paul looked at Faisal. The three men behind the desk looked at him. Leila looked at him. They all examined him as if he was a prize exhibit at a dog show.

"He's a tub of lard."

Leila must have translated. Faisal looked grim.

"I'm telling you, it's just not a good idea. A flight on one's own would carry enough risks. In the first place you have to have a good reason to go night flying." Preferably to be tanked up with whisky for a hover round Mount Leinster on a frosty night. He thought, if it had been just a straight flight I'd do it all right . . . without the pressures. The money would set me up. Maura and Tony would be okay.

"The whole idea is crazy."

The man and the girl talked together, and without understanding he caught a hint of menace. I told you so on the part of the man. A glance at the tape recorder. What would happen following his refusal? He felt frightened. Would they let Maura and Tony go? Sorry, a mistake, there's the front door. Would they let any of the Mooney family leave?

"You'd better tell me more."

"If you consent, yes, we tell you everything."

"How can I if I don't know what it's about? From what you say . . . it . . . it seems very difficult."

"My husband worked out how to do it."

"He was killed."

"He died in different circumstances."

"He was going to fly in double harness for a five-mile flight carrying a passenger? By night?"

"He would have gone alone. He was a good flyer."

Mustn't mention the word impossible. "Wouldn't it be a better idea to teach this one to fly?"

72

"Faisal? He has flown. He knows about hang gliding. But he is not good enough."

The little man must have understood because he laughed sourly. She talked to him again. Then she said "It is for a burglary."

"Burglary?"

"Not an ordinary burglary." They talked again. He was getting the knack of understanding the sort of things they were saying. It was easier because she was being persuasive and you could guess a lot. Also from the audience, the three hangers-on. They were silent, there wasn't a word from them. They listened and you could tell something from their reaction. She was saying: we've got the poor bastard hooked. His kith and kin are under wraps. He's fond of them. He wouldn't like to see them chopped. He'll co-operate. He was saying one way or another: there's no need to tell him anything until later.

"He says that once you know the details of the enterprise you must consent." How ugly she seemed, talking. Less than six hours ago he had been screwing her.

"How the hell can I consent if the thing is just not on?"

"I tell you it is quite possible."

"What about my wife? My child?"

She shrugged.

"If I refuse ... if it is just ... very difficult ... too difficult ... what will happen?"

"That is for you to decide."

"Can I see them?" She shook her head. "Can I talk to them?"

"You can, of course, give them a message. When you have decided." Stick and carrot. He thought about the money. With 50 grand he could set up Lacken Lift again. Pay off the hire purchase on the van. No more of those friendly letters written in typed capitals as if they were telegrams. THE ARREARS ON YOUR ACCOUNT AT THE CLOSE OF BUSINESS WERE AS ABOVE ... I HAVE BEEN INSTRUCTED TO APPLY TO YOU FOR IMMEDIATE PAYMENT ...

How could he be thinking of money? (But the idea of it would stick in the back of his mind.) Maura and Tony were what mattered. How could anything be guaranteed? If he did nothing

73

what were the chances they would be harmed? He hadn't any choice. He would have to string along.

The real problem was the double harness. Without that there was even exhilaration at the idea of swooping through the dark. Moonlight. You couldn't plan for moonlight. Ever heard of cloud? Could he talk them out of the dumb double harness? Like using an invalid carriage for a getaway car.

He said, "Okay I'll go along. I'll fly by night. Tell me more."

There was a collective sigh as the room full of people relaxed. They began listening as Leila lectured. They couldn't understand.

"We came to France as students before the revolution. When the changes came last year we welcomed the departure of the Sheikh."

Get on with it, bitch. Background. What the hell did he want to know about Almut's religious problems? The split between Shia and Sunni Moslems, that sounded like Catholics and Prods. He didn't give a damn about oil and oil revenues. What had oil to do with Maura? Or flying double harness by night?

More talk about the Sheikh. Leila was animated. Everyone knew something about the old bastard, of course. Even Maura knew about him, the way she knew about Princess Grace.

"The dynasty to which he belongs is probably the oldest royal family in the world."

"Anything to do with that ruler in Iran?"

"The Shah of Iran is the grandson of a camel driver. The ancestors of the Sheikhs of Almut were aristocrats when the ancestors of the English royal family, for example, were wearing skins."

He didn't want to know about royal families.

"The Sheikh's people were Seyid in origin and thus he is a descendant of the Prophet. He claims descent also from Saladdin."

Who was Saladdin?

"The dynasty has ruled since the twelfth century ... with only one short break when his father was sent into exile by the French. When the French mandate came to an end the Sheikh assumed the old power."

What about hang gliding?

She went on like a TV documentary. The Sheikh had been rich and cruel just like the papers always said. She mentioned one or two horrible things that went on in his palaces. She talked about him, half loathing, half with this note of admiration.

Even in exile he was rich. Paul had heard about his jewels. The loot his ancestors had gathered over the centuries during wars with Turkey, Persia, Mesopotamia Afghanistan, India and various khanates and emirates in what is now the U.S.S.R. had formed a reasonable base to start the royal collection. He had a passion for diamonds which he bought from all round the world through his agents. A small portion of his jewels ornamented his wives and mistresses. The Miss World finalist was said to have the world's finest collection of modern jewellery all in special settings by Cartier and suchlike. There had been the vulgar joke that she had the Miss World crown worn by her rival copied in real diamonds. The Sheikh also owned a number of famous old rocks with histories of death, misfortune or a sojourn in an idol's forehead.

He had seen the revolution coming in plenty of time to place a great part of his possessions abroad. In addition to the bulging Swiss bank vaults, he had secret investments in a couple of dozen cities in Europe, America and South America.

He had always planned to take his jewels with him. There had been problems about getting hold of the Crown Jewels since they were on public display in the capital's museum. However, a few members of the remnant of the army that remained loyal to him acted quickly when the mob was approaching the palace gates. They went to the museum, shot the guards, rounded up the museum's directors, shot them too, and hurried away with the crown, sceptre and the rest of the regalia of Lion of Kasvin in an airline bag.

The Sheikh departed swiftly from his country in his private Concorde. With him he took the jewels, his first wife, his beautiful wife and fourteen sons, mostly small boys. (Other sons had died in the revolution or had already gone abroad. Several were playboys; one drew social security in Southampton in England; another had become a computer operator in Trenton, New Jersey. Four had been assassinated by Almuti patriots, two in Paris, one in Frankfurt, one in Valparaiso.)

There was trouble finding a permanent place of exile. The Americans wouldn't touch the ex-ruler. At one time the CIA had given him support, but had stopped long before he was thrown out by Moslem Socialists. Fellow Arab rulers ignored him. Eventually he landed up in South America in a country with a dictator and a social life dominated by ancient Nazis.

But he did not lose touch entirely with the old world. His money was in Switzerland. So were his jewels.

The Sheikh had a chalet in the Swiss Alps where he used to bring his family for skiing holidays before the revolution. He did not ski himself, he was much too fat, but many of his sons did. He never went there now, Paul was told. He did not come to Europe where assassination was easier than elsewhere. He stayed safely in South America. But his first wife, a plain old lady, lived in this chalet all the year round.

"She has eight of his sons in her care and supervises their education from there. Most of them go to boarding schools, some in England, the others in Switzerland. They return to her for the holidays."

Paul remembered some heartbreak article Maura had read out from *Woman* or *Woman's Own*. "The Pangs of Exile."

"She keeps a selection of jewels at this place. The jewels that belong to the people of Almut."

"Crown and sceptre? That sort of thing?"

"Not the regalia. That is in a bank vault in Lucerne. And the modern jewels remain with the fourth wife. But the great parures, necklaces and tiaras and a number of the biggest jewels appropriated by her husband are in her possession. Jewels like the Coonoor Sapphire once owned by Tipu Sultan and the Nevski diamonds that Catherine the Great used to wear."

They hardly sounded like the property of the Almutis. Although jewels took on the nationality of their owners, like all the stuff in the Tower of London put on by the Queen of England when she wanted to dress up. Her crowns were stuck with jewels that came from piddling little Indian states or from some black man in South Africa who had handed in the day's find to the mining boss. And yet what had become more British than the English crown jewels?

"Why aren't these particular necklaces and things in the bank vault with the regalia?"

"While they remain in the old queen's possession there is no way that outsiders can estimate how many of them the Sheikh has stolen from his countrymen. The Swiss banks may succumb to the agitation among Arab nations about the facilities they have given him. The Sheikh's advisers felt that it was important to have a good deal of his wealth outside Swiss banks. He needs them for easy disposal. He'll use them in the future for payment for arms."

"What does he need arms for?"

"He has plans to sell his jewels and provide funds for a counter-revolutionary force. He hopes to be restored to power. His agents are in touch with the big arms dealers in Europe and America. Even Israel will supply him with arms. The queen is helping him."

"She doesn't mind about the Miss World finalist?" Leila made a gloomy face. "What do your lot want?"

"We wish to obtain these things which are the property of the people of Almut."

"Why? To hand them back?"

Ask a silly question. "We wish to equip our own counter-revolutionary force."

"What's wrong with the boys in charge?" Paul knew the okay people in Almut now were old men with beards and turbans.

Plenty, it seemed. At any rate Leila's lot didn't get along with them. These people who were trying to wreck his life were Marxist-orientated, anti-Zionist, allied to dozens of terrorist organizations throughout the Middle East. There were several hundreds of them, freedom fighters, scattered in half a dozen countries in Europe and the near East.

They had friends here in France. There was an Algerian connection. They were poised to start a campaign of violence in their own country directed towards the new regime. The theft of the Kasvin jewels would not only give them a stupendous propaganda coup but would provide them with the means to go shopping for rocket launchers and Kalashnikovs and perhaps a small jet fighter or two.

Paul asked: "Have you considered powered flight? A microlight? You might carry out your plan a lot more easily with something like a Ski Trike or a Soarmaster..." He didn't know any French equivalent.

"We examined the idea of powered flight very carefully. But the noise factor put it out of the question." Powered gliders were noisy, right enough, with a sound like a castrated helicopter. "A powered glider would be heard by guards. It would be a more decisive target on the radar screen."

"Radar? What else? Dogs, barbed wire, alarm systems?"

"They have come into consideration. The plan was very simple. Such precautions would be outwitted by surprise and silence. So my husband planned."

"He's dead."

"For a time the plan died with him."

"Let it lie."

"Then we found another way of carrying out his wishes."

"You mean me? You went round St Hilaire at a time when it was full of hang gliders looking for a fool like me? With a wife and child for you to bully?"

"Hassan had been dead for a short time. We had abandoned the raid. Then I met you again. I assure you we attended the championships with no precise aim — merely watching the hang gliding linked us with our dead friend."

Like hell.

"Destiny took a hand. Before my husband was killed there had been talk of double flight so that he could take a comrade with him."

"Faisal?"

"Yes."

"How much was this plan discussed?"

She shrugged: "It was at an early stage."

Paul said: "Look — just suppose — I won't ask for details now — that me and him do manage to land on this particular roof top. Suppose he manages to get hold of the jewels — it'll take time, I suppose? Safe cutting? Asking nicely for the key of the jewel case?

78

If he succeeds how are we going to make our escape? What about the guard dogs and the barbed wire and so on?"

She said blandly: "The chances of escape are good. There will be a hostage situation." She meant the poor old queen would be assisting their exit with a gun held to the royal ear.

"I may not be the world's greatest newspaper reader, but I've watched enough news on television to pick up one basic fact. He who takes hostages gets nowhere. Or gets to Libya if he is very lucky indeed." But Maura and Tony were hostages.

It appeared that Paul had missed the nuances of the plan. If an armed patriot waits around for the local police force and the army to muster he will be in trouble. Even in Switzerland. Especially in Switzerland where the Swiss judiciary is surprisingly tough when it comes to dealing with freedom fighters. But in this case the authorities would not have time to know. A few minutes in the chalet — an escort out of the compound with a very important person in tow. And a car waiting outside.

"All this action just to get at some jewels?"

"It is no more reckless than the work of patriot fighters who put on the black masks and hold up embassies. They are the sort who seize old women who are second secretaries and then ask for the sandwiches to be brought in. For what? To get the foreign papers to say that all is not right in their native country? Our purpose is more patriotic."

"Why bother with a daft scheme involving flying by night? Why not rob a bank?"

"Robbing a Swiss bank is tearing at the life blood of the country. The publicity would not be good. A daring raid — unique — would bring the world to recognize our cause. That is what my husband thought."

"I don't believe you. He wouldn't have considered it would be possible to find a target the size of a dinner table in the dark."

"There would be moonlight."

"What do you know about moonlight? Heard of clouds? You are flying by moonlight and you'll find your judgment goes to hell. And in double harness . . . what would I be doing killing myself that way? And receiving a bullet in the brain at the end of the day."

79

"It will be your wife and child who receive that treatment if you do not help us."

He lurched forward and gave her a great slap across the cheek. The three bodyguards helped the brother-in-law beat him up. They mauled and kicked him, mostly with little pointy shoes. She shouted something which could have been a warning — he must not be too stiffened or messed up if he was going to fly a hang glider for them. They took him out of the room and he heard her witch's shriek calling after him: "Think about it, Paul."

Chapter Six

THE SAME HOT bedroom, the bed with the sagging middle and phoney walnut bedends. Unmade. The wardrobe with the full length mirror and its image of his battered body. The only good thing was the bathroom next door with a shower. He showered in cold water for ten minutes. Blood rolled off him and swirled down the plughole like the scene in *Psycho*. Then he went to bed and slept for a short time.

He woke sweating, hot as ever. He got up and tried the door which was locked. He lay on the bed again and raged at Leila. Why did she have to sleep with him? He could have been trapped without that. He was easy prey. Had they thought to impose feelings of guilt on him as extra pressure? Or ... had Leila enjoyed having things her way? He stifled memories of pleasure.

He wondered about Madame at the *pension*. How about the unpaid bill, the unpacked luggage? But Leila and her friends would have solved that problem. *Mes regrets*, but Madame Mooney has had a slight road accident. Or, more convincing, Monsieur has had a *contretemps* with his *cerf volant* and Madame is by his hospital bed. Here is your account — they couldn't carry out a plan like this without plenty of funds — and you don't mind if we take away Madame's things and the toys of the little boy.

He felt sad, remembering the dressing table in the *pension* with the pile of little parcels, mostly wrapped in the distinctive polythene bags with the brown DF initials denoting Dames de France, the big store in Grenoble Maura had talked about such a lot. She had bought gifts for her mother and for the neighbours. Would the neighbours notice if they weren't back next week? It was summer and most of them would be away.

What about Henny and Ann? Ann, after all, slept in the same *pension*. Would they miss them, especially if Madame told them

Paul had suffered a hang gliding injury? There was some hope there. But knowing Henny and Ann, they would more likely be piqued than puzzled at Maura's failure to communicate. They would take it as a rejection of Henny's role as father figure. Especially since he and Maura had been expected to leave after his sacking from the team. They might well think that the Mooneys had gone off to somewhere like Mont Lachène. Had he mentioned Mont Lachène? And Henny had worries of his own. He still had the team to organize and all his family waiting for him back home. Not to rely on him to go chasing after lost sheep.

Maura's mother might wonder, but she and Maura were not great communicators. Maura had sent postcards of Alpine views and the *téléférique*, and also, he remembered, an uplifting card with a picture of a flower and a dew drop and a motto, *Le seul Fait d'Exister est un Veritable Bonheur.* Ann had translated it for Maura who had passed the message on to West Cork, exactly the sort of pseudo-philosophy the old lady liked. He had wanted to send her a sow nursing a large litter and saying in a bubble of thought, *Ah, si je connaissais plutôt la pilule!* (Ann had translated that as well. Since she had six children, the idea of the sow not knowing about the pill was not tactful.) Maura wouldn't let him. But the mother-in-law had received sufficient communication to keep her happy for a while. She might expect a phone call when they were due back, but not necessarily — they were always moaning about the price of long-distance calls. It could be a couple of weeks before she began to worry.

He would be missed at work, of course. He had taken the normal fortnight's holiday the building trade allowed itself and a few extra days as well. John Sheridan, his boss, hadn't been thrilled when Paul had asked for more time and mentioned the world championships. He had agreed reluctantly, eyes rolling, the usual rude remarks about hang gliding and the amount of time Paul took off work. When Paul didn't show up he'd do some fuming and planning to fire him. It wouldn't occur to him that his employee couldn't get to work.

For a moment Paul thought about prayer. He had annoyed and saddened Maura for years by skipping Mass to go hang gliding. Sometimes if the wind was too strong for flying he'd slip into church at Bunclody or Blessington on the way to a site. He supposed she was praying now; he should be doing the same.

He wondered how many more people besides the crowd he'd already seen were involved in this business. There must be more to capture and guard Maura and Tony. Very likely they were nearby. They could even be in this building. Sweat prickled on his skin. There must have been someone else who spoke English who made the call to Maura. Or was it Leila all along? He tried to remember her absences during that long night. Powdering her nose. Excuse me one moment, Paul. God, he'd been drunk. He felt the alcoholic dehydration now and went into the bathroom and drank water from the tap. There was so much of the night he couldn't remember. Had Leila's only job been to keep him happy? Or was the group larger, more organized? Why couldn't Faisal, the fat man, learn to hang glide properly by himself if he was so strongly motivated? Go night flying after the loot all by himself? Easier said than done, he knew. Such a flight as they wanted to achieve required talent. Talent of the sort Paul possessed. And Fatso lacked.

Speak of the devil, or think of the devil. Faisal came in with one of the other men who had mauled him. The bodyguard was carrying a tray. Minestrone and bread. Paul was hungry and glad to see it. He wished they'd go away and leave him alone. They stood and watched him drinking soup. No common language between them. What was the good of his limited number of French words? Faisal would be quite a weight to carry over a distance. Wherever they were going, the two of them in double harness would sink slowly towards oblivion. Shouting at each other as they glided downward. And Faisal would be carrying a weapon. It would be as companionable an aerial journey as the first one ever made with passengers — the balloon with the cock and the duck and the sheep.

The two men left, taking the tray and leaving a photograph. The brightly-coloured Polaroid flash showed Maura in her underclothes. She must have hated that. Sitting straight with Tony in her lap. She looked okay, a bit solemn, the eyes showing white which might have been the fault of the camera making the colours all wrong and lurid. Her hair was bright orange against the grey curtain behind. Tony's eyes were closed, but he'd probably been blinking while the photograph was being taken.

Photography had become part of the ritual of modern kidnapping. Your victim had his picture taken, usually carrying a newspaper with the day's date. These people had dispensed with the newspaper. A horrible photograph. No need for it either. He'd already decided that whatever damn fool thing they wanted him to do, he'd do. If he refused they'd get rid of him even quicker. He had a third option, which was much the sanest. He could persuade them that the idea was impossible, more risky than aiming astronauts at the moon. Or was it? So many times gliding by night among snow mountains. He examined his feelings. Part of his dilemma was the excitement that the challenge would bring. It was the logical outcome to those flights he had already experienced over Kilkenny and Wexford.

Would the Alpine flight accomplish anything apart from his death (and Faisal's)? Would it help Maura and Tony? There was no way to guarantee their safety.

He felt another surge of guilt. He felt guilty towards Maura for other reasons. For the way he had neglected her. For the way that he had let the hang gliding come between himself and Maura like a sword in the marriage bed.

He had been drawn to hang gliding from the very first moment he saw a glider. How long ago? Five, six years? He remembered clearly the day his life changed. Maura's life changed.

He had gone for a climb on the big Sugarloaf, that conical-shaped mountain that is a reminder to despairing Dubliners how close the countryside and the Wicklow hills lie beyond the city suburbs. There had been a soft wind blowing fleecy clouds across the sky. The fact that it was south-west, between fifteen and twenty knots, did not interest him.

From the summit he had caught sight of the giant black and blue butterfly spread out below him. It was being rigged on the ridge that ran beneath the peak. The first hang glider that he had ever seen. Without hesitation he hurried down the steep summit.

He found two men prepared to fly. They were both in their

thirties, one dark and stocky, the other fair and balding. As Paul approached, the thinning hair was being covered with a crash helmet made to British Standards BS 2495.

The sails threaded on the wings were flapping like sheets on a line. Later Paul would know that they were made of heavy-gauged sailcloth, heatsealed so that it was not porous, and waterproof and airproof with dressing between the fibres. Now for the first time he listened to the impatient sound made by the wind beating the terylene as the kite — a Wasp 229 — stood waiting for take-off. It was alive, struggling to fly away. The dark man held it down on its triangle while the pilot took off his rose pruning gloves and walked around the machine, running a hand along the edge of each wing, checking the leading edges, the nose plate, the control frame and the sailcloth. He inspected the joins of the outside triangle.

"What's that?" Paul had asked.

"That's the Jesus bolt. It holds the thing together. It goes, you go with it." The dark man took a hand away from the nosewires to hold a ventimeter towards the wind. A little disc danced up and down in plastic to indicate a windspeed veering between fifteen and twenty knots. He threw up a tuft of grass in the air for the pilot to see the wind direction.

The pilot slipped into the harness which had a small orange seat like a swing. The dark man stood at the edge of the steep ridge throwing up more grass. The pilot adjusted the angle of take-off very slightly.

"Go!" he shouted, and the dark man let go of the nosewires and ducked under the wing. The glider swooped off the edge of the ridge towards Calgary bog. Far below sheep grazed and the ground levelled off into heather and turf. The hang glider looked clumsy, like a bumble bee which flies against the rules of aerodynamics. Paul was not yet familiar with the famous comparison with "an incapable grasshopper". Although the wings were streamlined enough, the small squat silhouette of the seated man holding a triangle, his head enlarged by his helmet, his legs dangling against the sky, was faintly ludicrous. But he had jumped into space and the wind had thrown him up. He was in control. He was flying. He tracked along the ridge a few times, executing turns. Then he dwindled to a bright-coloured speck before landing on the distant turf.

Paul stayed on the Sugarloaf for the rest of the day watching the men take off alternately. Lugging the glider up the hill again took time, and by the evening they had only had three flights each. They were not skilled enough to attempt top landings, or perhaps they felt their machine was not up to such advanced techniques. He pestered them all day, bombarding them with questions. They must have found him maddening, a hang gliding groupie. But they told him what he wanted to know.

At dusk they folded up the Wasp until it looked like a huge golfing umbrella. He helped them carry it down the mountain to where their Audi was parked, and watched them tie it on to the roof rack. He looked after them, following the headlights as the car turned out into the land and turned again to begin the descent to Kilmacanogue.

He never saw them again. They might have been winged creatures from outer space flown in to lure him to his doom or, at the very least, to shape his destiny. Later he heard that the bald man broke his ankle badly on his very next flight. He did not know what became of the other, who must have lacked the strength of obsession that seizes dedicated pilots.

Maura had not been pleased when Paul arrived back home well after dark. But she had not been apprehensive. She did not know that already she was about to take second place to a heavier-than-air, fixed-wing glider. She had yet to learn that weather was no longer a matter of sun, wind, rain or snow, but consisted of wind speed and wind direction.

The windows of the room looked over a sombre yard whose faint smell of sewage trickled in through the louvred shutters. It was stifling with shutters closed or opened. Paul lay brooding, always on the same themes, obsession and neglect.

He winced when he remembered how when Maura went into labour on a Saturday he had been out flying at Lacken. A neighbour had to drive her into Holles Street. The sight of his son was great, but Paul couldn't help a twinge of impatience that he had ruined a perfect Sunday's flying, waiting in the hospital for him to be born.

He recalled the various stages of his hang gliding career. The Cloudbase he had bought from a Northerner; to save trouble he had met the seller on the main road just north of the border between Dandalk and Newry. The Cloudbase was set up by the roadside on the grass verge and drivers of passing cars slowed down and stared at the big kite as Paul carefully inspected it.

The prone harness. Learning to go prone and nearly killing himself. Not telling Maura.

Maura complaining about the expense. "Free flight, how are you? It's costing a fortune!" He supposed she was right. As his performance improved he seemed to get through a lot of money. The altimeter, the glide slope indicator and an airspeed indicator had been acquired. His vario was a good one. Besides having the usual audio with the different tone bleep telling you whether you were going up or down, it had an audio stall warning indicator and a visual unit. That had set him back a hundred quid.

Spares were endless. There always seemed to be a leading edge or something else that needed replacing.

He remembered how he had thought in for a penny, in for a pound. He had changed his Cloudbase — a good beginner's kite — for a Super Scorpion more adapted to his skills. Without consulting Maura, he had used his Christmas bonus which had been earmarked for a holiday.

This trip to France was in part to pay her back for years of neglect. Perhaps not the best way of saying thank you. She had put up with a good deal. For the most part, patiently.

He thought about Maura and Leila, alternately switching from one to the other without conscious effort, in the way that the eye changes the image of the optical cube if you stare at it long enough.

In the evening he was taken down to the same room where he had been tormented that morning. The same people were there and Leila was doing the interpreting.

"Will you help us?"

Help? He might be in their power, but they depended on him. They needed his skills badly. They had gone to a lot of trouble to obtain them.

"Let me see Maura and Tony."

She talked to Faisal who shook his head. Why? Had they hurt them too much? Were they too far away? He remembered Maura's crying and the way he had been kicked around. He gave in.

"All right. I'll help you." He wouldn't ask about his wife and son any more. Later.

They looked relieved. They must know something about the risks that were involved. Hadn't the husband been killed on a good clear day? They must be desperate for whatever this robbery entailed.

He must make them believe that the flight was impossible without putting Maura and Tony in further danger. They must know about the difficulties of combining techniques, two of which were at a pioneer stage. The cross-country part was okay in theory. Everyone with a high-performance glider knew about XC and could jog along five miles or so given reasonable conditions. But night flying to a specific target? One long downer? Okay, maybe night flying was just possible, given lots of leeway and luck and plenty of skill to be able to land in a small target area at the far end.

The worst thing was the prospect of flying dual harness. Dual harness was always something of a joke. A way of chatting up the girls, as he had found out. Some experts frowned on it even as a training method, although others argued there was no better way for a pupil to get the feel of ridge lift and 360 turns. But once you had got the skills of flying, there was no purpose in it. And going cross-country dual? He'd heard there was an unofficial record for a flight like that, something like three miles. The distance should be feasible all right. But two-manning, flying downward by night to that target? You must be joking.

"We'll give it a try."

They brought him into a private room off the main restaurant where the same redheaded girl brought in the same sort of food — a rice dish for variety. This time yesterday he could still have been eating with the Australians.

The bad thing about sitting here drinking Algerian wine in moderation — nothing like last night — was the air of enjoyment about the three of them, Leila, Faisal and himself. The other men stood in the background like waiters doing nothing, watching the redhead staggering in carrying plates piled high. Leila and the brother-in-law weren't drinking, but they were kind of jovial. Just the three, sitting round the table eating voraciously. Leila who had deceived him and put everything he loved into unspeakable danger. And yet . . . if it wasn't for Maura and Tony he would be feeling something like exhilaration.

If he got out alive he would read up that stuff about relationships between kidnappers and kidnapped. The dominant and the dominated. The women who developed a subservient admiration for their captors. Did it happen the other way around?

He watched Faisal eating copiously. More weight for the hang glider with every mouthful. Perhaps this was the moment to shout out that the task was impossible. You might as well ask the Wright brothers to fly the Atlantic a couple of weeks after they had done their stunt at Kittiwake.

Faisal left the talking to Leila. They covered a lot of ground. (Ho, ho!) Just the two of them would be talking and then she'd break off and translate for him. Sometimes he'd talk back in French. He seemed to have the idea that Paul understood a bit. Occasionally he'd grin and laugh as if he hadn't produced the photograph or the tape earlier on.

Paul's mood soon fluctuated back to despair. One moment he'd be cheerfully discussing the ways and means of meandering above snow fields. Then he'd dismiss the idea of success. He wouldn't exactly say the flight was virtually impossible, but he talked as gloomily as possible.

"We are as aware of the risks and chances of failure as you are." Like hell. Might as well put on the white scarf and gulp down the cup of sacred saki right now.

He struggled with the problem of his wife and son. "You've got to do something on your side. I can't take their safety on trust. I know what you've done to them already."

He got very little out of them.

"I won't let them vanish into oblivion. Their relatives will be on to the police very quickly." He knew how useless the relatives were. These people who had got hold of him didn't realize what an extra bonus his family was, and Maura's too. His parents struggling in the Midland town with problems associated with his father's alcoholism. After the big row they hadn't communicated for years. And on Maura's side one sister was a nun, not even a trendy nun, and the other was in Auckland, New Zealand. That left the poor old mother. How would a civil servant's widow with chronic arthritis begin to trace her lost daughter from a bungalow in West Cork?

The joviality ceased as he persisted. They thrashed something out, but it wasn't very satisfactory. They agreed that just before Operation Lunatic he would be allowed to post a couple of letters to anyone of his choice. There would be no police, no one in authority. No proper names mentioned, only a summary of the facts from which all precise information had been leaked out. It would be merely a reminder of their existence in an uncaring world. Who would he send them to? Henny, he supposed, for one. At least Henny had tried to be a father figure. Who else? Sean, maybe. They weren't great buddies, but over the years they had exchanged a good deal of hang gliding talk. And Sean admired his flying. And was attached to newspapers in some way. Didn't he work for the *Independent*? Even if he just laid out the litho type or whatever they did to newspapers nowadays, or sold copies on street corners, he must know someone in the business. The *Indo* might like to publicize the disappearance of an Irish family.

Once that was agreed they talked about money. They said they would open a Swiss bank account. A joint account for him and Maura so that if one or other of them survived they could use it. Fifty thousand, just like they promised. They'd bring him receipts before he flew. They'd get Maura to sign. Paul wondered if it was that easy to open Swiss bank accounts. Surely they'd need passports, for instance.

"There is no worry about that. We have everything of yours."

They must have retrieved the contents of the bedroom at the *pension*. They had another stroke of luck with the fact that Maura had taken charge of all the travel documents. Madame would not have minded them bundling out the Mooney possessions in bags and suitcases. No doubt she was pleased. In the height of the season she could find further guests without trouble. Not the sort that were perpetually asking for babysitters.

"We also have your hang glider," Leila said.

Paul was startled. The Scorp was kept outside the chalet with the other gliders belonging to members of the team. Apart from Joe's Cherokee which Paul had broken up. The Scorp would have been there when he came into Grenoble that night ... last night. Someone must have taken it knowing it was his for sure.

Coffee came in and one small harsh brandy for him. He must find out more about Operation Fruitcake.

"Has Faisal flown at all?"

"He has."

"How good is he?"

The tedious three-way exchange was more prolonged than usual.

"He has done about twenty hours ... over a long period."

When had he last flown? It appeared he hadn't been up for six months. Marvellous.

"He's able to fly prone?"

"Oh yes."

That was something. "Ask him what sort of kite he is used to flying." Three-cornered question. He named something called an Orage which Paul had never heard of. He deduced it must be some sort of beginner's kite, a continental equivalent of his own dear departed Cloudbase.

Faisal spoke again and she hesitated. "He has also flown an Atlas."

That was better.

"It belonged to my husband."

"Ah ..."

Silence for a time.

"Look ... if he's had experience handling an Atlas ... and he's really keen on doing this flight ... wouldn't it be better if he trained intensively and did it on his own?"

More gabbling and interpreting.

"This dual flight business is not good, you realize that, of course. ... You've gone to a lot of touble..." Ha! "I can understand that you believe a dual flight is the solution. But he'd be better off flying solo. He'd be his own man."

Interpreting.

"It would take time, but it would be worth it."

More interpreting. He felt hope. She said, "How long do you mean by time?"

"I don't know. It depends on weather. Ability. A couple of months maybe. A few flights in mid-winter would be good. There's plenty of hang gliding at ski resorts in winter. A calm winter's night with a bit of snow to light you would be the best. Wind conditions would be positive..."

"We only have three weeks."

He felt panic.

"The villa will be vacated at the beginning of September."

"How long had your husband been training?"

"Over a year. He had done night flying before his accident."

He had died and then the survivors had dealt themselves a new hand full of jokers. This little guy had minimum flying experience, just enough to handle the Atlas. A bit of spot landing, it seemed, ridge-soaring and so forth. He wasn't up to anything too strenuous. He needed a chauffeur.

Is your journey really necessary? How to convince him? Suppose the chauffeur got tired of his role while he was in the air? The passenger would have to shoot him. That idea would haunt both of them.

Take it easy. Plan it step by step and then perhaps nothing would happen in the end.

"How much does Faisal weigh?"

"Sixty-six ... maybe sixty-seven kilos."

What was that in pounds? Something around ten and a half stone. That was about his own weight. A combined weight of around 22 stone wasn't great, but it could be worse. He thought the pair of them could be carried by the Scorp. At least he would be flying his own machine — hideously modified. As for the sink rate flying at night, better not think about it.

One problem seemed easy to solve — or at least ignore. He would tackle the others one by one.

Harness.

"We need a standard prone harness, the usual sort. Two of them, modified." She looked blank. There was a pad and biro on the desk. Paul seized them and drew a dart from stick figures, one on top of the other.

The Arabs were taken aback.

Faisal clicked his tongue, took the pen and sketched a dart and two figures side by side in a seated position.

"No. Tell him it won't do like that."

"But of course, two people can travel beside one another as dual partners. We flew, you and I . . ." Blush you bitch.

"You don't understand. Dual flight side by side is fine for some people . . . beginners, pilots doing stunts, couples who can't bear to be parted for a minute. There was a pair lately in America who got married while sitting in dual harness . . . the clergyman was agile. Those are the sort of fools who fly in double-seated harness. When you get experience, if you must go dual and hope to do good flights, you go like that . . ." He pointed to the sketch. "One on top of the other. Like mating frogs."

Long argument.

"Faisal says side by side prone . . ."

"He doesn't understand either. Already he's asking for a miracle. A night flight across country. The problems of drag would be greater his way. They would be the final thing that would make the flight impossible."

Argument.

"Explain what is wrong with the double seating."

"If God had meant man to fly like that he'd have made him a Siamese twin. The sink rate would be drastic. If you have any hope of succeeding you'll have to go piggy back."

Faisal was still protesting and Paul could understand his objections. It would be Paul who would be doing the actual flying, steering and making decisions about wind and lift. And all the time on top of him, helpless, swinging in the second harness as if it was a hammock, would be Faisal, carried as an impotent passenger. Even if he had a weapon and felt obliged to use it on Paul he would have no means to direct the kite. After Paul, the pilot, had been disposed of, a very clumsy spaceship would inexorably tumble to earth.

The fool had been devising this dream of flying side by side, his gun in Paul's ear, while he did a bit of paddling himself to get the glider along. Like two rowers in a boat. You couldn't blame him if he was basically an ignoramus. You could tell that from the whole plan.

"Here." Paul did some demonstrating with darts, tearing pieces of paper and folding them into different types of flight profile. Simple stuff, demonstrating aerodynamics the easy way. He had seen old films about the Second World War, where paper darts helped plans for bombing Jerry. He made a clumsy dart with a wide, heavy bottom reinforced by paper clips. Then a high-performance paper with a deep rudder which flew across the room demonstrating its lovely smooth line and lack of drag.

Faisal broke off the conference abruptly. It seemed to Paul that all the involved bargaining and slow talk point by point appeared to have led to nothing. He was taken upstairs again.

He was confined to that bedroom for a long time. A day and a night. All that time to brood, apart from the periods he spent looking at tattered magazines they threw into him, filled with pictures of carousing royalty and the joys of motherhood experienced by pop singers and starlets. The door locked, nasty meals brought up at intervals. Time to brood.

If they abandoned the idea would they let him go. Dump him and Maura and Tony on some motorway and leave them to tell their story? Would they be believed?

It would be nicer to earn some proper money.

He had a vision of himself and Maura and Tony lying side by side in a French mortuary.

The heat seeped through the brown shutters. They brought him soup, a breadroll and a very ripe peach. He slept and had nightmares; woke and opened a magazine and stared at pictures of Princess Caroline at a fancy dress party. He slept. He hadn't shaved for three days.

What were Faisal and Leila doing all the time? He guessed they had gone to consult someone who knew about hang gliding. Someone who could advise them about Paul's ideas without getting involved or guessing at any preposterous plans. Who would tell them something about flying long distance in dual harness. The immeasurable benefits of frog fucking. Your man would have to be helpless in the hammock above. Better leave aside the whole idea. Find something else to steal.

Next morning he learned that they had found out Paul was right.

Did this mean they were going to abandon plans?

No, they were not going to abandon plans.

They wanted to consult him about supplies. Tomorrow they would be going off to obtain them. He, Faisal, had experience, and would make the right purchases after taking Paul's advice.

Paul lunged into wild argument, Leila translating as he shouted. They were not buying a dishwasher or a three-piece suite. How could he rely on two half-witted Arabs who knew so little about flying, they couldn't envisage the basics of dual gliding?

"Am-poss-eeble!" He knew that much French. Spending with the aid of a shopping list by two amateurs was pointless. He shouted that either he went along to choose the stuff he was going to break his neck with or they could forget the whole project. Skydeck instruments, harnesses, airspeed indicators were not things you find in a supermarket.

Amazingly Faisal gave in. *Bien, j'ai changé d'avis. Nous allons faire des emplettes ensemble.* Even a thin smile, and then, unbelievably, a handshake. It felt like the sticky touch of an insect-eating flower.

Chapter Seven

PAUL WAS GIVEN a throwaway razor. He couldn't wander about buying hang gliding gear looking like a wino or a hippie. He sawed away at his blackened cheeks.

Faisal did not do his shopping in Grenoble. He drove down an autoroute filled with maniacs on wheels. Roasting in the back of the Hiace Paul felt nausea and remembered poor Tony's trouble with car sickness when they crossed France all that time ago. A little more than two weeks. He looked out at tarmac shimmering in the heat at country he never wanted to see again. It was late morning when they got to Valence which resembled a deadbeat town in the centre of Ireland — the Mullingar of France.

Paul stood inside the barn-like hangar which was mainly devoted to manufacturing a hang glider he had never heard of. Downstairs they were turning out the metal rigging while up here the wings were being made on long wooden benches with the aid of a couple of Pfaff sewing machines. They were black. Faisal gazed at the rolls of black Terylene. Paul knew what he was thinking — black at night would be good camouflage. Most hang gliders aimed to be as conspicuous as possible. The rainbow wings of his scorp signalled keep away, keep away, like the bright colours of a poisonous insect. Paul had to argue, as always, through Leila. The spectrum colours would hardly be visible in darkness. No way would he play Batman on an unknown glider. Besides, the Pipistrelle was strictly experimental, and its exotic appearance would attract unwanted attention during practice flights.

The firm acted as agents for all sorts of gear, in addition to selling other types of glider. Faisal seemed to have plenty of cash. Would it be an idea to buy a number of gliders and try them out? An Atlas, for example, the kite most of the French team flew, the latest fashion, the glider of the month? But he knew that flying his own hang glider would be the best thing. Better the devil you know, even if it had to be modified for double flight.

By the way, he asked through Leila, had the French won the world championship? The stocky little salesman looked startled. (Funny how even on the periphery of hang gliding people were much of a type like a lot of Jack Russells.) *Mais oui, Monsieur*, flying high, nearly all in Atlases, including their best man, Thevenot, third in the individual. Monsieur didn't know? Monsieur received an odd look — a hang gliding enthusiast who had not been following the outcome of the *Championnat du Monde*. No more questions. Concentrate on directing Faisal what to buy.

Harness, webbing, spares. He indicated a couple of swing-type cocoon harnesses. Flying suits — they'd have to be warm. Night flying in Alpine conditions would be a dangerously chilly business. Thermal underwear and furlined boots were also supplied. A couple of *vol libre* cutaway helmets. Everything to equip the smart *delta planeur*. He directed Faisal to buy two each of different makes of flight deck. Here was a Thommen altimeter — nice to come across something familiar. Red goggles. Parachutes.

What about parachutes? Paul shrugged his indifference. He had a don't-let's-fasten-the-seatbelt attitude about the problem. It had not always been the case. Early in his flying career he had a bit of an accident, which was followed by regular nightmares about falling. He had invested over a hundred pounds for the joy of lugging an escape system into the air capable of function — a sprung drogue chute that threw out the canopy sufficiently to leap away from the back before the white silk was allowed to open. Curiously, once he bought it the nightmares ceased and he didn't wear it. He liked doing the trapeze act without the safety net.

The problem was Faisal's, and he could understand his point of view. During the flight he would be the one who was helpless. However much he loaded himself up with guns and grenades, he couldn't prevent Paul from being the one in charge. You could hardly blame him for wanting the only parachute. Him alone. Paul let him talk. He couldn't follow the French but he followed the reasoning.

Just the one American Briforce pack. The shute would leap

away from the pack in an emergency, catching the wind and pulling the canopy out of the pack vent hole first. One movement was all Faisal needed. One swift tug of the cord, if the pilot above failed him. Previously, he would have to do some slicing away at the harness beneath him. The harness with Paul's corpse; it would go down thud, thump, while Faisal drifted gracefully towards a snowy Alpine valley. He bought a German Martor Ruck Zuck, the sort of knife supplied to safety and rescue services for cutting through clothing in an emergency. Drivers who were nervous about being stuck in their cars when their safety belts jammed after an accident often carried them.

He was beginning to dislike Faisal more than he disliked Leila. Part of the trouble would be the language problem. It was bad enough having Leila struggle to translate information about response in varios and whether the audio was on up only, and battery life, and low battery warning indicators and self-zeroing. At least they had a language in common, even if it was only her prim, private-school American. He'd have to work on building up some sort of vocabulary in French to communicate with Faisal. And he'd have to struggle to overcome his antipathy.

He wondered what the salesmen in the hangar thought of their customers and their clutter of purchases. Were they odd enough to invite comment and enquiry? He guessed not. The region round about was full of hang gliding enthusiasts and must boast a fair measure of eccentrics. Faisal paid with wads of cash. There were no questions, merely a *merci, monsieur.*

The Hiace was filled up with gear. The heat was deadly. Another endearing thing about Faisal was his driving, which was fast and urgent. He overtook as if he was carryng emergency cardiac patients. Weaving in and out of traffic like a shuttle through a Persian rug, performing the fearsome *queue de poisson* manoeuvre with the thrust of a hungry shark.

Coming out of Valence they met traffic lights, braking with a scream and a shake-up of all the new purchases. There was a whole 50 seconds to wait before the lights changed, and nothing to do all that time. Faisal took out a piece of card from the pocket of his shorts and handed it behind him to Paul, who thought maybe it was a business card acquired from the firm they had dealt with today. It was another Polaroid of Maura and Tony, taken later than the first one he had been given. Maura was still in bra and pants — what had happened to the rest of her clothes? They looked . . . what was the word? . . . worse. Nothing you could see for sure. It was something like the way a corpse changes after a few hours. He felt very sick. The picture was taken against a different background. A dirty blanket. You could tell Maura was a worrier. And Tony looked really sad.

"*Gardez-le*," Faisal said with a smirk. Paul's impulse was to tear it up, unwind the window and throw out the pieces. Then he thought, I'll keep hold of it, write something on the back, and hand it to someone. If the worst comes to the worst I could even drop it from the Scorp. Maybe Faisal thought the same thing, because he changed his mind, took a hairy arm off the driving wheel and held out his hand over his shoulder. Paul would have liked to spit into it.

Even if he kept the photograph, what was the good? Like today. There had been plenty of times when he could have gone off and the only way they could have stopped him would have been to shoot him in the back. He could have gone and told someone, communicated with the gendarmes. There was nothing to prevent him except the fate of his wife and child.

The Hiace entered Grenoble through the austere urbaniza-tion of Villeneuve. Heat was something he had never associated with inland France. Surely nowhere in Italy or Spain could be hotter than these traffic-ridden streets at rush hour. Half a million sweating Grenoblois with the taunting background of mountains showing blobs of snow.

Faisal drove to a dreary section of the city near the station and down a side street off the Cours Berreiart. There was a garage which seemed to be well staffed considering the late hour. A crowd of men helped to take the things out of the Hiace. One with a shiny, tight, curled black beard talked to Faisal. He spoke authoritatively as the leader. Leila remained in the Hiace. Paul was summoned and got out.

Dark men, youngish, Arab. He followed Faisal into the garage, which smelled of spilled oil. There lay his Scorp. Old friend. Paul had to rig it for them. They stood around and watched like spectators on Killiney Hill.

He performed. Rigging out of the wind was simple enough, and he was used to being watched. Every time you took a kite out at home some old hiker or family of small boys would turn up. "What's that, Mister?" He ignored this lot breathing down his neck. When she was rigged, the 33-foot wing span taking up most of the length of the garage, the purchases were laid out like a military inspection. Faisal's bearded boss peered at the harnesses and varios and the rest like a visiting general with Faisal murmuring explanations. Paul was told to pack up again, watched by all the little squirrel eyes. Gestures. No Leila to translate. More gestures. Zip it up, pick it up, bring it out and put it on top of the Hiace.

The crowd watched the Hiace leaving.

"They are comrades," Leila said when he asked.

"Almutis?"

"Some. You must know that one freedom-fighting organization will help another. Our own group is very compact."

Could it consist of five people?

"Why did we go and see them?"

"They are helping us. They help many freedom-loving organizations. There are connections with E.T.A. in Spain. And of course your I.R.A. who regularly exchange weapons and expertise with other freedom fighters. The practical experience they gain from opposing imperialist forces is invaluable. Naturally you have sympathy for the struggles of the I.R.A."

"Fuck the I.R.A. I want to know about this crowd."

She wouldn't tell him. He coaxed to the point of whining.

"Are they holding Maura and Tony?"

Faisal spewed out a note of warning. The invisible chain that held Paul was enough to keep him in line. There was no need for him to know too much. What motive did the bigger organization have for aiding this little Almuti group on its wild mission? They must realize how hazardous the plan was. Perhaps not so much. Over the years Paul had never ceased to marvel at the layman's ignorance of the laws of flight. We hold this man's family, we help you and you do something for us in return.

"Why go to this trouble?"

"You must understand that the symbolic gesture of seizing the Sheikh's jewels will rally our supporters at home in the cause of liberation."

"Liberation from whom?"

"The religious leaders who are taking the country back to the Middle Ages."

"Why not invite the Sheikh to come home?"

Nothing like that. But it appeared that the forces which had brought about the revolution had broken up. The Moslem fundamentalists might hold power at present, but they were opposed by all sorts of people and the country was filled with dissenting factions. That was nothing unusual when you thought about Lebanon, where there was a political party for every twenty people.

"Many others in Almut would ally themselves with us. We wish to make the raid on the Sheikh's household to rally these people to our cause."

Paul nodded in Faisal's direction. "He is ready to kill himself — and me — for propaganda?" And some cash, of course.

"No one is going to kill themselves."

Her husband had died.

He didn't argue any further. Take it one day at a time. The first of these — tomorrow - he would spend in solo flight in his Scorp. His insistence i d to another quarrel with Faisal. So little time, a whole day wasted. Paul shouted he had no experience of Alpine flying. They should have picked someone else. Even flying around the area near Grenoble was not the equivalent of what it was going to be like in the big valleys. He had had one good flight in competition conditions a week ago. It simply wasn't enough.

Faisal conceded a day.

Paul had to approach them with another less pressing problem. He shouted about that as well. He had had no change of clothes for days, since he had first walked up the Rue de l'Arte, and after that hot sweaty session in the Hiace he was filthy.

It took almost as much argument to get clean clothes as it had to get a day's flying. Faisal didn't mind spending on altimeters but he was hard to convince that Paul needed new jeans, some Y-fronts and socks and a couple of shirts. They were not on the budget.

The clothes they flung into the bedroom in darkness before dawn the next morning were not new and did not fit well. But they were clean. His own garments were taken away, including Joe's jacket. When he flew the Scorp he'd probably go topless if it was going to be as hot as the sun at St Hilaire du Touvet. There was no question of going there now. The championships might be over, the tents folded, the caravans departed. But some of the competitors would have stayed on for the flying. It was a grand place for hang gliding. He might meet up with someone he knew or exchange a conversation with a pilot in mid-air. He might even run into Henny.

They started before dawn, setting off along the familiar Isère valley. Instead of driving the twisting road up to St Hilaire they branched off towards Theys where Maura and Tony had stayed. They took another of their people, the pockmarked man whose name was Yahir. He had beaten Paul with gusto that time. Yahir would be left at the landing target near the river to wait for Paul's descent.

The mountain chain with the pretty name of Belledonne was the line of snowcapped peaks he had seen day after day from the championship site on the far side of the valley. They were much higher than anything he had flown before. He would have a compass and a course plotted initially on a map, and this way he would get experience in catching thermals. Not that thermals were ultimately much help to him since there'd be few enough during that night flight.

At the river he set one of the new altimeters and watched it creep up as they climbed the zig-zag road through the pine forests. Through the gaps in the trees were impressive views looking down. They passed a large ski resort where white tower blocks were built into a hill. A rough track took them higher above the level of the trees until there was nothing but Alpine meadow and rock and walls of mountain. The altimeter showed they had come up more than 4,000 metres.

The van stopped where the track ended. Faisal put on a heavy jumper and gloves and handed another pullover to Paul. It was surprisingly cold — Paul remembered his earlier thoughts about flying half-naked. The shrivelled remains of spring flowers were still visible up here. They carried the hang glider between them and began climbing, Leila following. They climbed above a small glacial lake, its waters reflecting mountains and sky. A huge fissure separated them from the main range and its precipitous cliffs, patches of snow and thundering waterfall.

Handling the old famililar kite was always reassuring. In spite of his troubles he could not help feeling pleasure at the prospect of flying a high-performance hang glider with a better than one-in-eight glide ratio in these conditions. He set up the control frame, erected the king post and attached the leading edge tube to the cross tube on each wing. Faisal helped with some efficiency. He followed Paul's inspection with his own, checking the nose place, looking down the leading edges and checking the control frame. *Madame l'Interprète* was beside him as he gave out to Paul who was learning more French hang gliding terms than any other words of French vocabulary. He could understand when Faisal muttered about "*transversal . . . trapèze . . . saumon . . . bord d'attaque . . . .*"

They consulted the map and made a careful check on his direction. Taking off towards the north-west, climbing over a distant forested ridge, turning south, seeking to gain altitude and then making a last run down the valley for the target.

The take-off involved the usual zero wind as well as an unpleasant run past some nasty outcrops of rock. One wing almost hit. Paul sheered off the ridge, glancing back for a second at the pair of them, picking up speed fast and hoping for some response from the bar. Parachutists must feel the same way no matter how many times they jumped, the relief when you stopped falling and something braked your descent.

They'd given him a two-way radio but he switched it off even before he went in search of lift. He had made a clean take-off and now set off on the long flight to the ridge. For a few minutes he wondered if he would make it. The Scorp was sluggish, his vario showing a steady five to six down.

"Watch the birds —" Always good hang gliding advice.

Something like a hawk was circling ahead. Compared to it his own movements seemed earthbound. How many times he had admired the ease with which ordinary old seagulls varied their wing span, their angle of attack and nose angle by the slightest movement of their wings and feathers.

If he didn't reach the ridge it would mean a landing somewhere in the rocky valley below. And then how would he get back? A couple of hours' walk to the track. He concentrated. Each budge of wind meant a little more lift, but it wasn't enough. The edge of trees loomed ahead and he was about to head downwind when there was a bleep from the vario. A small thermal. He was flying at over 4,000 metres and began to gain height slowly. After a long time he was clear of the ridge and looking down on the far side of the valley. That familiar sense of isolation, the amazement that he was flying something so fragile as these gossamer wings and strings gripped him as usual.

The rest of the flight would be easy. He had worked out the course, the various dog's legs, and could pin-point the nests of habitation and the distant line of the Isère river. Across the valley were the cliffs where the championships had taken place. He could see flecks of colour. Other hang gliders. No use going across to join them. You'd envy the Europeans with their Alps and everything so much bigger and better and more roomy than the sites at home. He remembered the best flight he had had back home — beginning over a forestry plantation in the direction of Graighnamanagh. He remembered the thrill of hitting a great thermal, rising, floating on a mattress of warm air, very high and far away from the world. First-time thrill. He remembered the eerie silence, broken by the bleep of the vario, the hazy gathering of the Wicklow hills and the gleam of the sea. A once-in-a-lifetime experience. One that the guys who flew around here could emulate every summer's day.

Far below the pine trees fell away. He could make out squares of roof tops and louse-sized cars streaming down a main road. He felt like a hawk watching mice. As he hovered he suddenly thought — why not go into a deliberate spin and not come out again? It would be one solution. The perfect suicide. That would really make Leila and her friends give up. They'd let Maura and

104

Tony go. He was even insured against accident — no one would be able to prove anything else. Maura might even benefit. He'd have to direct a hard impact into one of those ridges. But would they let them go? Witnesses. Would they kill them out of pique? Would they kill them whatever happened? He looked down. He wouldn't die today.

He tried to figure things like the relative contrast between lift to drag ratio. What was the use, when he would be flying double? Handling was going to be all important. This wasn't a proper test flight. He was doing elementary flying — ridge-soaring on a grand scale. But he knew that once you started tackling chains of mountains and Alpine valleys conditions could go haywire. The wind flow became bewildering, and in places where you might expect to find lift you'd be facing a down current. Wind making its way through mountain masses and blocked valleys found the most direct route. The sun acted strangely in the creation of thermals, and snow and rocks played merry hell with wind conditions.

But he would be flying at night. In theory it would be calmer. It would be easier to glide down a moonlit valley when the sun had cooled, provided there was a nice little wind going in the right direction. The snag — always the snag — was the dual flight dragging them down. Most likely they would end up on a bare mountain.

Meanwhile he was going down fast. All his mind was concentrated on looking for the landing target. There was that man Yahir and the white rectangle of towels he had laid out in a field. Paul lazed around letting the wind hold him for a few more minutes like a swimmer treading water. He could stay up longer, just riding the ridge, paddling out towards the cumulus cloud that promised lift.

He would go down. The fields of maize were there, just like St Hilaire. He had to make that line of poplars, dive down, then turn into the wind and flare out. All a matter of timing. Over the small field of cut grass, then the maize, then the corn. Yahir waving. A burst of sink and a quick push out on the bar. He was standing holding the wings in the centre of the target.

How would he do aiming for a target by moonlight or perhaps

by starlight, looking for scale indicators? How big would a helicopter pad be?

"It was okay," he told Leila when she and Faisal drove down. The Scorp was a darling machine, finely tuned, and they were going to dismember it and destroy its potential.

He was scolded for turning off the walkie talkie.

He flew again that day, not from the same site but from another more accessible place above the Col de Coq. Less high, less far — at about 1,500 metres. Other flyers were gathered on the ridge and the place was crowded with French nonks. He looked around for familiar faces, but it seemed this site wasn't spectacular enough to attract the international people. Even so, there were almost as many flyers here as at the championships, taking advantage of the evening breeze, a nice little south wind lapping the ridge which measured twenty kilometres on the wind scale. Paul rigged, surrounded by his little court like a knight with squires. Faisal, Leila and the new helper, Yahir, were all handing him stuff.

"Faisal says give it minimum flight. Just do some ridge-soaring and then land."

Further along the slope he could see a hang glider rigged with a double harness. It was some sort of beginner's kite being used for a joyride. Two figures were running hard and then taking off. They ripped through the air, going sideways along the ridge. His heart sank as the glider sank to its ignoble bottom landing.

There were a number of Atlases ridge-climbing or moving off feeling for thermals. He thought he noticed a German Wings Scirocco and something like an American Seagull which could have remained over from the championship.

He made a good clean take-off and tracked along the ridge close enough to take every advantage of the wind. He flew in a tight figure-of-eight course, keeping height and maintaining a little extra above minimum sink. He found a thermal and did some soaring. He could have made for a bank of cloud above the valley that promised to lift him out of sight if he liked to chase it. He did a couple of 360s and a practice stall.

Strange how quickly conditions could vary. The heat was off the bottom and the wind carrying him down was on the increase.

A lot more than you'd expect for an evening breeze. Many of the pilots were giving up. Surely this could not be katabatic wind, the cold evening air that whooshed down Alpine valleys in the evening when the sun's powers withered. That would be more like a gale. He knew so little about the practicalities of mountain flight, and needed weeks of work to learn it. Time, however, was not forthcoming. Meanwhile he took no risks. Just as the light faded he came down like a vulture swooping after carrion. There was no target to aim at, just his captors.

He was very tired when he had packed up the Scorp and they drove back to Grenoble. He should not be feeling so good. With his situation he had no right to any feelings of relaxation, pleasure and satisfaction such as came after good flights.

They had a quick meal at a snack bar somewhere in the west of the city. Then, when all he wanted to do was to climb into bed, they drove through the darkness to the garage near the Station.

"*Au travail!* "

There were some of the men he had seen the day before, the partners, the comrades, who must know about Maura and Tony and where they were imprisoned. Three assistants were ready to hand him tools when he called for them. They treated him like a top surgeon operating on a royal patient. Faisal was hanging around glaring and watching, ready to make some contribution or to offer some criticism. And Leila was ready to translate.

He wished they'd all clear off and leave him to work on his own. Modifying the Scorp for dual flight was like gelding a thoroughbred. It would have been a lot better to get hold of a hang glider built for the job. Hi-way, the people who built the Scorp, did a special reinforced hang glider for dual flight. These people should have obtained some Continental equivalent rather than let him hammer away at building this bicycle for two. He had thought he would feel more comfortable flying his own kite, even after it had been converted. But as he worked away, constructing a new frame, replacing the existing down tubes and widening their angle, he began to wonder if he had been wrong. It was no use consulting these people. The man who died had been the expert. They would have to see for themselves that the task was impossible, then they would give up for once and for all. He and his family could go home.

The alterations meant the wing wires were the wrong length so he spent hours making a completely new set. A hang strop had to be fitted for the man on top. Keep the bastard and his bad breath as far above him as possible.

The drag would always be the problem. It would have been a difficulty even with a specially made dual-flight glider with strengthened struts especially to take tubbies like Faisal. In theory, two flying one above the other would make the flight angle less grotesque. He had never seen a serious dual flight in a machine adapted like this, but had read perfunctory reports about them in flight magazines. There was nothing to stop them taking place, he supposed. It was just that no one in their right mind would want to go in a long XC flight on the double. Unless the passenger lacked experience in hang gliding.

"You'll need a sewing machine to make a new hang strop," he said to Leila. No problem. He had only thought about that while he was working on the bars, but she came up with one as if she habitually carried it around with her. Ten minutes out into the night and she returned with a neat little Japanese electric machine which was set up for her in a corner of the garage. Bought? Borrowed? She sat down to do a woman's job under his direction, whirring away until he was satisfied.

He tested and fitted the new harness carabiners. It took until well after midnight to get the thing finished. When they left the converted Scorp at the garage for the night and drove back to the house in the Rue de l'Arte, he was exhausted. He wished he was not going hang gliding tomorrow.

Before he went to bed they had a tape for him. We're all right, Paul, really we are. I'm okay, Daddy. Do what they ask Paul. Even after listening he slept deeply, the sleep of exhaustion.

Up at dawn. This project would founder because he was so tired. They did not go back to where they were yesterday, but in another direction altogether. Forget about the Isère valley. They collected the Scorp and drove west towards a resort called Allevard Les Bains which turned out to be yet another place devoted to invalids. A little wholesome town, not quite so hung with ski lifts as elsewhere. Maybe too many pine trees were in the way.

They took him far beyond the town to a valley where the trees were less and a long ridge of limestone rock promised a good height for a head on wind. The place was relatively quiet, probably because the approach road was so bad. It was being improved; bulldozers were at work. Next year or the year after the ski *pistes* and the tourist hotels would come. Europeans would never rest until the whole of the Alps were hidden under a web of ski lifts. Now in midsummer not too many people seemed to be around this particular part of the Alps. Those who had come here were flat earthers, hikers, botanists, picnickers with screeching children. The scene was pretty, the sort that Maura would have liked.

The Hiace crossed a river torrent and made its way upwards. No other hang gliders were in the vicinity; like the site yesterday morning, the ridge that Faisal had marked out for take-off could only be reached on foot. They carried the Scorp between them up a steep path, a twenty-minute walk.

Yahir, the bodyguard who had assisted yesterday, had come to act as dogsbody once again. He would be noseman when they started their double act. Now he was hung like a pedlar with helmets and audios. Leila followed behind.

They were sweating when they reached the ledge that was pronounced to be suitable for take-off. What a place to choose. It was quiet enough.

One reason for the heat was the total lack of wind. Paul peered over the edge and pronounced it unflyable. Nothing at all to aid the flyer, not even a stir at his back like the beat of a butterfly wing. They stood overlooking the edge, Paul sweating, while the others persuaded him in three languages that there was no problem. Faisal was firm. A man whose appearance was ludicrous suddenly turned menacing. Paul had to obey orders. They were urgent. So little time. More time, and they might have recruited someone of their own persuasion instead of a reluctant mercenary.

At least he persuaded Faisal that this wasn't the best moment for a double flight. He would take off and test the converted Scorp on his own.

Twenty minutes of sweated argument had him prepared to rig.

Suppose he died right now? He had never felt this much fear. Strange when he remembered that this time yesterday he had seriously contemplated killing himself.

"I have to trust you," he said to Leila as he buckled on his helmet. "If anything goes wrong I must trust you about Maura. You'll see she's okay." He was shocked to see tears in her eyes. She wasn't crying over him, that was for sure. Then he thought that perhaps he was about to take off at the place where the other guy had been killed. It was quiet here, a good spot for practice. No one to interfere.

He rigged and checked, taking particular care to inspect the bits that had been changed, and testing the new adjustments to the bracing wires. Faisal also did his checking. Then he stood there waiting with Yahir, little people like rats.

Keep the nose down, run like hell and don't pull out until you feel the lift. The only way of getting a clear take-off was for Faisal to hold up the nosewires and let them fall. The edge of the cliff was sharp, a clean fall into space.

A last glance at the rigging and then he swung into the harness. Christ, what a drop. Faisal stood with his back to the abyss, a nosewire in each hand.

"*Allez-y!* "

Paul shouted, then jumped or rather, pushed off. A fleeting impression of a small scared man leaping under the wing and then . . .

Remember to keep the bar in, forget about your feet. The white cliff face brushed past as close as death. Far below he could see the green tops of fir trees, a dense, ragged carpet towards which he was falling. This is what it is like for people who leap off skyscrapers. They have plenty of time to think. Heartbeats hurt. Straight down and then the wings caught the air, held, and he gently pushed out. Suddenly he felt that familiar and always wonderful sense of going up — why did he always disbelieve that it would happen? The vario blipped in the rising air. He let it rise until the altimeter showed a 400-metre gain. He played around a bit, testing the new handling of the scorp. It was pretty dreadful, but not as bad as he dreaded — a bit sluggish considering the conditions, but the change in the frame had affected it less adversely than he had anticipated. Nothing he could not manage. But wait until the passenger was installed.

There had been such an argument about take-off that they had made no real provision for landing apart from a cursory glance at a map. They'd be watching him from high on the ridge. He would have to avoid the electric cables, cutting across the far perimeter of the valley. When they flew by night very likely they'd be bumping into electric cables like a thumb across guitar strings.

He did two 360s, lost height and came in over the trees. There was a field, a natural target. Some cows in it, hopefully all female. The Scorp would be a rainbow-coloured rag to a bull. He turned into the wind, easing off height, flipping his wings, and he was coming down fast. His feet were out of the stirrups holding on to the bars, the altimeter was zero, he flared up and his feet hit the ground. The quadrupeds fled, cow bells jangling and a group of hikers cheered.

Faisal and Co. joined him half an hour later, hot and puffed and depressed. They sat down in the meadow to a picnic of hunks of bread, peaches and Coke, and Leila began talking about the accident that had killed her husband. Paul's instincts had been right — he had died here. A couple of fields away. Today was the first time they had come back. The way he died sounded very similar to what happened to Gordon back home beside Mount Leinster. Some dragon of wind turbulence had gobbled him up. The risk of erratic thermal current carrying you up to hell was a lot likelier in these parts than in County Kilkenny. The usual way experienced gliders died was the result of an unforeseen freak of wind and weather. This man, Leila's husband, had been expert. You'd think they'd all be put off the way fate had got him. Bad luck had killed him, not bad flying, Kismet. It was as if he had been struck dead by a thunderbolt. God didn't want them to go ahead with their plan.

This place had bad vibes. But it did not put them off. Their motivation was strong enough to drive him crazy. Stealing diamonds, they said.

111

They waited for hours for an evening breeze. They had learned patience. When they got up the slope again in the cool of the evening, there was a peachy little eighteen-miles-an-hour wind blowing in his face. For a few seconds he anticipated a joyful flight. Then his pleasure died instantly, as he realized that he had flown solo for the last time.

Here was Faisal swanking around in his prone harness looking like a blacksmith whose apron had got tangled with a horse's bridle. The rigged glider flapped like a wounded bird. He had to be strapped in, then Paul had to take off, all flailing arms and legs, carrying the weight above him like Sinbad and the old man of the sea.

It could have been worse. Even Faisal called down "*Bien!*" from his perch above. He must be brave, Paul acknowledged. He had not flown for months, maybe years, and he had trusted himself to Paul.

They did nothing spectacular. Incredibly, Paul found some lift and was able to accomplish a bit of wind soaring. The drag was formidable, but not as bad as he had feared. Great credit to the manufacturers. What more could you ask from a three-, or was it three-and-a-half-generation glider?

He came in safely to the same field where he had landed in the morning. Again the cattle scattered — they'd be ripe for spontaneous abortion.

And then there was a half an hour sitting with his loathsome passenger waiting for Leila and Yahir to make their descent. They practised some pigeon conversation larded with words like *accastillage* and *instrumentation* and *pompe*. That meant lift — it pomped you up, didn't it? You couldn't call their exchanges communication. He hated Faisal as much as ever. Surely the feeling must be mutual? How could he trust himself to Paul and become his helpless passenger. Talk died and dusk gathered as they stood side by side near the dirt track waiting for the Hiace.

And so the drive back to Grenoble and bed. For a night cap there was the usual taped message. He may have been trying to reassure himself, or it may have been his imagination, but he thought that Maura and Tony didn't sound so frightened. They sounded bored. Hard to tell. At least no one was hurting them for the moment. He slept fitfully, his dreams full of images of cutting away at a harness and watching a hideous figure fall down, down on to razor-sharp rocks. Scream, you bastard.

Chapter Eight

THEY HAD PRACTICE flights for the next three days. What these proved was that performance was erratic. You couldn't predict a good flight. Nor could you predict that they would hit the target. Paul endlessly hinted through Leila that they needed months to attune themselves to the strangeness of dual flight and night flight. However, the attitude continued to be, "It'll be all right on the night".

He concentrated doggedly on his Sinbad role, learning the nasty business of adjusting to a good machine whose handling characteristics had been loused up. Never in all his misfortunes did he think he would actually come to hate hang gliding. If I survive this I shall take up darts and snooker. Days of dangerous drudgery. Not that he could entirely blame Faisal, who on the whole wasn't a bad partner, responding well to the twists and turns of flying. Except that he was growing like a monster with his guns and grenades.

The big one was a machine gun. Paul's knowledge of such was confined to the line in the ballad about the rattle of a Thompson gun. He learned now that Tommy guns were still in existence, revamped and updated. Faisal had something superior. Paul had thought vaguely that Armalites and Kalashnikovs were the last word in smart gunfire, but Faisal preferred a Heckler and Koch, the sort favoured by the West German police. It was good at plastering a lot of people with bullets very fast. For a robbery?

Then there was the automatic revolver that Faisal carried in a special holster. This turned out to be far more frightening. Knowing it was for keeping him in order when they were flying, Paul had to get used to the concept that the man over his head was armed. On the ground there was no sign of the automatic; in the air his passenger took no chances.

There was one good flight on the second day when they were

able to take advantage of a nice steady evening breeze for ridge flying that took them the distance that Faisal had in mind. It was their second flight — the morning outing in semi-windless conditions had been hopeless. This evening flight might even be a record for going dual. Leila had driven down to a spot in the meadow where she laid out a target while Yahir, the little weasel, stayed up to do the job of noseman. Paul flew as easily as if he had been flying alone, and landed the two of them slap in the middle of the square of towel.

Unfortunately he did not improve. The next two landings were way off target. You would think that Faisal would get the message about hit and miss.

The third morning presented a very slight tail wind. Paul was so frightened at the idea of dropping like stones, the two of them dragging the glider down to earth, that he forgot all about Faisal above him. The tops of the pine trees were very near before the merciful lift pulled them up. This sort of movement was not only too dangerous, but it was quite useless. There was no point in flying in such conditions in order to simulate the atmosphere they would be dealing with during the projected fly-by-night. Sink was taking over. "*Merde, c'est déguelasse!*" as the French boys shouted when their kites began obeying the laws of gravity. A kilometre or so and Paul made it over the pine trees into a green field considerably short of target. Landing was hellish, almost as bad as the take-off — up with the bar, and then swinging down, legs braced to absorb the extra weight in the hammock above him.

When the harnesses were off and they waited to be collected by Leila, Paul noticed a change in Faisal's demeanour. You had to hand it to him — he was tough. The part of his brain that registered fear was wiped blank — but now he kept looking at his hand gun, the one he kept for controlling Paul. He was trembling. He was examining the parachute pack tied to his belly below the prone harness. Much good it would have done him during the flight. Sprung droge and all, it would scarcely have had time to open.

When Leila and the little creep Yahir came up they all had an almighty quarrel. Paul had no idea what the shouting was about. When he learned he began shouting too.

It appeared that the automatic Faisal had for his protection was something special. It was an American-made Mac-II whose production had been stopped by the United States Government after fewer than 200 had been made. The Americans considered them too dangerous to be in circulation. They went off too easily. If the Yanks considered them dangerous, that meant they were not the sort of things to be distributed carelessly. However, various Algerian and Libyan diplomats managed to get hold of 50 or 60 and smuggle them out of the U.S. in diplomatic bags. To have one in his posession made a terrorist or freedom fighter feel good. The great advantage of the Mac-II was its silence — even the safety-belt click of the conventional silencer was eliminated when it was fired. That was why Paul had not heard it go off. He hadn't felt the bullet go past his ear as he strove for lift. The great disadvantage of this particular type of automatic was its instability. That was why it had gone off in the first place when Faisal waved it around.

Even Faisal realized that you needed more than silence and status to protect yourself when you are up in the air. When they next flew, he had swapped the Mac-II for a Polish WZ 63, seemingly the favourite weapon of international terrorists. He wore it for their first night flight.

They went up to the ridge well before sundown to save having to carry the kite up in the dark. Leila and two of the bodyguards remained down at the usual landing area rigging a target which they would light up.

But he was told that this was a rehearsal for the real thing and there would be no flare path at the end of the rainbow.

He had wanted to have a solo flight first of all to get him into the feel for night flying. No time, they said. So he flew off at dusk, with Yahir shouting "*Quand tu veux*" and his mad passenger hovering above him. The flight was easier than he had feared. He found the wind steady and in no way gusty. Adrenalin contributed to his confidence as he forgot the fool overhead and made for the bottom landing. The sun was still throwing up a few lemon rays about the mountains as he hovered above the target. Visibility was still clear enough for him not to be misled by night-time illusions and problems about perception of depth.

116

There was no real need for the torches they played on the target area. He sped in and made a spot-on landing.

The second flight gave him more trouble. Under the quarter moon the problems of sight became more menacing. Carrying the hang glider in the dark lit by torches was a long and tedious job.

The rods that picked out night vision at the periphery of the eye were hard worked. Faisal handed him a pair of red goggles and gestured for him to wear them. (Leila had remained at the landing area.) That meant a long, chilly delay. Rigging a hang glider with subdued red goggles is difficult enough, but inspecting it is worse.

"Oh, to hell with it!" Paul tore off his goggles and accepted the destruction of the white light from Yahir's torch on his eyeballs. That meant waiting another 30 minutes in the darkness for the eyes to adapt again, waiting with growls and curses from his passenger and the feeling of growing cold which the flying suit could not keep out. Faisal lit a cigarette and smoked impatiently. Would do him no good. Diminished the oxygen in the blood. Carbon monoxide inhaled with cigarette smoke combined with the blood about 250 times more easily than the oxygen is displaced. Faisal's visual acuity would be considerably less than it should be. He wouldn't be able to see to shoot the driver.

Possibly this knowledge made Paul fly well. He handled the restricted range of vision that made speed close to the ground seem greater than during daytime because close objects are visible. He was prepared not to be fooled by this illusion which can bring good pilots to stalling speed. The stall approaching landing is the hazard that night pilots dread. He overcame another problem, the perception of depth. The human figures just outside the lighted area, visible in silhouette, provided scale. He landed light as a bird square on the target, and couldn't help feeling pleased, or to put it another way, over-confident.

In this quiet valley they hoped the flight would be unobserved. There was no discussion of the hang glider carrying night lights or the pilot observing visual flight rules. Back home visual flight rules come into effect half an hour after sunset and last until half an hour before dawn. Night flying without correct glider lighting was illegal. Paul was sure that there were similar regulations out here a lot more stringently observed. However, none of the Almutis mentioned the desirability of steady red light of at least five candels showing in all directions. They flew dark as a pirate ship.

He was even more dead tired than usual when they got back. The clear night and cold were energy-sapping and he was more than ready for sleep. The contentment that followed achievement was drained out of him abruptly by the usual grisly bedtime reminder they had ready for him. This time they produced another photograph. He found the photographs much worse than the tapes. The visual evidence of their subjects' helplessness and degradation destroyed his self-satisfaction, while the physical tiredness he felt as he stretched out on the bed dissolved in misery.

He didn't have to fly the next day, which was as well, since he felt he had done two days' work in one. He'd have liked to stay on in bed, but he had to get up early and prepare for a journey. They were leaving Grenoble and going towards Switzerland. There would be no more peripheral flying in Alpine foothills. They were going into territory where the real flying took place and he would meet the real problems of Alpine turbulence.

It was bad that he was leaving Maura and Tony behind. He couldn't even tell whether they were in Grenoble — in theory they could be in any foul place in France under guard. Except that the tapes and photographs arrived so regularly. He felt certain they were in the city under the care of the comrades, and now he was abandoning them. Wherever he was, there was little he could do for them, and he had felt no comfort when he had believed they were near to him. But now, all the same, he was sad.

He got back his clothes, including Joe's jacket. They had been cleaned, and extra shirts and a new pair of jeans were provided in addition to a pile of mountaineering clothing. Someone had gone to trouble. Not the Almutis, who, so far as he could make out, had not had a minute to go shopping.

They set off with the rolled Scorpion on the roof of the Hiace. Four of the team came, Leila, Faisal, Yahir, and another man whose name — Achmed — Paul only now ascertained. Faisal drove; they travelled north along the Turin-Geneva motorway towards the higher mountains and the tougher flying. Five hours of boredom, brooding, misgivings, regrets, second thoughts and fears passed before he saw the big mountains.

"*Voilà Mont Blanc.*"

A queue of cars for the tunnel, signs for Italy and Switzerland. The Almutis were making for Chamonix. They lunched near the village of Le Fyet at a Routier. Paul remembered the last place like this where he and his family had had breakfast the morning before they drove into Grenoble. Now Faisal and the rest escorted him past the entrance hall with its pictures of lorries and accidents towards the dining room. The window had a great view. The sight of Mont Blanc put him off his food as he thought about winds and cross-currents and storms which blew up in a cloudless sky.

His companions were unusually cheerful, acting as if they were on holiday like everyone else here. Maybe in Grenoble they felt oppressed by the other comrades, the ones who held Maura and Tony and the purse strings. Now they were out of school. Whatever the reason, they were in good humour and from time to time a wintry smile even crossed Faisal's lips. Paul wasn't included in the jokes.

The Chamonix valley was only a short distance away. They drove past the curling edge of the Glacier de Rossons into the town and parked near the statue of Horace Bénédict de Saussure. Leila, still in her good mood, informed him that Horace was the first man to climb Mont Blanc.

"He had sixteen porters to help him."

They made their way on foot through crowds of holiday makers to a small pension by the river Arve. They must have booked months ago when the other guy was going to do the flying. Chamonix appeared to be booked up and every little hotel had its *Complet* notice like this one.

He shared a room with Achmed. Not a word of a shared language between them. The roar of the river and the snores of his companion kept him awake together with the knowledge that his room-mate carried an automatic. Paul had a good look at it and ascertained to his dismay that Achmed had taken over Faisal's wicked Mac-II.

Next morning he was instructed to dress warmly and donned a heavy pullover and padded blue skiing jacket and boots that he hadn't broken in which hurt him. The others were all dressed in mountaineers' clothes as they sat at a table overlooking the river drinking hot chocolate and eating croissants and jam like other holiday makers. While they ate they indulged in some animated decision-making which concerned him, he could tell. He asked Leila what it was about. A shrug. Plans for the day. Were they flying? It seemed not. Tomorrow, but today there was an alternative programme.

They drove to the aerial cableway which started just outside Chamonix. Although the time was not yet nine o'clock already there were long queues for tickets. Climbers with rucksacks and coils of ropes lounged in the sun, while in the café opposite a group of Japanese were taking pictures of one another holding up cups of tea. High overhead above the valley the Mont Blanc Massif shone white in the sky.

They had to queue for an hour, a period of squeezed bodies moving almost imperceptibly towards the *caisse*. Something more than just the crush was making the Almutis unhappy.

"*On sera en retard!*" Leila kept muttering. There was another queue for the cable car. When they finally reached it the crowd charged in until the cabin was packed. No animal welfare association would have tolerated such conditions for cattle. A door slammed, a bell rang and they were away.

Crush, nausea and a frenzy of people swaying from one side to the other to take mountainy pictures out of the window. Chamonix disappeared beneath them, then came forest far below and a view of the Glacier des Bossons streaked in blue. Pardon ... pardon ... a small boy being sick. Young Germans talking loudly. An elderly Japanese strung with cameras wearing a straw hat with the ticket of his tourist group struck in the hat band. Only a thin layer of steel between this crowd and a whole lot of pine trees beneath them. No Frenchman that Paul could see was making the weird journey.

It was curious that people who thought this climb a thrilling

120

experience and one of the world's exciting journeys regarded hang gliding as madness.

At the summit of the Aiguille du Midi the great rust-coloured column of granite under the summit of Mont Blanc attracted so many people circling the viewing station and crowding the lifts that it was difficult to move. On the ridge of snow outside scores more visitors were putting on climbing crampons. The scene was like old photographs of prospectors in the Klondike. Had they paused to read the notice warning that the Société de Téléfériques would not be responsible for their foolhardiness if they tripped and fell high in the snow?

Faisal, Leila and the others weren't here for the snow. Onward to Helbronner. The Helbronner cable cars were small and red and came in threes. Three little cars were slung on wires across the abyss of the Vallée Blanche like beads on an abacus. Then another great pylon and loop of wire spun them into Italy in their little tin box. Thirty minutes in mid-air without the pure thrill of flying. Down below the lines of climbers moved as small black dots across the snow. Just before the car reached the Punta Helbronner the passengers saw skiers for the first time, making the mountains more of an ant heap. They were angling down towards another serrated ridge of red-brown rock where France and Italy met.

More queues at the other side waiting to show passports at the French and Italian customs. Faisal handed Paul's, the one they had grabbed when Maura and Tony were taken. The passport showing was a busy tedious formality — Arab, Japanese, Irish, German, Arab, stamp, stamp. There were too many in the milling crowd for the blue-uniformed, debonair officials at the Controllo Passaporti to seek out trouble.

The five of them made their way to the Bar Belvedere which was crowded with noisy Italians dressed in flashy ski clothes. Paul was given a cup of coffee from the bar where the mob of skiers and tourists could buy key rings, postcards and cuddly dolls. Did they carry the dolls inside their anoraks as they skied? Faisal and Leila were waiting anxiously; whoever they had come to meet was not here. They found a table for three, which meant two of the party had to stand. Paul chose to wander round restlessly with Yahir following, keeping silent company. He allowed himself a few thoughts about skiing. How did it compare with hang gliding? Would there be something of the same pleasure sweeping down the high mountains at Courmayeur and Chamonix? Always supposing you could get away from the crowds.

More coffee. Faisal and friends became increasingly agitated as they watched the cable car from the Italian side. They were too unhappy to pretend to look like a holiday party. They trooped miserably outside, up the steps, past the lavatories to the viewing balcony. A giant statue showed Christ with outstretched hands over an inscription meaningless to Paul. "*Se tutti i popoli del Mondo Vulessero la Mano.*" Here was another opportunity to watch skiers, a chilly pastime out in the snowy atmosphere. Lines of beginners were learning to cross plough, their skis turned in.

A hand was placed on Faisal's back. A blonde woman who was pretty if it weren't for her sulky face and moody expression. Or did that look show fear? Her fair hair and slim figure made Leila look particularly dowdy by comparison. She was too conspicuous to be the ideal conspirator — even as she stood under Jesus and talked briskly to Faisal she attracted casual comments from passing Italians involving words like *bella* and *buona*. She was quick to hand over a cardboard roll, the sort you put maps into. Faisal pointed out Paul to her, but did not beckon him over. Her eyes inspected him briefly, just long enough to recognize him again.

The meeting was over in less than five minutes before the strange woman disappeared into the crowd towards the Cormayeur cable. Then for the rest of them there waited the same journey in reverse back to Chamonix by cable car, the same sweep over valleys in overcrowded tin boxes. The magnificent views were a mockery in that discomfort. Every now and then somewhere in the world one of these cable cars gave way and dropped people down in the snow far below. Like everyone else, Paul had seen the newsreels. He could do without the swaying glimpses of mountains. Someone once said that "the prospect of the Alps fills the mind with an agreeable kind of horror". That guy should be up in a cable car.

The others didn't think to tell him what the whole day's journey was about. They had wasted precious time when they could have been training. The stranger must be a contact . . . perhaps at the villa itself. Handing over a map or a blueprint. He could make an intelligent guess as to why he had been taken along, to be vetted, inspected, his face filed for future recognition.

Somewhere behind Chamonix was the route in the high Alps where they would be flying when the test came. Tonight they were too tired for a night flight, but tomorrow they would resume serious training. So Leila deigned to tell him.

"How long do we have?"

"Not so long."

In the evening he was called in for a conference in the bedroom which Faisal and Leila shared. The embarrassment of invading intimacy was on his part, not on theirs. Yahir and Achmed crowded in as well while maps were unrolled on one of the twin beds.

A map of part of Switzerland meant nothing to him. Massaccio Monte Bianco with a scale of 1:5000 — large enough to mark small foot tracks. Faisal's stubby finger pointed, Leila translated. Morgex, La Thoille . . . the main range . . . the lake of Petra Rossa cradled by the mountains. The take-off point on the Becca Poignenta.

Emphasis on foot tracks. It dawned on Paul for the first time that in addition to its other insuperable difficulties the flight involved an initial long walk. Like a good many pilots he had got lazy. He liked to restrict himself to as little walking and carrying as possible. At home the reason why Mount Leinster was the most popular take-off place in Ireland was that it had a road leading to the television mast at its summit.

How many kilometres? Something like fifteen to walk, carrying weight. Firearms for starters. Food and stuff. The hang glider.

"Shouldn't we be doing some training in mountaineering?" The trek seemed to be almost more appalling than the actual flight.

"We have been over the route a number of times before." Before her husband died. "And you . . . you are in good shape."

Paul had his doubts. They would be hard put to it, lugging the great glider over the Alps, bringing rations for several days, tents, and all the paraphernalia, flying helmets, harnesses, altimeters and the rest. And the arms had to be carried as well. He wondered if they wouldn't be needing porters by the dozen. They'd have to climb over a track that would probably be crowded if today was anything to go by. Wouldn't a hang glider so far from the usual routes of communication attract attention from passing hikers?

"We will be going at the beginning of September. Most visitors will have finished their vacations by that time. The enthusiasm for hang gliding is comparatively new in the Alps. There are many pilots who wish to fly down from different peaks. To say they are the first to have done so." Paul knew this was true; only recently someone had flown a hang glider off Mont Blanc for the first time. He remembered how he himself had sought out mountains all over Ireland from which to fly.

"It will soon be the most natural thing in the world to see an adventurous hang gliding pilot seeking to fly off the Becca Poignenta."

He concentrated on listening instead of worrying about basic imponderables — Alpine winds and downdrafts that made mockery of distance. Always remember, always comfort yourself that at night there was less turbulence and smoother air. At least it appeared that if the wind was right and the sink did not defeat them, direction would be no difficulty. Always provided they could see something with the aid of moon and stars.

Faisal pointed out on the map the line of electric pylons across the valley which would have to be avoided. They would be lit with red lights by the careful Swiss. A village — it would have minimum lighting during the after-midnight hours when they would be flying. A house here, a house there. Most of them would be unlit. And at the head of the valley he pointed out the crude swathe cut through the trees when the chalet was first built in order to bring up materials. A rough track remained, suitable for only the toughest vehicles. Elsewhere new trees had been planted which were nearly grown. The nearest road was five kilometres away.

Behind skeins of barbed wire spaced with security towers stood Shangri La.

"It will be floodlit?"

"Of course." A blaze of glory.

Faisal brought out the cardboard tube that the blonde had given him at the Courmayeur cross.

"Who is she?"

"She is the wife of the caretaker at the chalet. She acts as housekeeper."

"She looked too pretty to have such a dull job."

"It is not dull at all. She and her husband live there three weeks out of four. A helicopter flies them out for a week's holiday at their apartment in Geneva. They are paid very well."

"Why is she putting her job at risk by helping you lot?"

"She is a patriot."

The blueprint in the tube showed the plan of the chalet with the layout of bedrooms.

Paul asked about security.

"Those who guard the chalet have to be discreet. There must be no aggravation to the Swiss government."

"How many guards?"

"Something like two dozen."

"That's practically an army. Why so many when the Sheikh is never there?"

"His sons are always under threat. Several have already been assassinated."

Faisal interrupted. Enough, conference over. Tomorrow we fly. Sent to bed, Paul had to listen to the breathing of his companion while he pondered problems of security, guards, positioning of jewels, ways of escape and other insoluble questions. He also had the latest photograph to think about, showing Maura and Tony gaunt and frightened.

Even at dawn Chamonix was crowded. As they wound through the tourist developments at the outskirts of the town Faisal pointed out a small field hemmed in by buildings which seemingly was the landing ground. Paul was reminded of the football pitch at Kilmacanogue. He didn't like it at all, the contrast between flying in the wild mountains and landing in the suburbs. But this flight, Leila assured him, would be no trouble, and since it was his first in the high Alps, they had chosen the simplest route. They would go above the glacier at Argentière to Les Grandes Montées, 4,000 metres up. He would see there would be plenty of room for flying.

The station for the mountain at Argentière was in the trees about seven kilometres on. (He must think metres.) Leila and Achmed stayed behind while he went with Faisal and Yahir to the *télémécanique* pushing behind the day's quota of mountaineers trailing ropes and icepicks. Paul was interested to see a few hang gliders, too, putting their kites into the carrier. Who was it who said that the essence of sport is the invention of an artificial problem for the fun of solving it.

They piled into the cabin of the *télémécanique* for yet another famous flying view — once again, the nubbly face of Mont Blanc, which must be about the most easily recognizable mountainside in the world, with the possible exception of Fujiyama. They sat in another crowded cabin and endured watching pine trees, snow, rocks, falls of ice and the Argentière glacier, while Chamonix and all its tourists wedged into its narrow valley receded into the distance.

Anticipation of a flight in the high Alps, his first, gave him a pleasant feeling of excitement. He couldn't help it. The scale of flying here would be as different to flying near Grenoble as Grenoble was to the old Sugarloaf in County Wicklow.

The glacier was slashed with mud-coloured crevasses. The cold was a shock. Of course it was bound to be colder 9,000 feet up. Those mountaineers picking their way across the ice had come up here for fun. The crevasses were frightening. They'd swallow up a Scorp. Rigging with gloves on was tricky and he took a far longer time than usual to fix the king post, check the rigging wires, put in the batons and reach the stage where he could inspect the hang glider spreading its wings on the ice. Mountaineers plodding their way upwards stopped and stared at the rainbow wings and the double harness. After making his inspection Paul thought about the wind. There wasn't that much, but there was cloud. He looked up and took note of the clouds that had suddenly sneaked across the main ridge of Mont Blanc. He pointed them out to Faisal in his great French. "*Pas bon. Trop. Non.*" Faisal was impatient, snapping at Yahir, but even he

126

realized they couldn't fly with that much cloud about.

They waited for an hour, consulting the map much of the time with shaking hands. All shade, no sun to warm things up. The cold was a continuing problem. The chill seeped inside him in spite of all the stuff they had given him to wear.

Suddenly the great rounded crest of Mont Blanc appeared. They had better get on with the flight while the going was good. The time was only eleven, but he felt he had been up here for ever.

Mountaineers stopped to watch as they prepared for take off. He buckled in, Faisal above him, and Yahir holding up the glider — hard work for one man. Some of Paul's good spirits returned as he concentrated on the problems of flight and of crossing the ice into the wind. If the Scorp fell into a crevasse the wings would keep them up. The drop before levelling was the usual huge fright, with the addition that Paul's gasping lungs were seared with icy air.

The cross-country took time. He didn't know how long, maybe twenty minutes of flying with Mont Blanc beside them. Too short — even the passenger above couldn't spoil the joy of it. There was a road. That must be the main road to Martigny on the Swiss side. Trees, the line of the river, houses. Their extra weight now meant extra speed so that the ground was rushing up. There was a cable wire to avoid, there was the landing field. That little figure waving a red scarf must be Leila. Someone standing beside her. Other faces looking up. A little more speed and his belly was scraping the tops of trees. Leila had marked out the usual target with towels. Then to come in to a perfect landing.

A crosswind caught them just as they came in. He felt a surge of fear, just like at take-off only more so. A bad landing only takes a second. Disaster comes as swift as a shot. The Scorp was knocked on its side. The impact was fierce. He was stunned. The other guy lay beside him.

Silence. A long silence. Then screams, a long-drawn-out series of screams. For a moment he felt sorry for her. She was seeing something like a repeat.

Chapter Nine

FAISAL LAY IN his prone harness. Paul felt nothing about him — no pity or satisfaction or revenge. All he felt was annoyance at the way the landing had gone. It was hardly his fault that he had been spooked by an Alpine crosswind. It could have happened to a bishop, as they say. Faisal was not in good shape. The leg sticking out at an angle. The snore like a death rattle.

The crowd gathered, as Paul stood up and peeled off his harness. Here was an officious gendarme coming up and shouting at him. Leila was still screaming. Here was a doctor or someone like bending over Faisal. Amazing how people like that sprang out of the ground. The poor old Scorp looked bad, and Paul figured that no matter how much work you put into her she would be a write-off. She'd go no more a-roving. He felt sorrier about the Scorp — a lot sorrier — than he did about Faisal.

He was giddy. Shakily he began to derig the mess he had made while people continued to crowd around Faisal's prone form. Leila had got over the hysterics and was suddenly directing people here and there. An ambulance speeded up, its siren neighing like an electrocuted horse, and spat out hurrying men and a stretcher. Paul figured concussion and a broken leg. He himself had been lucky, taking up the ground with the neatness of a ballet dancer as the thing had pitched forward. Faisal had been helpless as a bag of cement.

The gendarmes would be back for him after the neat Frenchmen had packed Faisal away into the ambulance. He didn't want to get involved with questions and statements right now. They might not do Maura and Tony any good. He'd slip away with the rest of the onlookers.

He wasn't going to find his exit easy, since he was chief actor with the role of dying gladiator. Even with harness and helmet off he attracted attention. However, suddenly all eyes were on Faisal's prone form as it was being wheeled towards the ambulance.

At the edge of the crowd he found a little English couple in a Metro.

"Do you happen to be going into town? I want to get back and tell his sister . . ." Funny how respectable and cosy the mention of a sister always was. They had been on their way to inspect the brown wastes of the Mer de Glace, but now they were all eagerness to help. They turned round as Paul sat in the back uttering the occasional groan to discourage talking. Are you all right really? Shouldn't we go to the hospital? No, I'm fine. I'm fine. They drove into Chamonix and deposited him in the Place de l'Eglise, conscious of having been helpful.

Tourists were wandering through the old square, inundating the Office de Tourisme with requests for accommodation. He passed by the Hôtel de Ville with its forlorn notices of people looking for employment. Horse-drawn carriages filled with holidaying fools trundled past.

He didn't know what to do. Get back to the hotel and wait for Leila. They'd have to let Maura go now, the whole project was aborted. How long before Leila would be back? She'd be holding the hand of your man and waiting round the hospital to learn how bad he was. Suppose he was dead? Poor girl, it would be miserable for her, husband and lover going the same way. Serve her right.

He peered into shops at lines of cuckoo clocks, cow bells, stuffed St Bernards and T-shirts emblazoned CLIMB A ROCK. He wandered down the pedestrian Avenue Michel Croz. Shoppers and tubs of flowers filled up the street. His head ached. He had a cup of coffee and a Danish pastry at a café.

He was going into a museum of mountaineering. It cost money, the French didn't let you do anything for nothing. He hadn't much left from what he had taken from Joe's jacket all that time ago. Most of it was yellow coinage embellished with cocks and ladies in liberty hats. And yet here he was paying to see photographs of bewhiskered guides, old inns and charabancs. Tourists and crowds from early times, the women twirling parasols as the men prepared to climb. Here was Horace Bénédict de Sassure again, surrounded by his porters. Here was Michel Croz, the man who gave his name to the Avenue. Old

Croz had been a guide, like 90 per cent of the male population of Chamonix. He was a pioneer who went up the Matterhorn with Whymper and the rope broke. Poor old Croz and several others went with it. Someone did not do a proper pre-flight inspection.

The thought brought him back to the morning's happenings. No way could he be blamed. Not like the other time he had an accident — years ago, when he had been learning to fly prone. That time he had definitely been at fault. He had been too cocky, ignoring the fact that the transition from flying seated to going prone is well known as a dangerous period in a pilot's life. He had been lucky then, too, falling in boggy ground so that the triangle of the A-frame broke his fall. He had been left hanging by the Jesus bolt six inches from the ground like a parrot on a battered perch.

He was wasting time. He must talk with Leila and explain how the circumstances had been beyond his control. He hadn't been responsible for the blast of crosswind any more than her husband had invited the Alpine fury that had killed him.

He and Maura and Tony could go home now.

He must find Leila. He made his way in the direction of the *pension* and came across it more or less by luck. At the reception desk was the smug, spruce moustached proprietoress. Perhaps something in the climate made mountain people look alike, resembling the unglamorous Swiss. Polyglot lady. Your friends, those Arabs? No, they have left no message.

He was at a loss. What to do now? Go upstairs and wait in the bedroom for developments? He thought of the hospital where Faisal would have been taken. He was about to return to the desk to ask the horse-faced woman where it was when he felt a tap on his shoulder. Here was his silent roommate. Achmed had been down on the landing field with Leila when they came crashing in.

He had awful French, but what he had to say was simple stuff. *Venez*, Madame wishes to talk to you, *vite*.

Paul followed him out of the *pension* and down a side street near the river. An alleyway more like. The Hiace was parked awkwardly beside a loading bay. Achmed must have come quickly because no one had yet objected to where it was, taking up room. This was the first street in Chamonix that Paul had seen that wasn't jammed with people.

If Paul had been planning the killing he would have fudged for a good bit longer before producing the gun. He would have let his victim climb into the van and driven him out to some quiet place in the mountains among pine trees and shot him there. Paul would have had no suspicions — how was he to know the location of the hospital where Leila and Faisal had gone? He was already used to seeing hospitals and sanatoria located out in the countryside.

Instead Achmed made a mess of the whole business. He was sweating with excitement and his eyes were bright. He slid open the door of the van and motioned Paul to get inside. In the back, he beckoned with his gun. That flashy Mac-II. He'd shoot him when he was inside. The Mac-II was known for its silence. The street was empty.

Paul hit out, his reflexes fuelled by hate. He felt no fear, leaping off a cliff in a no-wind situation was more frightening. He caught Achmed's arm and it went up as the automatic demonstrated its two characteristics, instability and silence. Paul heard no noise of firing, only a zinging sound and then a thud and a tinkle behind him as the bullet hit a window somewhere in the alley. It was hard to associate the volatile toy with death. He had the other fellow's wrist and was wrenching and shaking with his hands while trying to get his knee at his groin at the same time.

Achmed had started off tops, holding the Mac-II and preparing to kill. Now he got killed. Paul squeezed his wrist hard enough so that he dropped the gun, and it was Paul who got to it first. And he shot him. Achmed gave this big sigh and then relaxed. He slid to the ground, his eyes open, brown eyes, not all that dark, the amber colour they put into teddy bears.

Silence. Miraculous silence, except for the distant rush of the river at the end of the street and a far-off car horn. Midday in a town packed shoulder to shoulder with people, and not a sound in this alley. Paul did not pause but picked up the little corpse quickly and thrust it into the back. The shattered remains of the Scorp were already there.

The keys were in the door. He pulled them out, climbed into the driver's seat, remembered to fasten his safety belt, and drove off, not too fast. Was there a shout behind him? He crashed the gears, but got the hang of driving before he was out into the main stream of traffic.

In the past he had sometimes wondered what it would be like to kill someone. For the moment he felt nothing, not even the fulfilment of a mild curiosity. His self-disgust came for quite different reasons. He had spent hours wandering about looking at tourist souvenirs and old photographs without a thought as to how disaster was building up. He could put some of his behaviour down to shock at the accident and the blow to his head. But it didn't altogether excuse his stupidity. It didn't excuse it at all. He should have worked out what would happen minutes after he saw Faisal lying there.

No more hang gliding for Faisal for the time being, if ever. The Scorp was wrecked. That meant mission cancelled. Discouraging the way things had turned out.

Of course, these people would cut their losses. They would dispose of the debris. The debris was himself. Very embarrassing having him around. And Leila must have felt rage at what he had done or failed to do. He was responsible for the accident. She may even have thought he would go to the police, now he had so little to lose. Instead he had hung around looking at plush St Bernards. She had decided quickly, and told this little dead guy lying in the back of the van to kill him.

If he were disposed of, what about Maura and Tony? Why should they be released to go out and moan and groan about their experiences?

He must find the hospital. He didn't dare slow down and ask in his French. He caught a glimpse of himself in the mirror, wild eyes looking back at him. He drove around aimlessly keeping to the outskirts of the town. Nowadays hospitals were usually in the suburbs. There were traffic jams, cars braying, drivers with their hands on their horns. After about twenty minutes he was lucky and caught sight of a sign — HÔPITAL GENERAL —and an arrow. For all he knew it could be for maternity cases. There might be two or three others around.

He found a modern-looking glass palace geared for dealing

132

with shattered limbs of skiers and mountaineers. A concrete car park sloping away in front was packed with cars. You'd never think so many were associated with the sick in one small town. It was as if tourists were dying of plague like that film about Venice.

A car quite near to the steps moved off, and he parked. He closed his eyes for a few minutes. He was trembling. He'd have to calm down before he went inside and tried tackling the porter or concierge or whoever. *Pardon, Monsieur, un accident,* and flap the arms like a bird's wings. He didn't know Faisal's full name. *Le vol libre, le delta planeur,* those were the words to use. Probably they'd speak some English. He must stop trembling. Find a comb to make himself a little more respectable. There was a blood stain on his sweater. The corpse in the back had been wearing a sweater. The bullet had made a star design like an unusual logo.

The gun was beside him on the passenger seat. He picked it up and fiddled with the mechanism, lucky not to shoot off his foot or shatter the windscreen. The thing opened, revealing the barrel. He took out the bullets. He didn't want to shoot anyone else that afternoon.

He was about to make his way towards the entrance when Leila came out of the glass door with the other henchman, Yahir. They caught sight of the Hiace, turquoise, conspicuous. They came towards it.

He must have looked fierce stepping round in front of the snubby bonnet and pointing the Mac at them. They figured out what had happened long before he bundled both of them into the back and made the man lie on the floor. There wasn't much room with the dead man and the remains of the shattered Scorp in there as well. A measure of how badly it was damaged was the way it was folded in a bundle of steel struts, wires and Terylene.

He remembered how Yahir had kicked him around that first time at Grenoble. He searched him and took his automatic off him — a Walther. He searched Leila — unarmed. It was difficult tying Yahir up while having the Mac handy, and now the Walther as well, but it was a pleasure. He made Leila help. There was plenty of rope and wire lying about. Yahir's hands were tied with spare wire used for the Scorp's wing wires. He was gagged with an oily rag. He lay beside the corpse and the other stuff.

There wasn't much room to seize Leila by the wrist and shake her and hurt her.

"No, no your wife is fine, she is well, no one has touched her. No one has touched her yet. I promise, trust me . . . Ahh . . ." a scream as he battered her head against the tinny sides of the van . . . "we planned bad things . . . but they did not happen . . . I swear it . . ." Her eyes followed the gun which he was waving breezily in her face. "I could telephone . . ."

"Telephone?"

"To Grenoble . . . to where she and the child are staying."

"What good would that do? I can't speak French or Arabic."

"You could talk to them."

He savoured the idea of hearing Maura's voice.

"You'd have to talk first. And I wouldn't understand what you were saying."

She gave her shrug. He had his choice.

In the end he locked up the van and took her into the hospital. He didn't cover her with a gun, but carried the both of them, the Mac-II and the Walther, in a carrier bag he had found beside the driver's seat. It was white scattered with brown initials — Leila had done her shopping at Dames de France. They found the public phone booth where a fool girl kept them waiting minute after minute with a wretched long giggling conversation that appeared to involve her whole family. Then more delays from the infamous telephone system. He watched Leila feed *jetons* into the voracious call phone. He couldn't threaten her with guns while nurses clopped past in white lace-ups and patients shuffled by. But the invisible whip moved her the way it had moved him these past days.

Then she got through and there was a spate of Arabic. Was it persuasive? Informative? Hortatory? He'd give a finger, an arm to know what she was saying. A pause. A long pause. Five minutes. She handed him the receiver.

"Hello?"

"Hello?"

"Who's that? Is that you, Paul?"

"How are you, Maura?"

"Paul, what's going on?"

"Are you all right?"

"I'm all right."

"What about Tony?"

"He's okay as far as it goes."

"Listen Maura, don't build up hopes. It's just I got a chance to talk. Hold on and be a brave girl."

"What's it all about?"

"I'd better go now. Take care of yourself."

He put the receiver down before Leila could speak again. He had tears in his eyes.

"Who has the authority to let them go? Faisal?"

She looked bewildered.

"Okay ... we'll go and see Faisal now."

She shook her head. "He's not well."

He seized her arm and hurt her. An old woman in a dressing gown in a walking frame came by with a relative or someone beside her. They didn't notice how she was in pain.

"We go to Faisal."

It was bluff, of course. She could have stopped any of the people in the polished corridors and shrieked for help. She had seen Achmed dead, Yahir helpless, and knew that he carried two hand guns in a carrier bag. She accepted the rules that he was the aggressor now and led him up two flights of stairs and down a corridor. She stood beside a spyhole and gave a little sigh as he looked in.

He looked in at a unit with three or four beds in it. You could see the nearest bed. A drip, a heart monitor, bandages. A gorgon nurse came towards the glass partition and shooed them away.

He had hoped that Faisal wouldn't have been so badly hurt. That it had been him, not Leila, who gave the orders to kill Paul.

They went out of the hospital into the sun which was glaring and relentless. There were more people around. He made her drive away. Find somewhere quiet. She drove badly, the bound man and the dead man bouncing in the back. They stopped once, and he and she got out to get some lemonade. He was very thirsty. They went on, silent, as she continued her appalling driving that brought them to the edge of the town again. A tourist notice. An arrow pointing upwards to Pierre à Ruskin.

"Stop. This'll do."

He should talk to her here, sitting in the van, but he couldn't bear to.

He checked Yahir in the back, removed the gag and let her give him a drink. He trussed him up some more, tying him to the steel struts of the seats so that he couldn't hammer at the sides of the vehicle to get someone curious. He locked him in with his friend.

"Come."

Leila trailed after him as he walked quickly up to Ruskin's Rock, just like dozens of other pairs of smiling tourists. They walked for twenty minutes up above the rooftops and into the trees. He wanted a respite from word and action. Maybe she did.

"An Englishman. A philosopher who believed in the perfection of beauty. He thought the mountains beautiful. He brought the first tourists. The English middle classes . . ."

All matters of life and death and here she was chatting away like a guide. Here was Ruskin as a bronze relief near three park benches and a green garbage can. The view was good, facing across trees and hotels the old boy wouldn't have known about when he gazed towards Mont Blanc and the glaciers on the far side of the valley.

Paul sat down on one of the benches and she obediently sat beside him. He thought, I've killed a man. She had been silent after her funny nervous little lecture on the English sage. "You have made racecourses of the cathedrals of the earth," Ruskin said when the people of Chamonix fired off guns to celebrate some conquest of Mont Blanc. He'd be mad now if he saw the way the town was wrecked. He could understand Leila's rage and despair. First the husband, then the lover.

"How bad is Faisal?" He tried not to sound pleased.

"He is unconscious. They think a fractured skull..."

He could hear the hate in her voice. Blaming him for the crosswind.

"I want my wife and child released."

She was silent, looking across at the great wilted wave of the Bossons glacier.

"It is too late."

"I'll do ... whatever was planned."

"There is no way now."

"I'll go stealing all the jewellery you want. I'll fly across Switzerland."

She said sharply: "What was planned was not stealing."

He took the Mac-II out of his carrier bag and the bullets from his pocket and began to load it. She watched impassively.

"We want the Sheikh to be killed."

The Mac was loaded again. He pointed it casually towards Mont Blanc.

"Is that a fact?"

"Assassination. We have already killed three of his sons."

He had always known in his heart there was more to the plan with its wild risks than mere theft.

"What about the queen?"

"She is not there at present. She is in London having an operation." These people were forever sick, bringing their troubles to Harley Street.

"No jewels? No stealing for propaganda?"

"The death of a tyrant would have been the best possible propaganda."

"You said he was in South America."

"He is coming to Switzerland for three days."

"I thought he never came this side of the Atlantic. Because he was afraid of people like you."

"He has to come."

"Why?"

"It is a matter of money. In the usual way his Swiss bankers or their representatives would fly over to South America to confer with him. This time the mountain must come to Mohammed. In secret. No one knows."

"Except you?"

"We have a contact at his court in exile."

He knew instantly who this must be. "The woman we met yesterday?" She nodded. "You said she was a caretaker's wife?"

"You were not told everything."

"Why is she willing to betray him?"

"She is with us. Also it is courting danger to have too many mistresses."

"Why should he have to come here? What's wrong with his money? Isn't he still one of the richest men in the world?"

"He is no longer an absolute ruler, and that makes him vulnerable. Even the Swiss have been worried by the demands of the new government in Almut for the repatriation of his money. Of course, he has much real estate around the world. But the bulk of his liquid assets is in Switzerland."

"Would the bank people want to start that sort of thing? Every time they opened a bank vault they'd be opening up a can of worms as well."

"There have been precedents — cases when the accounts of proven criminals were revealed. Especially if they were involved with drugs. God knows, the Sheikh is a criminal."

"Do the Swiss think so?"

"They have given him their support. They are poison."

Paul had always thought the Swiss were merely disliked on account of their thrift, their bourgeois habits and their image as smug, clean clockmakers.

"They permitted the initial transfer of his private fortune from Almut to their banks long before the revolution sent him into exile. And now ministers of state have been opposing any request for his money to be repatriated."

"So what is his problem?"

"He is afraid that someone will yield to pressure from the Almuti Government . . . that circumstances may arise when even the Swiss would allow for a portion of his funds to be frozen."

"Which would mean less pocket money?"

"They know he is trying to gather support for a counter-coup."

"So they want him to come over and open up the bank vaults?"

"Nothing like that yet. These pressures take time — perhaps years. But high-ranking government and banking officials insist on a conference where the Sheikh is present. They are tired of meetings with his financial representatives."

"How did you learn all this? About the problems of Swiss bankers? Or that he would be coming to Europe? And you . . . your husband . . . has been training for months."

"We knew from our contact he would have to come . . . in the late summer. Now we know at the beginning of September. For a long time he has been very anxious to conceal from the dictator in South America who offered him sanctuary that the Swiss could be contemplating changes in his financial circumstances. His status as an exile would be in jeopardy. So he has agreed to come here in his private Concorde for a conference."

"Your contact has been a useful girl."

"Her information has encouraged friends to support us."

"What friends?"

"Our comrades. They give us money and arms."

The P.L.A.? Possibly. More likely some maverick anti-Zionist, anti-Imperialist group named after a sad date in Middle East history.

"What do you have in common with your comrades apart from the fact they are fellow-Arabs?"

"They think the same as we do. That tyrants should be eliminated. There are others — world leaders — they wish to bring to justice. But of course they wish to bring retribution to the butcher of Almut."

"Are they happy that you only want to kill him?" Paul had seen interviews with Almut fundamentalists talking about kidnapping the Sheikh and bringing him back to Almut to face trial.

"Kidnapping is not feasible. We considered the idea."

"You are only good at kidnapping the defenceless."

They were silent, looking over the valley.

She talked about the plan with plenty of could-have-beens and might-have-beens. The Sheikh's well-justified paranoia made him virtually impossible to approach. In South America he lived

139

in a fortress and in Switzerland too his villa was considered impregnable.

"Few people knew it belonged to him. Anyone who enquired was led to believe that the owner was his cousin, General Siri. Siri was arrested and executed by the revolutionary council in Almut. But the house had always belonged to the Sheikh who commissioned it as a safe hideout many years ago."

"I suppose other people have tried to kill him?"

"Plenty. There is the scar of a bullet wound in his neck. In the old days he would point it out if he wanted to make an effect. To a female Western journalist, perhaps, or a group of army recruits. The last attempt on his life was just before the revolution. Now in exile he is very careful. He has a sense of destiny that he will return to his kingdom."

"Is that why you want to kill him?"

"The idea of the arch traitor backed by the United States and the CIA bringing back the old Imperial regime made patriots of my husband and his brother."

"You were all that desperate? You knew the mission was suicidal?"

"Anyone who is prepared to commit assassination is prepared to die."

"You really hated him?"

She wept as she told him how the Sheikh's secret police had arranged for the torture and death of her brother. How her father, a respectable provincial judge, had been publicly beheaded five years ago. The savage deaths of her husband's parents. The little guy Yahir — terrible things had happened to his family. The others . . . each member of the group wanted the death of the royal exile, not only for political reasons. They burned for personal revenge. Any means would do . . . anyone's wife and child.

"Now it's over, the plan has failed. Now you must let me and my family go."

She said that it wasn't in her hands.

"Whose then?"

"Naturally, our comrades."

"I don't believe you. You wanted to kill me because you hated me. You thought I was responsible for the accident this morning.

Once I proved useless getting rid of me wasn't unreasonable. But Maura and Tony are different."

"I tell you, what happens to them is nothing to do with me. When our partners learn what has happened, they will decide."

"What do you think they'll decide?"

"I do not know."

"I'll kill you if anything happens to them."

"It will make no difference."

"If things had gone well . . . if Faisal and I had made the flight . . . would they have been released?"

"Oh yes . . . there would have been this big publicity. Perhaps a secret press conference . . . the world's press . . ."

"And now?"

"Maybe they will be let go."

He remembered the way Achmed had tried to kill him a couple of hours back, on her orders. He had accepted risks for Maura's sake. He thought over the story about jewel robbery. He had let himself be strung along — hold up, seize the jewels, take the old royal lady hostage — he hadn't sought details. He let them tell him whatever lie they wished and accepted the chauffeur's role. He was like FitzHarris, the man who drove the cab for the Phoenix Park murderers.

He hadn't let himself consider he was on a death mission. They didn't spell it out and he had agreed for Maura and Tony. He had kidded himself into believing he was not committing suicide.

He looked down at the gun he was carrying. The tourists walking nearby peering at Ruskin could have spotted it. He put it back in the Dames de France bag with the stylized df, df, df, covering the surface. Damn fool, damn fool, damn fool. He pulled out the Walther and stripped it. He had the hang of these things.

The accident this morning was bad luck. It was not because of his flying. It was the way her husband had died. You could never predict the outcome of a flight. He asked: "Would you be prepared to kill the Sheikh yourself?"

She said nothing.

"You hate him. Would you shoot him if you had the opportunity?"

"Of course."

He had an idea that "of course" was a translation of a simple Arabic affirmative. It was less emphatic than English.

"How badly do you want him dead?"

"I told you."

"I could take you there. I could take you in double harness instead of Faisal . . ."

"What are you talking about?"

"I agreed to fly with Faisal before."

"The difference is now that you know if you make the flight you will be dead at the end. Before we gave you no details. It was an adventure. Now you know that you would have to face a private army."

"I always knew about the risk. The flight is as much a risk as facing the guards."

"The idea was impossible. A dream of my husband's. It is better to forget all about it."

"Suppose we still made the flight. Suppose you gave me a machine gun as well. An automatic. Grenades. Fragmentation grenades. Two of us going in, firing, throwing, surprise . . . we could do well."

The evening sun shone gloriously on Mont Blanc. Somewhere beyond was the Matterhorn, equally menacing. Ruskin may have believed that mountains were created to show us the perfection of beauty, but they could just as well be forces of evil.

"Why?"

"The reason is the same. For Maura and Tony. I don't believe your friends will let them go now. I don't think you want them to be freed."

"I will see they are released. I swear it . . . not only because of those . . ." The guns. "I want an end to this."

"Of course they will be released. I won't do anything until I know they are safe."

"I have already said they will be set free."

"Isn't that a change of heart from this morning?"

She was silent.

"I'd fight for the money."

"We have no need of mercenaries."

He wanted to persuade her. He thought of mercenaries, ageing men in tropical bars on the lookout for insecure black dictators. They didn't fight solely for the money.

He remembered how shaken he had felt after the shooting today. Self-defence. It reminded him of something in his past. He remembered suddenly the day when he had left off the Sugarloaf in a hang glider for the first time. Exhilaration. The feeling that gripped him now.

He looked at the Walther again. With two well-armed people flying in unsuspected before dawn carrying plenty of lethal weaponry, the chances were good.

He'd get his money. He daydreamed a moment ... enough to restart Lacken Lift.

Flying among the snow mountains under the stars to adventure.

An image came into his mind of Charlton Heston as dead El Cid leading his troops into battle.

He remembered how Leila had wanted him killed a few hours ago.

Her cold voice. "You would not be taking me on this trip. I could not do it."

He was surprised. He had imagined her in the heroic mould. "I thought you wanted him dead?"

"Yes, I want him dead. But I could not do that flight or the shooting."

"You like others to do your dirty work for you? Like Achmed shooting me?"

"Perhaps."

Could he offer to go in alone? "I thought you wanted him dead," he repeated almost sulkily.

"I tell you I do. So do others. I know of two who would have been willing to make this flight. They suffered very much because of the Sheikh. They lost members of their family. They hate him. One is dead. They are both lying in the back of the Hiace."

Chapter Ten

IN THE GARAGE near the station at Grenoble Paul surveyed the crushed frame of the Scorp which reminded him of the fossil remains of archeopteryx. It was like Humpty Dumpty. All the best engineers and welders and men capable of fixing new leading edges and Terylene and framework could not put the poor old kite together again.

For the first time he felt a twinge of guilt. Perhaps, after all, it was not the wind that had brought it down. Although Faisal and he had flown well enough in the Scorp with its double harness, it was possible, he had to admit to himself, that there was a basic weakness in the conversion. Plenty of people converted ordinary single gliders to carry two people. But for long-distance Alpine flying something stronger would have been better, something made for the job.

Ten days from today the Sheikh would be flying in from South America to his mountain fortress where he would be staying three days and three nights. Paul and his new flying partner — they sounded like a pair of acrobats — would be poised to try the flight on any of those nights should wind and weather be favourable. There would be a waning moon, one which rose later and had a chip bitten out of it.

This clapped out Scorpion could never do the required task. They would have to get another, stronger glider expressly constructed to take a heavy weight. Yahir was a lot lighter than Faisal. That was one advantage. He would have to test the new glider with a couple of solo flights to estimate its capabilities. He would have to take on board a passenger who had initially ill-treated him and on whom he had inflicted humiliating torture and almost killed.

When he and Leila had climbed down from Ruskin's seat and got back to the van Yahir lay beside his dead friend choking in his gag. This was the man who would have to learn to fly with him.

Paul had checked in the back of the Hiace for weapons, prodding the debris in a cursory way. Meanwhile unpleasant noises continued to come from the live figure on the floor. He left it to Leila to undo his bonds and inform him he was not joining his friend. As she revived him with Coke she was presumably telling him that Paul had become an ally.

He couldn't keep her under cover for ever. He left her in the back to do the talking and comforting, went round to the front, consulted a map and drove off.

The details of the rest of the day were vague. Practicalities. Stopping and shouting at Leila to get out and buy a packet of large black plastic rubbish bags. Two of them fitted over head and feet of the little corpse. Finding a rubbishy place to leave him far out in the countryside at dusk. It proved surprisingly easy — a turn-off through a mountain glen, a little stream with a picturesque bridge and plenty of muck and cans and suchlike thrown into the sparkling water. Just like home. It seemed the French weren't like the Swiss. He made Leila and Yahir carry out the shining black bundle and wedge it down below the road under the bridge. He should have searched him first for identity leads, but couldn't bring himself to do so. The big watch on his wrist and his bloodstained wallet would give clues when he was found. Paul hoped at least the corpse wouldn't be found for several weeks. Better still, not until the winter snows hid him for months.

There was a rag in the car. Yahir wet it in the stream and mopped up bloodstains.

When they drove back to town they called at the hospital. It seemed Faisal was stirring and would soon be back to consciousness. The prognosis was hopeful. Leila wanted to stay, but Paul, standing outside the door with the glass peephole, said they must go. He still carried the heavy Dames de France bag like a demented shopper, and she knew he wouldn't hesitate to use it. Yahir was silent and acquiescent. Shaken by Faisal's condition. Not to mention the death of his friend. How much a friend? How would he ever consent to fly with Paul?

They drove back into the centre of the town in the dark. The flowing heart of Chamonix was warming the glacial valley, a golden ingot and electrified bubble of prosperity. The mountains rose high above it, the crested wave of glaciers seeming to menace the prosaic tourist life far below. Chamonix was still *en fête*, beginning its night-life phase. What to do now? Eat. He was hungry and dead tired. Before he slept he had to make out his future, which depended largely on the inclination of this bruised little Arab. They went and ate in the Hotel Savoy, which retained a tinge of old-fashioned Victorian comfort, as if Ruskin and Whymper were staying. Paul had no money, only his bag of guns, and Leila paid. They had a queer dismal meal in a spacious dining room where Paul tucked into a bloody steak while Leila worked on Yahir. All Paul wanted was to make some sort of peace and get Yahir to look at things his way. He had acted in self-defence — it wasn't him who drew the gun first. Self-justification had to be conveyed in another wretched three-way conversation, Paul cursing the legacy of Babel while he tried to guess reactions and comment. There was a fairly likely chance that if Paul didn't get his point across they would try and kill him again. Was there a relaxing of tension towards the end of the meal? How close had Achmed been to Yahir? A brother? Not a brother, a friend. Paul remembered when Gordon had died.

They slept the night in the guest house and he shared a room with Yahir. What else could he do? He slept with the guns in the bed with him. Yahir beside him took two sleeping pills. Before lights out he caught Paul's eye. A half-smile. Paul made a thumbs-up gesture and looked at him quizzically. The Arab shrugged in the way Leila shrugged.

Paul slept deeply without worrying whether his neighbour would get up in the night and smother him. It was light when he woke. Yahir was awake, staring up at the ceiling. They dressed and went out to find Leila had gone, leaving a message at the desk that she had gone to the hospital. She must have taken a taxi since he had the keys of the Hiace. They followed her at once. Faisal had been moved out of intensive care since he had recovered consciousness. The X-rays showed the skull was not fractured. The right femur was in a nasty mess.

Paul sat in a waiting room furnished with tattered magazines. As always he carried his hardware. You would have thought that Faisal wouldn't be in the mood for decision making. But seemingly they badgered him for advice. Something he said or nodded evidently meant go ahead. When they came back their attitude was — how to put it? — positive. Yahir seemed less crushed and rejected as Leila explained that he was ready to be Faisal's replacement.

Paul had second thoughts by this time. The prospect seemed infinitely depressing. "How much experience has he had?" he asked, as they drove back to Grenoble. Regrets clamoured in his brain. He remembered asking the same question about Faisal.

Leila was preoccupied. She was returning with great reluctance, leaving Faisal in the hospital.

"Not so much," came her glum and expected answer.

When Paul questioned her more closely he learned that all the Almutis in this group had some training in hang gliding. What about the one that had stayed behind in Grenoble? Hassan? Oh yes, he had flown as well. Would he be prepared to make the flight? He was less able to fly than Yahir here. Also, Leila threw off, dead Achmed was his brother.

How good was Yahir? Difficult to gauge by indirect questioning. It appeared he had gone prone a few times. He had been required to learn, but had never been enthusiastic. Paul was interested — he had not come across a reluctant hang glider before, a pilot who had flown without being seized with the madness.

"I never wanted to fly myself," Leila said. "My husband wanted me to learn while he was in Dublin. He insisted I should go to your flying school. That was even before he had made his big plans."

He had been an odd sort of visionary, seeing hang gliding as an aid to guerrilla warfare. He had forced his brother and associates to learn. In the early days of the sport there had been other revolutionaries who had thought that hang gliding might have some specific military use. The P.L.O. used powered gliders successfully in a raid against the Israelis. But there was nothing a squadron of powered gliders with all their inherent risks could do that one helicopter full of armed men could not achieve more easily.

As for pure hang gliding of the quality envisaged by Leonardo da Vinci, developed by the Rogallos and practised by the birds, it had never been considered to have much practical use. As a means for getting from A to B a hang glider was rather less

147

reliable than a messenger-bearing pigeon. Maybe if you were the Count of Monte Cristo stuck on an island and you got hold of some tubing and Terylene you might build a glider and escape from your prison.

Leila's husband had romantic ideas. Magician's plans aided by the knowledge that he was a good hang gliding pilot and there was no other way of approaching the Sheikh's mountain fastness. He had conceived a corps of efficient flyers, a silent raiding party. He had insisted that his brother and associates should train as hang gliding pilots. And then, after weeks of training, he had concluded that none of them possessed his own blend of skill and madness.

Paul could not blame Leila for being unenthusiastic about renewing the project. But the half-conscious Faisal had seized on one last chance to fulfil his brother's wishes.

Paul had got himself into this mess, not once, but twice. After the accident when Faisal was hurt and he had killed Achmed, he had the guns. One way or another he could have worked for Maura and Tony's release instead of volunteering yet again for the role of sacrificial lamb. He had resumed the role of mercenary with eagerness.

Grenoble and the dirty old house in the Rue de l'Arte seemed almost like home, a pleasant place without Faisal where he could now move around without a gun. He kept his guns with him, although they were as much use in directing his future as if they were children's toys. While his wife and child were held these people could do what they liked with him. They could still decide to cut their losses in spite of Faisal's go-ahead. What would become of Maura and Tony then? If things went badly there was not much Paul could do besides indulge in revenge killing.

Leila and Yahir had to tell Hassan, the other Almuti, what had happened in Chamonix. Paul wasn't there when they did so. Then they had to go and meet their contacts. He was undecided whether he would accompany them, arguing feebly that without him the plan was useless. He might suspect that where the contacts were, there would be Maura and Tony. But he couldn't be sure. He might endanger them still more by insisting. He let Leila persuade him that his presence among his shadowy allies was unwise.

148

He thought the comrades wouldn't mind a change in plans as long as the violent theme ran through the new campaign. He speculated on their identity once again. Were they the group that had concentrated on killing Jews in Paris and Antwerp? Were they the P.L.O. proper who were behind Yasser Arafat and had quarrelled with their Iraqi allies? Were they some Libyan-backed group bearing the blessing of Colonel Gaddafi? Arab terrorists, like Irish terrorists, split and resplit like amoebas, usually for the same reason — rejection or otherwise of violence. If this lot, through his agency, could achieve an extraordinary Arabian Nights' feat with djinns and magic carpets flying through the night skies, terrorism would be given a fantastic new publicity boost.

He himself would get publicity too, if he survived. He day-dreamed for a few moments, seeing his face on the cover of *Time Magazine* with meticulously drawn hang gliders and machine guns placed in a pattern behind him. He would make hang gliding an international craze like skate boarding. He would be responsible indirectly for more people dying than he would ever kill with bullets, as wild boys followed the fashion he set and threw themselves off mountains. . . .

He was a fool. He should be worrying about Yahir. They would have to trust each other with their lives, like Faisal had to trust him. He wondered again how good a friend the dead comrade shrouded in black plastic had been. Perhaps it was as well he could not talk to him in any known language. Never apologize, never explain. What about persuade? On the drive back from Chamonix, Leila and Yahir had talked a lot. About what? Paul had been unable to pick up any vibes.

Now he saw them off, watching them climbing into the van, and wondering as he watched them whether he should change his mind and stop them. He had his guns with him, carried around like a spinster's knitting.

They were away for three hours. He was solitary in the big house even though other people flitted about. The Algerians seemed to have nothing to do with the little core of Almutis, confining their activities to the restaurant and the filthy kitchen. Hassan, the other Almuti, the last of the bodyguard, stayed behind and sat in Faisal's office. At one point during the long afternoon Paul broke in boldly. There was a pile of papers on Faisal's desk and Hassan was working out figures on a pocket calculator. When he heard the door open, he raised his head with a look that Paul interpreted as hatred.

After the red-haired Algerian girl gave him an omelette, he went upstairs to the bedroom. Once again he wondered if he should seek out help. Would he be better off spending the afternoon at a French police station? He could hand over the burden of responsibility to authority. There would be people who would know all about international terrorism and ways of dealing with a kidnapping.

In the end he came to the same decision as always. He wouldn't put Maura's and Tony's lives at risk.

He turned his attention to the arms he had with him. Two guns were one too many. One would be sufficient to allow him the option of changing his mind. He couldn't fire two at once if they tried to take him by surprise and disarm him. He would keep the Walther and get rid of the Mac. He found one of the French magazines they had given him to read in the early days and wrapped it up in that. At the back of the house, in the black heated yard behind the kitchen, was a garbage can singing with wasps and flies. In the heat of the afternoon when customers had departed and the kitchen was deserted he went out and stuck his parcel deep into a mass of garbage and broken glass.

He needed a holster for the Walther. He went upstairs again and tore strips off the bottom sheet on his bed to improvise a sling. When he was flying he'd find some webbing and mock up something better. It was hardly comfortable carrying a bulky firearm under his shirt but he could hardly trade it in for a pearl-handled revolver.

Leila and Yahir returned with news. The others had agreed and the plan would go ahead. Maura and Tony would be freed when the flight was completed. He swore and tried to get tough. The usual statement he had half expected and would have to accept.

If he got killed he would have no chance of killing Leila.

He listened to her. It is not my decision. I am telling

150

you what I have been told to say. If you agree to carry Yahir like you were going to carry Faisal no harm will come to them. They will be safe.

Even if the flight goes wrong?

Even if the flight goes wrong. Was there a note of hesitation?

Later she asked if he would carry a firearm. He misunderstood, thinking she was referring to Mac the gun or the Walther. But she meant would he be prepared to help shoot the Sheikh and his bodyguard. Would he have agreed before he had been blooded by his first kill? He did not refuse now. He felt briefly a surge of exhilaration at the thought of battle.

Maura and Tony. He tried again. Let them go before we set out. Once I know they are safe . . .

"It is not possible."

So without any guarantees except the promises of people whom he had hurt he agreed once again to the most unlikely flight since that first one by Wilbur Wright at Kill Devil Hill. He had ten days to work out a relationship with Yahir and achieve a form of communication. Release! Run! *A gauche! A droite!* I am going to lose height! He had to teach Yahir about flying while Yahir taught him about weaponry. He tried to read his mind. The face was immobile as a poster of a politician.

He said, almost pleading, that he must be in touch with his wife again. For all he knew she might be dead. I must talk to her.

Perhaps the business with the instant camera and tapes was too difficult to set up again. Perhaps he was allowed to talk because Faisal was no longer in charge.

When Leila handed him the receiver he could hear the two of them. Tony in the background, sounding a good deal more cheerful than his mother, humming away with that note Paul remembered so well. Like a Kentucky tobacco auctioneer.

They have given him toys, he is a lot better. The conditions here are really terrible, Paul. You should see the dirt. No, they don't tie us up. They did at one time. They make us take drugs. It's not good for young children to be given big doses of tranquillizer. Paul, what's happening, is there anything you can do? Rabbiting on, poor woman. At least she didn't sound as if she knew she was going to die.

151

They were in Grenoble, that was for certain. A city about half the size of Dublin. If he drew his gun on this lot... or would he go on believing all that Leila said, that he was working for their safety?

Ten days to work everything out. And quite possibly at the end of it the weather would be wrong and all this anguish would be wasted.

It will be all right on the night.

The first difficulty would be the replacement of the shattered Scorp. One day out of the ten would have to be wasted obtaining a new glider and fixing a double harness. He tried once again to assess how much flying Yahir had done. Did the Almutis all fly together like a little flock of birds, an engineless air corps? Apparently not. They had never been that good. Yahir's glider had been some sort of low-performance rogallo something like a Wasp, if his crude sketch was to be believed. Some unfamiliar continental make. Paul was hardly surprised. If Yahir or any of the other Almutis apart from Leila's husband had shown talent and inclination for flying, there would have been no need to bring in a stranger. But it was essential that Yahir got some modicum of experience at flying double if he was not going to act like a drowning man pulling his rescuer under.

Paul suggested he should go out tomorrow and find himself an instructor. Practise on the nursery slopes somewhere. Practise going prone. There would be difficulties, Leila said. After several years in France Yahir spoke about as much French as Paul did. Oh, for God's sake. Let him go, let him break his neck.

So Yahir went off with Abdulla under orders, while Paul went out with Leila and bought a hang glider.

Once again he was tempted to buy and fly an Atlas. As far as he had heard, the firm that made the Atlas, La Mouette, was the only really established hang gliding manufacturer in France. Atlas was the best thing it had come up with. The guy who had designed the Atlas had built other fancy gliders like the Jet. But the Jet had come up with a few problems like being blamed for killing people. It earned a reputation as a rogue after a couple of fatal accidents. Then came the Atlas, the super bird . . . now in demand all over the place in top competition. Any French *homme volant* worth his salt flew an Atlas, and Paul was tempted to do the same.

He must not. This was not the time to fulfil the old glider's ambition to fly the current fashionable kite. He would have to obtain a proper double glider, something like the Gemini, the model made by Hi-way, the people who made the Scorp. It was purpose-built, very big and very strong with proper stresses. No more conversions for him.

Leila took him back to the supplier at Valence. She wouldn't listen to the argument that there would be no problem about shopping in Grenoble. Hang gliders sold in this region like hot cakes. Why did it have to be Valence? She wouldn't say; maybe the Almutis had contacts with the guys there. Or maybe it was just to spread the plan around and dilute suspicion.

He had them rig an Atlas just for the hell of it. The sickle shape had similarities to the Scorp; she'd be a good thermal eater, no doubt. *Magnifique* . . . he made Leila ask about hang gliders built for two.

They came up with a double version of the Pipistrelle, the black-winged experimental kite he had seen the last time he was here. He told himself everything to do with hang gliders was in the way of being experimental. He examined it and it seemed strong, capable of carrying a big weight. What would have happened if they had bought it in the first place? If he had believed in destiny the way Leila did, he would have said that this thing was waiting for them. It didn't look all that different from high-performance kites when it was rigged. Higher, bigger, stouter, maybe, with a perceptible lack of elegance. On the wing was a logo showing two little Greek guys, Castor and Pollux. They'd been twins, the same people who came under the one name as the Gemini. The Castor and Pollux double hang glider did not have a double prone harness, but two seated harnesses arranged side by side. That would have to be changed.

The kite had been a special order from a Grenoblois who had never collected it. Some little mystery there. Not an uncommon one among enthusiasts of a dangerous sport where inclination fluctuated. Very likely the purchaser or his partner had broken a limb and had to give up. He might even have been killed. So here lay his uncollected goods in this little hangar waiting for another rash pair of fools.

When they had brought it back to Grenoble Leila got on the phone at once to Chamonix. She rang the hospital three or four times a day. Paul brought himself to ask how the invalid was faring, A lot better, it seemed. Faisal had a telephone by his bed now, and was able to offer a stream of agitated advice. The concussion that had seemed so spectacular couldn't have been bad. Paul wished him headaches and double vision. His broken leg would keep him out of action until long after the proposed night flight took place in the high Alps.

It was like a persistent dream, to be driving once more through the long tunnel looking for the turn-off for the Col de Coq. What was really holiday was not having that toad with them.

A little evening breeze welcomed them on the ridge. There were scores of pilots taking advantage of the perfect conditions for flying. The place was almost as crowded as those flying sites in England that had shocked him when he went over to fly during the early part of his career as pilot. Ireland might not be the best place in the world for hang gliders, but at least there was no jostling for place at take-off and very little risk of crashing into some other flyer.

He togged up in the same gear he had worn three days ago when he and the wind had brought Faisal down. Leila stood watching while he rigged the kite. He liked being in charge, no Faisal hanging around to boss or to make a fuss when he declared that he'd be flying alone at least for the first time. The rigging was simple enough. The designer had got rid of a lot of wires and pulley systems, which meant that like the Scorp there was a minimum of string. *Fabriqué en Suisse*, he read on the corner of one of the Terylene wings. Was that reassuring, a good omen? The Swiss were careful people. Wasn't Switzerland the first country in the world to insist that hang gliders had licences? He'd be flying unlicensed over Swiss territory during the big flight.

Yahir helped him at take-off, although the breeze was light enough. Not too much pressure on the front wires, if you please, or it'll pitch over the ridge. A nice fifteen-knot wind, not too little, not too much. Just right for flying an unknown kite for the first time. He would not like to be taking off with the Castor and Pollux without wind or something that was too breezy altogether. It was a clumsy name for a clumsy machine. Perhaps it was known as C et P, like Canadian Pacific.

He ran, Leila vanished, he flew. Feeling his usual idiotic self-confidence once again, he was on a high, half drunk with the joy of moving through the air. Even now, the experience of flying made him forget his problems. Hang gliding was the best thing. Hang gliders get it up higher. Hang gliders do it again and again and again. Hang gliders do it in select circles. Hang gliders do it when they've got the wind up.

He was brought down to earth almost literally by the diabolical performance of the C et P. There were other flying problems. For one thing too many other kites were flapping around, so that he felt like a swimmer in a crowded bath. He'd heard plenty about accidents from collision. He tried ridge-soaring, keeping an eye on other pilots. He picked out the sickle shapes of Atlases swooping through the skies and felt envy as he turned his attention to his own flying machine. The sink performance was hardly great. He caught a bit of updraft by the ridge and she moved up clumsily as if she had been blown by a bellows.

It was a matter of learning how much of a performance he could get out of her. The design appeared to be efficient, the structure taking advantage of the latest theoretical aerodynamics so that the drag wasn't all that bad. He took her up and down the ridge again and tried a 360. Not quite flat, but not too far off. He looked with envy at the Atlases around him flying like swallows after flies.

He stayed up for nearly two hours as the kindly Alpine evening wind blew him around. He began to think, maybe if destiny is with these people the thing is possible.

He brought her into a neat ridge-landing just as dusk began to change his vision. It seemed a pity to waste the wind. Leila was anxious to get back to her wretched telephone and communicate with the loved one, but Paul insisted on staying until nightfall. One by one the other gliders came in, derigged and went away down the hill while he waited for his night flight, adjusting his eyes to night vision. Leila, protesting, went down to the valley beneath and put on headlights beside a target area big enough for anyone, a football pitch. He instructed her to direct the headlights into wind from the downwind end so that he wouldn't be dazzled.

A gentle sink straight down on to the target. The wind was sweet, and lifted him up very soon after he could see Leila's headlights go on and her signal of six blinks. He launched himself and flew down in the darkness, the C et P sinking with dignity like an old lady seating herself on a throne. Down he went. There was the target. There were the lights. All it needed was judgment.

He could fly fine on his own by night, but he had to take a passenger. Yahir had obeyed Paul and spent the daylight hours doing bunny hops on some little slope dedicated to teaching five-year-old children how to ski. Paul went to look at him next morning and watched him take off under the eye of an apoplectic French instructor with a wicked RAF moustache. He did not seem to have made much progress. It was a case of shutting the eyes as he came in to land to the accompaniment of torrents of French abuse from his mentor.

Paul understood why the boss had decided against forming his little flying corps. Faisal had not been a good hang glider pilot, but he had been a bird compared to Yahir. The feeling of confidence Paul had built up after his night flight evaporated. He went off with Leila and all that day flew the stately galleon on his own.

The next day rain poured down on Grenoble accompanied by a wind of well over 25 knots. Summer was nearing its end. At first Paul felt relieved as he listened to the patter of raindrops falling on the dank pavement outside. Then he became panicky. How many days would it take for this wind to blow itself out? Had the September equinox come three weeks early, bringing storms? He had got used to bland French weather forecasts.

"*Bien mais froid le matin. Des nuages se dévelloperont en course d'après midi, nouvelle aggravation le soir. . . .*" Henny had done the translating. For all the aggravation it had never turned out bad enough not to fly. No complete day wasted. There had been a consistency about the summer days here in this part of the world quite unlike the weather back home where every day was a surprise. Too often in Ireland wind speed and turbulence kept you from flying, stuck on a take-off site hour after hour waiting for the right conditions. No dedicated hang gliding pilot should live in Ireland. He should travel to the breathless Alpine heights or to the thermals of California and New South Wales.

Leila, ringing Chamonix every spare moment, took Paul's own calls to his wife so much for granted that when she got through she handed the receiver to Paul and went off.

The first occasion he took advantage of her absence.

"Maura, listen, I'm alone, no one is listening . . . tell me where you are."

"I haven't a clue, Paul. We were blindfolded . . . we haven't moved out of this one small room since we were brought here. What? Only now we are taken downstairs to the phone. They remain, the two who bring up food . . . just the two . . . haven't seen any others . . . of course I would recognize them anywhere. . . ." Leila came back, and if she listened hard she could hear the tearful complaints pouring through the earpiece. No exercise, nothing . . . the light is terrible . . . nothing to read . . . always in this one small room . . . shutters on the window . . . nailed . . . you can just see outside through the cracks . . . a yard or something . . . an old house I should think . . . no certainly not one of those new apartments . . . the smell is awful . . . poor Tony has been having a stomach upset . . . The mournful litany went on without revealing any hard fact. An old house? How near here? Could it be some corner of this very building?

The wind blew, the temperature dropped and rain poured. There was even thunder and sheet lightning. The weather turned inside out. *Nouvelle aggravation*.

They could only ignore it and make the best of wasted time. In fact, that day spent in Faisal's study was useful, even vital. He and Yahir studied the maps — Leila as ever beside them translating. They went over the length of the Grendelbach valley and the clearing in the fir trees where the villa would be blazing in light. You couldn't miss it for search lights. There would be no problems about judging moonlight landings.

157

He examined the plan of the villa handed over by the contact they had met at the Courmayeur junction. Also a couple of photographs. The place looked like a North Sea oil rig stuck in snow.

"How many guards, do you think?" He'd asked that question before. It was important.

"I have told you, about a dozen. The contact could not be sure."

"Wouldn't it be a lot easier on everyone if she did the shooting?"

The idea was frivolous.

There would be a heavy guard at the perimeter of the villa, backed by electric fences, dogs and the like.

What about the roof?

It would be guarded, of course. But not too heavily, they thought. There would be someone on the lookout for a possible helicopter attack. No one would anticipate hang gliders flying in silently with speed and surprise, ready with a blast of gunfire before they landed. Paul wondered how he had ever contemplated flying without a weapon. Part of his old take-it-one-day-at-a-time philosophy. It was increasingly obvious that ruthlessness as well as speed was vital for any chance of success.

"How did Faisal think he could do this on his own with me carrying him there and standing around while he did the shooting?"

"He would have put pressure on you. You would have realized that your life depended upon your willingness to use a gun."

Paul remembered Faisal buying one parachute and one German knife for cutting his way out of the harness.

Speed was the essential. They would have to come in silently, prepared to fire at the last moment. He remembered a film about soldiers parachuting into Holland. The Germans on the ground looking up and picking them off as they floated down. Some guy with a parachute stuck in a clock tower.

They drove to the hangar by the station. Rain pounded on the tin roof as they rigged the harness and practised all afternoon. Take-off. Landing — the way Yahir would have to descend when Paul hit. Getting rid of the awful butcher's apron of harness before they sped on with the task.

Yahir was neat in his movements, but his inexperience was discouraging. The hours with the moustached instructor hadn't helped very much. It took Paul the whole afternoon to teach him the basics of the manoeuvre of take-off and swinging into a prone harness.

He would have been more depressed except for two things. One was Yahir's enthusiasm. There was no doubt that he was not only willing, but proud and excited to be taking part. The other was his humour which came across the tedious net of interpretation. He joked, he laughed, he acknowledged his clumsiness.

Paul used to admire Faisal's courage. He thought his fearlessness in allowing himself to be a passenger under these circumstances must be unique. Yet here was Yahir willing to undergo the same ordeal with the man who had killed his friend. If he was wary it didn't show.

Paul couldn't trust any of them after what had happened in Chamonix. Even so, he couldn't help liking Yahir. It wasn't only that he was a contrast to Faisal, but he liked him for himself. As they smiled and clapped each other on the back, it became difficult to reconcile him with the role of killer. Perhaps every terrorist laughed and joked and played tricks to relieve tension.

Leila's role as interpreter meant that they had the same working relationship as before. He remembered their brief sexual encounters with bewilderment. Would he mind seeing her dead? His antipathy for her was fuelled by his despondent telephone talks with Maura.

A week was spent getting basics into someone of nil ability.

Even though Yahir was a dummy to be carried about, it was essential he should understand what was going on, learn take-off and landing and have something in his head about theory. They had some nightmare flights. During the morning Alpine wind or the calmer evening breeze the two of them threw the clumsy dead weight off a cliff and clawed for lift. Paul fought the deadly sink rate, managing the odd ridge soaring or staggering to a thermal in a machine that behaved like an asthmatic climbing stairs.

The flight was possible, he conceded. It was just possible if Allah provided the right wind conditions on the night in question.

That appeared to be as likely as an eclipse of the moon. Sometimes he felt that all each day's training achieved was keeping Maura and Tony alive for an extra 24 hours.

He pondered alternatives. He still had a gun.

They kept on doggedly. On the fourth day they went up to the St Hilaire du Touvet take-off and began night flying under the same moon that would guide them to their target in a few days' time. How many weeks since he had made the moonlight flight with Simon? I gave up my boyhood, he had sung, to drill and to train, to make myself part of, the patriot game.

Hassan acted as noseman when they took off. They had spent the recommended half-hour getting used to darkness, but still Paul could hardly see a thing. Down below Leila had headlights at the ready. The wind was nice and Paul let it take them on a minimum flight. He felt almost blind, but brought in the kite surprisingly smoothly, his legs and boots suddenly illuminated by the lights from the van. And the other smiling little chum, brave to the point of lunacy, came down neatly beside him.

They'd managed well. Perfectly. He felt a little encouraged until the flight next evening. The wind was less and carrying the weight above him almost defeated him. There was a terrifying moment of stall when Paul tried to concentrate on the dark ground beneath them and misjudged airflow by flying at air speed instead of ground speed. It was a daytime beginner's error that nearly sent the pair of them clouting into one of Isère's limestone cliffs. The silent struggle out of stall in darkness had him lost for several minutes until he glimpsed the headlights far below. Leila knew nothing about his difficulties. Only what his passenger could tell them about the capricious movement of the wind.

The comrades took to coming out to watch. They were with Leila after that night flight. They came out by day, three or four of them, not always the same. Paul made no attempt to identify them, just as previously he had made no effort to learn the names of the Almutis. He didn't enquire their nationality — Syrian, Lebanese, Iraqi, Palestinian, Libyan — he couldn't care less. They were cool and courteous towards Leila and jovial with Yahir, which made Paul like him a little less. They were the ones who held Maura prisoner. With him they were polite and helpful, and one of them even spoke a few words of English. Paul didn't ask his name.

September had come and suddenly the hills were much emptier. The insane, feverish August was over, and holiday makers were swept back to autumn duties, school, jobs and suchlike. A few times Paul had recalled with something like nostalgia the nine-to-five routine of his job at home. For years he had moaned how work took up valuable hang gliding time.

He was driven to yet another valley in the Massif de la Chartreuse, which was unbelievably empty without manic vacationers. They walked for an hour away from the road until they came to a disused quarry. Two men mounted careful watch while Paul was taught weaponry.

No one referred to the Walther which they knew was in his possession. Instead, he was offered a selection of weapons to try out. He was reminded of early days training with a hang glider. Back to the basics. Except that learning to shoot with a Kalashnikov was a lot easier than flying. There was no time to give him training for guerrilla warfare, all the bits about running for cover and the manoeuvres of soldiers searching for the enemy. If and when they reached the target area, the actual shooting would be crude and simple. Yahir, smiling so pleasantly, would be responsible for the heavy slaughter. He'd be loaded down with grenades in addition to the automatic weapon that he carried as they prepared for their last training flight. Paul would help with his Kalashnikov if he liked. It was optional. He wasn't issued with his weapon now. After they had taught him how to fire it they took it back.

That last training flight at night worked well. The wind carried along the heavy double harness and they glided gently downwards as if a stream was carrying them along. They made the five-kilometre journey from the limestone ridge to the target where Leila and the comrades had three cars making a ring of light. They simulated firing in case the inhabitants of the Isère valley were disturbed. They did well that night. If it had been the real night they would have landed all right on the target.

When they returned he found that Faisal had come back. Everything that happened to Paul here was a surprise, a result of the language barrier. Not that he was involved in the old-fashioned bustle of the invalid's return, except to observe Leila's almost hysterical concern and the addition of a uniformed nurse to the grubby household. Faisal had been brought back on a five-hour journey to convalesce. The nurse would be taking care of him while Leila was away.

You'd think that English being an international language they could find one other person who could communicate with him properly. Not so. She'd be tagging along with Yahir, Hassan and some of the other comrades to act as bearers.

Faisal summoned Paul to his bedside like a dying monarch bestowing blessings. It was a nervous sort of meeting with Leila making her translations which included no word of reproach. Ironically Faisal was the only one among the lot of them who knew that the accident at Chamonix had not been Paul's fault. He would have felt the crosswind. But very likely he remembered nothing about it.

Paul remembered that somewhere back in the past they had said he could write a couple of letters to people of his choice. He had lain awake sleepless for hours composing clever letters to Henny and Sean. In the bustle for departure nobody remembered the promise. He thought maybe they had genuinely forgotten. There was the business about money. Money in the bank to start a new life. He couldn't bring himself to question Leila about any of these small side details. It was difficult enough making telephone conversation to Maura. That was terrible. He had a word with Tony and that was bad, too, listening to the irritable tears.

When he got upstairs he took down the Walther from the top of the wardrobe. If he was carrying the machine gun, he'd hardly have use for it; but he'd take it along as some sort of talisman. He lay awake listing volunteer missions of violence that ended badly. Assassins — John Wilkes Booth, Lee Harvey Oswald and the man who tried to kill one of the French kings and got himself torn to pieces by horses. Fools, cockleshell heroes, Robert Emmet and a good many other Irish patriots, and various recent men of action masked in black talking from embassies or standing beside grounded aeroplanes swimming in heat.

Chapter Eleven

WHAT WAS IT Ruskin had called the snow mountains? Heavenly castles. He had walked on a late summer's afternoon all over the Alps oohing and aahing at the sun shining on grassy knolls and through fringes of pine. He was a romantic Victorian who saw in the Alps the Divine Hand at work and didn't have to lug a hang glider along on his shoulder.

They were taking turns, naturally. Except for Leila who was carrying an over-large rucksack containing something useful — grenades or packets of soup. They all had rucksacks strapped on to little ladders. They all had sleeping bags of the superior kind in which you could sleep in the snow. They had three tents, radio equipment, varios, altimeters, harnesses, machine guns and other odds and ends. In addition the hang glider was heavy. The time might be early September, but the weather was hot.

They passed a lot of wholesome-looking cows. Ruskin had commented on the gentle sound of cow bells. Twenty minutes had passed and it was time to change. Sweat was pouring down Paul's face; his body was soaked in it. The track they were following had shot upwards and was climbing an edge of rock above a glacier. Higher up, below the dominant slope of mountain were great ridges that traversed the sky. The grandeur that Ruskin extolled was tempered by signs of man. Notices were everywhere. ATTENTION! DANGER! IL EST DANGEREUX SUR LES ILES ET BANCS DE GRAVIER.

Looking down they could see the glacier, a broken mass of melting ice scoured and corrugated beside the last scattering of trees before it stopped at the head of the valley. Further down were houses with pitched roofs and balconies. They could hear the roar of a mountain stream.

They were making for an Alpine hut where they could spend the night. Except for Paul, the party was familiar with the route; evidently these people had explored it earlier in the summer.

Leila had explained to him the route they would go, pointing out objectives on a map. In the normal way, if they hadn't been carrying so much it would take about two further hours to climb from here. But they were going to be a lot slower. Soon they would change loads again, and then, after another twenty minutes — timed with precision — it would be his turn again to carry one end of the hang glider.

He remembered the time when he had carried the Scorp up Croagh Patrick. That had been a few days after the pilgrimage on the last Sunday in July. He had walked all the way up carrying the hang glider on his shoulder. Like today, the weather had been warm. He must have been crazy. He had met two men who asked if he was carrying a penitential crucifix. That had been a good flight ridge-soaring off Patrick's holy mountain and Clew Bay scattered with islands below him in the fitful sunshine. Why the hell had he ever left Ireland and sought to fly elsewhere? Here the Alps looked a little less like Croagh Patrick on pilgrimage day. The number of people climbing and sporting on the mountains had dwindled significantly with the end of the holiday season. On the way here they had passed through Chamonix, and that blighted town had seemed positively empty. Europeans everywhere were back at their jobs in hardworking places where rush hours began at seven o'clock. President Mitterand had not yet introduced the five-week annual holiday.

But nowadays you can never be wholly alone in the Alps. Every so often on the footpath a couple of hikers or some mountaineers would pass the taciturn group of men and one woman carrying the hang glider in its black jacket. They attracted curiosity and sometimes a raucous question in one of several European languages. Where in God's name are you taking that thing? The answers were vague in broken French — we are seeking new places to fly, we are looking for a new Alpine record. . . . Then the hasty move on upwards like the traveller in the poem. Beware the pine tree's withered branch, beware the awful avalanche.

When and if they flew the thing and if it made headline news for one reason or another, these hikers and climbers would remember the painfully odd group sweating upwards. Yahir and Hassan, small, unsuited to their Alpine gear, their anoraks and boots. Their stern Semitic looks were out of place on this particular hillside; they belonged to a barren desert slope rounding up fat-tailed sheep. The three Syrians or Iraqis, or maybe Palestinians, were contrastingly tall. One wore a neat beard and both looked reasonably well organized. Leila staggered along with them. Her face was pitted with perspiration and her hair was greasy. Paul was as dark as any of the Arabs. He was wild-eyed.

As the climbing got steeper the problem of carriage increased. One of the Syrians or whoever, had a walkie talkie and preferred hanging on to that rather than doing his proper share of the big burden. It was almost dark by the time they reached the hut wedged in a scree of rocks just below the snow. The neat wooden structure built of oh-so-picturesque logs was lit up. That meant they would have to share the place for the night.

If the group with the hang glider presented an odd sight to passers by, they were more of a puzzle to the two young Germans already installed in the hut with sleeping bags, gas cooker, icepicks, boots and a lot of rope spread around. Nine in the hut was a lot of people. Language difficulties were increased. The Germans spoke a little French — very little — and Leila, as always, was interpreter.

They were filled with curiosity. They themselves were planning a light climb on Mont Blanc. Late in the year and skill and luck were required. Like the flight with the *delta planeur*. You are taking the hang glider up Mont Blanc? You are too late, *n'est-ce pas*, to be the first to fly off the summit? Some intrepid flyer had already done that marvellous deed.

Leila hedged with plenty of *peut-êtres*. There were other peaks in the Alps from which to fly. Invigorated as well as exhausted by his long walk, Paul suddenly felt that the most wonderful pastime in the world must be flying from one or other of these snowy mountain tops. Mont Blanc and the Matterhorn were not emblems of menace but of challenge. No one had flown off the Matterhorn, as far as he had ever heard. The ordinary ascent was hard enough. He day dreamed that perhaps he might achieve something like that. Those hills in Ireland were miserable compared to the great waves of snow around him here. The only drawback to peak flying was that it had to be a team effort. How he hated team work. Here it was all round him.

The Germans had a transistor tuned into weather forecasts and *Schuplättler* music. They were noisy as they sorted out wreaths of rope and all the bits of tin that helped them get up the ice, put stuff on their climbing boots, hung clothes out to dry and got the gently hissing butane to heat water for instant Kaffee Hag.

Questions about the hang glider . . . about the walkie talkie . . . about what they were doing and where they were going had to be fielded by Leila. No privacy. Tired plotters with heavy events on their minds had to listen. Leila was short-tempered, the others silent while the Germans continued jovially.

There were eight bunks in the cabin, two already appropriated by the Germans. A sulky Arab would have to sleep on the floor. As chief participants in the projected enterprise Paul and Yahir automatically received the choicest sleeping accommodation and were excused cooking duties. They had climbed for ten miles and more and were ready for an exhausted sleep. The room smelled of sweat. Leila curled up modestly in her sleeping bag like a caterpillar in a chrysalis. Yahir's snoring was a familiar rhythm remembered from Chamonix.

The shot was loud and vibrated through the hut. It brought Paul up through his four levels of sleep like a speared fish dragged from cool dark waters to the surface. Torches flashed in the darkness and someone lit a butane lamp whose sharp white light illuminated the hump of the body on the floor. Like everyone else in the room, the other German had woken. It took three men to drag him off the top bunk and take him outside the hut whimpering, where he was shot too. The staccato of the automatic weapon rang among the glaciers.

Paul heard it as the tall comrade with the beard lunged towards him where he lay in the bunk. Would he whimper too? His teeth were chattering; the air outside the warmth of the sleeping bag was cold and stuffy. "He wants your gun." Leila's voice. He was not going to die stupidly now. He hadn't thought of the Walther when the shot was fired. If he had the right instinct he would have brought it out and saved the other man's life. Mowed down

166

the whole lot of them. No stomach for a fight. One day's training in terrorism had not been enough to instil new warrior qualities in him. He knew nothing yet about killing, really, which was strange, because he had killed. He handed over the gun abjectly — his talisman. The man who took it was trembling as well.

The others came back into the hut and tidied up with morose energy. They put to one side the sack of arms that the German had inadvertently discovered. Paul's automatic went in among them. They gathered up the things belonging to the dead men — the pathetic damp socks, the boots, ropes and tinkling metal gadgets that would have helped them up rock faces, and took them all outside bit by bit. Leila boiled water and dashed in powdered coffee, freeze-dried milk and heaped spoons of sugar. When Paul was handed a cup his hands were still shaking so much that most of it spilled.

No more sleep. Not the best preparation for any flight. They talked — nothing he could understand. Leila listened silently making no contribution to what they were saying and no attempt to translate. Paul strained to get the drift of their voices. Argument? Decision making? Reproach? Hard to say. Easiest for them now to abandon plans. Abandon him. Add another body to the two outside. Time passed slowly with muttered exchanges.

Light came and then sun. They got dressed. He had to get dressed too. He was needed as a porter. They did not make him carry the bodies. The others, two to each body, tackled that while he and Yahir carried the Germans' equipment. The descent of the mountainside was perpendicular. All around them the sunrise painted the high mountains rose pink and illuminated the clumsy progress of porters and ambulance men. Weights almost as heavy as the hang glider, the bodies kept threatening to slip and escape to slide downwards towards the glacier. Twice Hassan let go his burden and a blond head bumped on stones and snow.

They crawled down to the glacier, taking about an hour. The edges of the crumpled sea of ice which Victorians had swooned over were a dirty mottled brown. Further out the great white band resolved into a moonscape of humps and hollows of ice.

The bodies were clothed in the thermal underwear they had

slept in. When they were thrown down on the ice the limbs stiffened and bounced. Then they were dragged along the puckered slippery surface by their own rope until they reached a crevasse. The bearded man who was directing operations knew where it was, a deep blue-green cavern about a metre and a half wide. Scraping and thudding and slipping they threw in the Germans where they would be preserved like mammoths. The first corpse stuck and became wedged against walls of ice. The second, thrown in on top of him, sent him down into infinite blue-green space. Then clothes, rucksacks, ropes and a mountain tent disappeared after their owners. Yahir kept back a knife and a compass until the bearded man made him throw them in as well. Paul was hot with exertion. He thought about trying to escape, slipping over the ghastly ice. Was he to follow them? Please God, if he did go down, he would go down dead. His companions had thought about it. Sweating and swearing in Arabic, as the last crampon disappeared with a tinkle against the icy walls, they paused and grinned and made a parody of pushing him. They'd probably done worse things.

They continued to grin as they watched his humiliation and fear. He'd always thought of himself as the brave man. The fellow prepared to throw himself into space each time. He was let live, and they went back up the hill. Their laughter subsided into muttering when they noticed a little line of climbers in red anoraks way off at the end of the glacier. Too far to see anything. Unless one of those red dots had been watching through a powerful pair of binoculars.

The sight made them hurry back up the hill to the hut. The return journey didn't take very long, but they were behind schedule. Leila had packed up their things and the hut was tidy. They ate some hard white bread and drank coffee while the bearded man tuned up the walkie talkie.

He got through — staccato chatter. Paul wondered whom he was talking to. Arabic equivalent of "over". In this law abiding world you needed a licence for a walkie talkie just as you needed one for hang gliding. Somewhere in these snow fields they would be crossing over into the land of order and rationality and money-making.

Perhaps the high altitude affected him so that the early-morning events took on an air of unreality. His mind was exercised with a basic problem. The rest of the day would be spent climbing and night time would pass bivouaced in little tents. Tomorrow they would reach the take-off place and wait for nightfall. All the time he would be carrying weights for slow miles up icy mountains. The problem was twofold — his boots.

He had spent plenty of time with Leila before they set out looking at maps and being told about the painful three-day journey and the camping. He set aside the horrors of the morning and concentrated on footwear. The boots had taken him up plenty of Irish mountains and had done him well enough this morning. When he had been fitted out with warm waterproof clothing he had not asked for them to be changed. No time — it took weeks to break in new ones properly.

He continued to worry as Leila erased all traces of occupancy. The bearded man listening on the walkie talkie gave out an 'Ah . . ." and a little dribble of talk which activated the others from the depression the morning's events had inflicted. More exchange and rattling signals before the antenna was pushed back in. Talk. Movement. Suddenly the silent group became cheerful and animated.

"Why?" he asked Leila.

"He has heard that the Sheikh has flown into Zurich. The helicopter is taking him to the chalet at this time. He will be there in about half an hour."

In theory they could attack tonight, if they hadn't so far to walk.

What was the wind like? This morning, even during the horrors, he had done the usual hang glider's check of the wind. A nice little easterly, around eighteen miles an hour. Even as the lads had been carrying their terrible weights he had been thinking that you could do a take-off from outside the hut towards the glacier. What effect would glacial ice have on wind drift?

Leila wasn't coming with them. She was going back to prepare the pickup operation that was supposed to be the conclusion of their plans. She was too weak, too fragile, to go up among the

169

ridges of the Courmayeur. She was about to leave him in the hands of a lot of murderers. When she departed the only communication he would have with these people would be the hang gliding terms he had imparted to Yahir and his French phrases. *Ça va* and *Pas bon* and so on. He had a minuscule French dictionary among the things he was carrying. Would he be looking up terms for wind force in the moonlight?

She had nearly killed him. Without her, Maura and Tony would not have been kidnapped. But she had been a link with normality. Now he must rely on Yahir. He didn't think Yahir had taken part in the morning's carnage. He hadn't dragged the second German outside.

The hut was clean. You wouldn't know anyone had stayed here last night. They were on their way with their burdens. Leila was going down by herself. Not a pleasant trip with the wind rising. No hang gliding in this wind. The Almutis made a formal farewell, kissing her on each cheek, holding her by the shoulders as if they were French generals. Not kisses of affection, but of brotherly camaraderie. She had the heart of a man. The others shook hands.

Paul shook hands.

He didn't remind her about Maura and Tony. He didn't plead. He let her go and before they had picked up their loads she was on her way. A dumpy little figure like a witch, like an old woman going about picking up sticks. Her anorak was the same blue as bluebottles.

High above their heads was a buttress of ice and snow that led to some sort of summit with the crest of Bianco de Courmayeur beneath. They would detour around a knife-like ridge, high up over there. Paul knew from map reading that the point which had been marked out for take-off was on a spine between the two peaks of Luigi Amido and the Aiguille Blanche de Peuterey. They should have had practice flying in a wilderness of snow and ice. The only real snow flight he had experienced had been the Chamonix disaster.

Icepicks, crampons, orange snow glasses. He should have had training as a mountaineer. They were as heavily loaded as Whymper's men approaching the Matterhorn. And for

170

Whymper's men the rope had broken. Was there a twinge from his boots? It was high enough to be breathless. Looking back he could see the folds of mountain falling away into the trees and the glint of the glacier. Far away was the head of the valley leading to Courmayeur where Italy and France met in a tangle of ice and snow. They were roped together — a murderer in front of him, another behind. They seemed to know what they were doing. Why hadn't they learnt how to hang glide as well as to climb mountains? Then they could have done their own dirty work.

An occasional shout from the bearded man who had taken upon himself to be leader and they would stop, swap burdens and gain their breath, and change places in the rope line. The ones who were carrying the actual glider came last. Its weight kept them very slow. The distance they had to cover wasn't that great, but they had to creep along. Already the sun was taking its afternoon dive. From the top of the ridge they crossed another plateau of snow and then came to a mass of rocks.

A ledge gave a small shelter and protection where they would camp. Three small bivouac tents were pitched in the snow. The conditions were bad enough for mountaineers, while hang gliders could go home. He shared a small tent with Yahir while the comrades, and the armoury piled themselves in the other two. He was alone for a lot of the time while Yahir went over to the middle tent where the bearded man was trying to get sense from the walkie talkie. One of the comrades came over from time to time with soup out of a packet tasting harshly of monosodium glutamate, rolls, lukewarm tinned stew and chocolate. Afterwards he was thirsty. When he had to go outside to relieve himself, he scooped up a handful of snow and ate it. The wind was lively.

He lay with the flight deck, his helmet and some of the harness gear wedged by his side. Yahir's breathing made time with the wind's rhythm. There were things they should be discussing, questions he wanted to ask that he should have thought of while Leila was around. Once he looked out of the tent at the moon with clouds scudding strongly over it. The hang glider lay in its shroud out on the snow. He prayed for the wind to increase. What was the fierce Alpine wind called, the unpredictable killer? A föhn? He would have done his best. The cold, the horrors of the morning, and the wind licking round the shelter of the rocks inhibited sleep. If he was to fly he would be flying tired.

He dozed, dreaming terribly, and woke in the dark, cold in spite of the cosiness of the down sleeping bag and the stuffy shelter shared with Yahir. Cold was another factor. The thermal underwear, the two pairs of woollen socks and the heavy black climbing suit, would they keep the cold at bay? Yesterday it had been the boots he worried about. They had stood up to the walk yesterday, although he had a small blister, which would not affect his flying.

What was different? Yahir's breathing was more pronounced. The wind had dropped. He lifted the tent flap. Stars, not many, fading out with the glow of dawn. Another magnificent pink sunrise was building up. The wind had died down. There was stillness.

Once again as they packed and set off with their burdens he cursed the climbing part of the expedition. He had been unprepared, and he rather suspected that the others were also taken aback by the effort required. The climb was easy by mountaineering standards. They were familiar with the route, Faisal and his brother had mapped it out very carefully and they were all in good physical shape. He was healthy enough himself. The tensions and expertise demanded by hang gliding tended to keep you fit. But the porterage had been underestimated. They should have had a lot more porters, something on Himalayan lines — a string of Sherpas. Six people were not enough to carry easily the ugly weight towards the top of the ridge.

He hadn't really understood about the climbing. Leila's English was fine and subtle, thanks to her high-class American education. But it was one channel, so to speak. There had never been time to cover the whole range of problems, to rage, to curse, to instruct and to catch pieces of information outside the two-way conversation.

The others were quiet enough, puffing and blowing and resting as they went. There were compensations to the limitations of the language. They helped to blot out the horrors that had happened and those in store. People hardly talked to each other. Here it was his turn to carry half the glider, sharing the weight with a tall, strange Arab, taking turns to go to the rear and front during the long twenty-minute shift that would hopefully get them to the top of the ridge.

The murders and the fact that his companions were murderers had become almost unimportant. Fatigue and the basic problem of moving upwards anaesthetized the vividly recent memories, the blurred apprehension about the flight and its goal. His judgment was obviously faulty. He ceased to feel hatred towards his silent companions. They were allies, blessedly silent, faces and expressions invisible behind goggles.

They reached the top of the ridge. Paul had been expecting a great view, but as so often with climbing, there was another barrier ahead, a long sloping plateau of snow glaring and sparkling in the sun. A small breeze enticed them along. They crossed the snow easily towards another cluster of rocks beside a deep gully. Then suddenly there was the valley stretching in front of them.

With the glare of the snow it was difficult to focus his gaze properly. Mont Blanc was the distraction. The great peak loomed superbly, catching the eye, controlling the wind, Queen of the Alps. Admittedly it was miles away to the east with a wave or two of mountains in between, nothing to do with the valley below. He shifted his gaze nervously. Wider, much wider than he had visualized from the map. And the target must be far beneath them. He knew that the fall was something like from 4,000 metres to about 2,500. He could thank God for every metre with the sink rate there was going to be on the travelling bus.

The scale and magnitude of the journey was frightening, seeing it under his eye on this way. The wild dream was possible — he could see that. But the preparation had been grotesquely inadequate. The feeble succession of training flights they had undertaken over the last three weeks bore no relationship whatsoever to the task ahead. You could blame circumstances for that, the series of incidents as unpredictable as the Alpine weather.

And yet — in one way all that was needed was the basic skills. These he had. The rest was luck. Destiny, Leila would have said. A gentle night breeze that did not relate to the usual complex behaviour of the air in mountains. A visible horizon. The horizon was there all right, scheduled to be lit by the stars or the moon. Snow on the mountains would reflect the light. The moon — at a fairly robust stage in its cycle — would rise soon after midnight. Time for all the erratic thermal upcurrents and mass of wind movement through gaps in mountains to sort themselves out. That was the theory if Allah was willing. They were making the journey on a wing and a prayer. The prospects of flight were so formidable that it was easy not to think about the landing.

In an hour of slow walking they reached the place that had been marked for take-off. The ridge was a king-sized version of the drop from St Hilaire du Touvet, a vicious precipice dropping into space below. He looked for the wind and found a gentle tail wind that would carry them towards the target after take-off. The good omens were eerie.

No sign of the target from here of course. It was hidden far away, in what looked like forest from this angle. He was handed a pair of binoculars and left to look out all he wanted while the rest rigged the little tents and prepared something to eat.

His importance loomed large now. Yahir was also resting before the big performance. Paul handed him the glasses, and he, too, tried to make sense of the wide valley and the smudge of trees in the distance. But it was Paul to whom they deferred. They treated him with a respect that verged on gentleness. He was given privileges due to a sacrificial victim. In his little tent he could sit and brood over the map. When Yahir came inside they studied the route together, achieving depressingly little in the way of communication. The pair of them could only hope that most questions had been dealt with during the time when Leila had been around. They pointed to take off and agreed with signs about the alternative take-off spot a few hundred yards away where the ridge curved. That could be used in the event of a wind change.

Oxygen was a problem. They were about 6,000 feet up and breathing was slower than normal. Their slow progress up to this spot had been a reflection on altitude. Lack of oxygen affected night visibility. No point in worrying. They had brought up a cylinder and he would be taking a few breaths before take-off. If

174

there was a take-off. At least he wasn't a smoker. He'd need all the night vision that was going if Allah continued to provide a favourable wind.

The afternoon passed with painful slowness. Every small step was exhausting, and the couple of trips he made out to the ridge to inspect the take-off filled him with fatigue. He dozed for an hour and had nightmares of hallucinatory vividness that were forgotten the instant he awoke. The cold seeped into his limbs and his energy was sapped before evening came. After darkness adrenalin would have to take over.

The needle that he invariably felt before an important take-off, the blend of anticipation and anxiety, grew Cleopatra-sized. It took over his conscious actions as he had to accept that the monster plan was now more than a possibility. All along, even with the melancholy proofs of these people's intentions, his mind had failed to admit that he would have to do what they had planned for him. So much had depended on chance or whatever they believed in. It seemed that a malevolent force was channelling the winds and keeping the sky clear.

At various times weather forecasts were relayed to him from their walkie talkie. They were tuned in on one uncertain and most likely illegal wave length over which someone crackled far away. This source kept telling them about the weather. "Ça va" would be communicated by Yahir and Paul's stomach would turn.

They rigged the hang glider while it was still daylight. The sun was already hidden behind the mountain and shadow brought a new kind of cold. For days they had argued about rigging by night. The trouble about setting up the glider now was that someone would have to keep watch beside it the whole time. They worked out a rota for every member of the team, apart from pilot and passenger. A half-hour watch on the exposed bare ridge. Before the actual flight — there was going to be a flight, his beating heart told him — he would have to make a final inspection. He didn't want little nagging worries about some invisible rigging pin coming loose or some link in the cross boom. He had already given the kite a thorough once-over before they set out two days ago. (Before those Germans were shot.) He would look at it now after he had rigged and then leave it to one of

175

the lads to guard. Like a tethered goat with a shepherd. And he would check it again minutely in darkness just before . . . But the final check would of necessity be subject to the unreliability of his visual deficiencies.

Rigging was automatic, he'd done is often enough. Unzipping the long black cone on the snow, erecting the control frame with the nose plate to windward, checking the cross tube was free to rotate, putting up the small upright of the king post and brace to both ends of the keel tube. Leading edge tubes spread and attached, one to each wing. Bracing wires done up from king post to ends of cross tubes, from control frame to nose. Nuts locked, wires tensioned. Four sail batons in each wing. All done slowly in the high thin air. One of the comrades stood by with the oxygen and several times Paul went over, clapped the mask over his face and took a few breaths. They helped, but he worked slowly, very slowly. Hands in thin leather gloves lined with woollen gloves moved carefully to lock bolts and bracing wire attachments. Last of all the nosepin.

The inspection was hardly pre-flight, since the time was only six o'clock. The sky was amethyst as dust began to change the contrast of its darkening colour and the white mountains. Take-off, weather permitting, would be made after midnight, six hours away. But this first inspection must be thorough; it would be the one that found out the mistakes that night vision would miss. The reflexes instilled during the first days of training made the instinctive checks — the gloved hand feeling its way down the leading edge, across the fabric of the sail seeking scratches or the small signs that could be a crack or an abrasion. No wires snagging on projections. Above all, testing the bolts that held the flying frame with its great weight.

It was as if he and Yahir had never flown together in double harness. The rules were new rules. No amount of practice, even if he had years of training in the Grenoble area and Chamonix, would have prepared him for something on this scale. There was a word for all that pre-flight preparation — pathetic.

He looked at the angle of the take-off which they would make with the wind blowing down — a shelving slope of snow that ended in precipice. They would dive into a gaping beautiful view.

176

In the distance, about a kilometre ahead at the entrance to the valley, was a ridge of rock standing up like a dinosaur's back over which they would have to fly. In daytime, given the right conditions, it would provide lift, but by night it was merely a feature of the landscape unless it mysteriously affected Alpine wave lift in some way. Paul couldn't tell. Had anyone tried anything like this before? Would they end up down there in the snow, building snowbanks, burrowing out hollows against the wind and making a tent out of the hang glider? It was strange how the prospect of failure filled him with disappointment.

Because of the snow, which made every footstep sink in eight or nine inches of fluff, they wouldn't be able to run at take-off. They would have to dive over the edge. Someone, Hassan most likely, would hold the nosewires at the brink. Then the plunge, the gathering speed and raising the nose, praying for lift. For God's sake, he'd done it often enough.

He studied the view again and the ridge, so menacing, so different from the line on the map. The area of forest — what changes would it make to the behaviour of the wind, any more than the positioning of the surrounding mountains controlled and funnelled it? He looked out for the electric pylons that would link the villages along the valley, but could see no sign of them. They would only be dangerous in the case of uncontrolled sink. No signs of ski lifts and other marks of civilization.

The scale of the mountains was oppressive. Down below, when he had allowed himself to be persuaded into this flight, it had never been the flying itself that was the challenge. The hang glider's supreme self-confidence, the amplified general belief of mankind that nothing could go wrong in his own case, had helped to suppress doubts. (The target and what happened after the flight were different problems.) Somehow he had never allowed himself to believe that any flight he set himself to do was impossible. When Faisal had loaded him down with the prospect of double harness and gunnery, he still felt in his heart of hearts that he could achieve any flight he set his heart on doing. He had flown well in the championships, he had flown many times at night. Now up here, with Mont Blanc mocking and menacing, he felt different.

Not a cloud. In the distance a few bland lights appeared in the valley before darkness closed in. There was no sign of the evening star hidden behind a frieze of mountains.

He went back with Yahir to the tents, leaving one of the others to guard the glider. He hated leaving the bulky old carrier. These guys were not to be trusted. You never knew after the way they had behaved. Suppose one of them wanted the mission to fail? Just a loosening of a bolt pin. He'd bear the thought in mind doing the pre-flight check. In the dark.

They gave him a meal, the same damn meal. They had only brought the one sort of soup. You'd think, with it being France, or was it Switzerland at this juncture, that packet soup would taste better. Now he really missed not being able to talk to anyone. No small talk, no calming the nerves with a joke. He had always been a person who liked flying on his own, but there were limits. Hang gliding was a group sport in many ways. He'd give a lot for a laugh right this minute.

Instead, when half the endless night had passed, Yahir had brought him the walkie talkie and let him have a talk with Leila. It was useful, he supposed, to be told the weather forecast again. It was grand. Any problems, asked the crackling voice. He could think of nothing immediately and anything that cropped up later would be too late. When they had blasted their way out of the place she would be waiting to pick them up with a couple of others. That was the general idea. They had been over the map three nights ago. The night before they set out and those people had been killed. She reminded him again how she would be waiting.

How could he say it again, about Maura and Tony?

"Leila, you'll do the right thing if things go wrong this end?"

He couldn't hear her answer through the static. Minutes of crackling and incomprehension passed. She said something like when you have flown they will be safe. He could imagine the shoulders shrugging.

Yahir was interrupting. He wanted to check on arms. Paul was irritated; they had been through this routine numerous times already. He was unarmed now, and would like to continue that

178

way. He'd never use a gun again. He'd never wanted to carry a weapon while flying. He had enough to think about. Nor hang himself about with grenades.

Once again Yahir was trying to press a machine gun on him. He'd brought enough weapons to choose from like a golfer playing with a bag of clubs. Paul said, very well, he would have the old automatic. Nothing else. They could give it to him at take-off. Or better still, right now. In good time to fit the holster comfortably. They could give him the bullets at the last moment. He might or might not use them.

A joke at this point would have cleared the air. As it was they had a three-way fight over the walkie talkie. At the end of it adrenalin sagged and confidence vanished. To hell with it. He shoved the radio back into Yahir's hands and walked out of the tent. There were stars overhead now in a velvet sky, and the snow around reflected their light. He wouldn't fly. He had done everything he could for Maura and Tony. Now he would walk away. Walk down the mountain back towards Chamonix.

Yahir came out and shook his hand. What for? He went over to one of the other tents and said something to the man inside. It almost seemed to precipitate another quarrel. He brought over the automatic with the holster and handed it to Paul. Another handshake. Paul had a look by starlight. It was loaded. We trust you fella. Licensed to kill.

They went back to Paul's tent. Yahir pushed up the aerial. *Encore parler? Pas maintenant. Plus tard.*

Time continued to creep. He went up once more to take-off point, and had another look at the glider and the valley under the stars. Back in his tent he referred to the flight plan and nothing seemed easy — the forest, the ridge and valley, and somewhere tucked away in the pine trees the villa, hopefully lit up for him. He was brought coffee in a flask . . . midnight was coming. The moon had risen, and now it was so light that when he stood outside he could read his watch. A quarter past twelve — getting on. A piece of old pilot's advice slipped into his mind. Never fly at night unless you know the site.

They had brought red goggles because of all that stuff about night vision and chemical changes and vitamin A. He wore them

179

for a time and then gave up. In these circumstances their use was a load of bullshit. There was no need for adaptation since the light was so clear. To hell with the problem of landing and all that business about restricted range of vision and speed closer to the ground seeming greater than during daytime since only close objects were visible. The moon would take care of that and lessen the chance of illusion and the danger of stalling when coming into land.

Take-off came before landing.

One last contact with Leila. Meaningless. He could say goodbye, mention Maura, say he was giving up, abuse Yahir. They didn't exchange more than a sentence. One more time she said I will be waiting for you on the road below. That was one last little twist to the plan. If he and Yahir did manage to get out they had two miles to walk at the end of it all. Probably pursued by Dobermann Pinschers.

He felt lonely walking up to the take-off site with these murderers. They talked among themselves in a subdued way and now and again one of them would laugh. He had no one to laugh with. The worse thing was to be flying with this stranger. Yahir was beside him as they trudged upwards. He was a pleasant enough little guy if only he spoke a bit of English. Paul and he exchanged grins in the moonlight. Yahir put a gloved thumb up.

Paul felt the automatic over his flying suit. It had to hang outside, like the knife, and both were in his way. He could see fine in the moonlight, but he worried over whether they should have worn the red goggles. He shivered and rubbed his gloves before putting on his helmet. Yahir was ready. He was taking a machine gun and some grenades. They weren't too heavy; Paul had checked on the weight of the lot of them. It was cold. Paul began to worry about the cold more than anything, although he was layered in woollens topped with a flying suit. The visibility was unbelievable. He could fasten the harness fitting in the steel clip with the naked eye. He could see the pin holes in the wing bolts. Without any difficulty he screwed the flight deck with its vario and altimeter to the frame of the glider.

The higher slopes of Mont Blanc and the familiar melted dome looked beautiful. The wings of the glider cut a sharp black shadow on the moonlit snow. He did another check. The light was clear enough for him to be able to stand back and take a critical look at the whole aircraft. Close up he went through the same inspection that he had made six hours ago. Check for this, check for that. He could see everything. He had left the kite alone all that time with these people. In the moonlight he went over every bolt and pin.

If she flew wrong they could try for a straight bottom landing after a quick scratch around. Suddenly he felt drunk with adrenalin as the prospect of this massive flight with its quality of uniqueness gave his mind a lift. He didn't care any more about having to fly dual. He looked into the half-light towards the valley so clearly visible from the snow reflections on either side. Again he was aware of the quality of moonlight exaggerating the clarity of what he could see. It was like looking through another medium — clear water, perhaps.

Was the wind dropping? They had better be off before they got any colder. He'd better have a bit of oxygen. He clapped the mask over his face and took a series of breaths. Disastrous. The result was depressing as realism overtook his euphoria. He'd have preferred a gulp or two of Paddy to cheer the memory of the Angler's Rest.

His helmet went on over the balaclava. It was a straightforward helmet to some French specification which was near enough to his own BS5361. Cut away at the ears so that he could hear the sound of airflow as a check on airspeed. The balaclava would hopefully prevent his ears from freezing. The automatic hung outside his flying suit. Yahir ready, machine gun at his back, grenades on his belt. The hang glider ready, a delta shape where the stars should be. The others were not talking or laughing now.

Paul crossed himself, something he hadn't done since his first days of flying.

"*Allez . . .*"

They were over the edge instantly . . . at a nose angle of about 80 degrees. Pointing down. He held the bar tightly in. The heady take-off brought instant fear. They were falling like a stone. He tried pushing out gently, but there was no response. The hang glider was plunging towards ice and snow.

The dreadful sink pulled them down inexorably. He had spoken to other pilots of downdraughts, when the bottom seemed to fall out of the sky. This was like an elevator in a skyscraper block that had broken loose. Most likely thin air at a high altitude was its cause.

The metal of the alloy tube control bar was icy cold through gloves, leather and wool. Another push and this time a minute response. Concentrate, concentrate. The controls felt mushy. The altimeter was reading 2,500 metres which meant they had fallen something like a thousand feet since take-off.

Then it happened. First a mild buffeting on the wings and the nose suddenly pitched it upwards, yawing wildly from side to side. The effect was instant. One moment it seemed that nothing would save the hang glider from impacting. The next they were being jerked up into the sky. There were no thermals at this time of night, or what was the term? — orographic lift. More like a ghostly wave on top of which they were balanced like a lonely surf rider under the moon. She's too high, he thought, and put on more speed to avoid stalling. But the kite kept going up. Then a sharp tug knocked the right wing into a tight 360 turn. Even this didn't seem to affect the climbing performance. They were over the take-off point — little figures below, standing still and he heard a faint cheer. They were killers, but he liked hearing them.

The vario was still sounding up. With all his strength he pushed the bar to the right, at the same time keeping it wedged into his stomach. His arms ached from the seesaw motion and tugging. The problem was no longer height to cross the ridge, but to break out from the lift.

Anyone who has flown hang gliders knows that one of the problems is the basic one of weight shift control. How do you control a runaway that you are only clinging to, that has turned you into a passenger rather than driver? He was as helpless as Yahir above him. The ungainly glider was still going up in darkness. The icy wind biting his face made tears run. He should have worn some sort of face mask.

He glanced at the sack above him which was Yahir in his harness, a helpless bundle. He called up and heard no reply. Was he mute with terror? One more sharp 360-degree turn and then as it came out the hang glider suddenly fell out of lift. Paul felt as if he was coming into harbour. One moment there had been turbulence and the constant buffeting, and then the wind was smooth as glass.

"*Ça va?*" he called up again and heard a faint "*C'est bien*". He ceased to feel that he was carrying a mummy.

At least the problem about height ceased to take precedence. The ridge over which they had to fly was just a line hundreds of feet below. Again the warning bleep of the vario, showing that now they were falling. For the first time since take-off he did not feel anxiety. He was in control. Far below, small as a mouse, the black shadow of the glider was visible on the snow. It hardly seemed to be moving. He wondered if they were near stalling speed, or was it an effect of night vision? Pull the bar in . . . even push your feet forward. He was now halfway across the valley and could see down to the other side. The glacier that flowed down Mont Blanc had its birth somewhere here in the snow. The crevasse and broken surfaces looked like embroidery. Small indentations, pinhead- and thread-sized, could swallow up a man. Like the two Germans were swallowed.

When they crossed the ridge there was still a good deal of turbulence. The wings were pushed up and down by an invisible claw and the alloy rods creaked as they buckled with the pressure. Yahir shouted something and they were over and going down.

Paul searched to find the neutral or optimum position for normal flight that pilots call L/D — the ratio between lift and drag which gives the distance gained for height lost in still air. He looked for the right glide angle, the right balance between the exigencies of flying and the inevitable sink that was pulling the machine down. The wind or that pretence of wind had veered south-east. This meant it was crossing his bow and gave a little more lift and nose angle. He had anticipated sink all the way. His hands were getting cold. He lifted them momentarily one at a time off the bar and wriggled the fingers. The cold was also getting into his arms and legs, but the hands were the important thing.

183

He glanced at the stop watch that was fitted into the flight deck. They had been flying for seven minutes, but it seemed so many hours. The glacier was like a white road and for now all he had to do was to follow it as he had been shown on the map. Easier said than done to play about with this little breeze in order to follow a straight route. He and Yahir were the only things that moved.

"Okay?"

"Okay."

The idiotic limitation of communication was probably just as well. Everything around them was still. They were moving very slowly, crawling along on this vacuum of frozen air like a flying tortoise. They had covered about half of the glacier. Way beyond he could see where the snow ended in a dark area of shadow which must be trees. When he reached there he would have to turn to the north-west, getting the angle as exact as possible with the aid of the compass on his flight deck. He could see the needle with ease.

He would be keeping an eye on the time. Leila had been full of time checks when she was helping him to locate landmarks. Five minutes? Trees, the first things with which the moonlight deceived him. They didn't look like trees at all, they looked like a spread of black velvet. He made his turn. Pressure on the bar, pushing out and the inner wing beginning to dip left. Straighten out, nose down . . . no fear of stalling . . . and the smaller valley opened up beneath his frozen legs thousands of feet below.

The lights he had seen from the take-off ridge showing villages and roads were behind him. Now they should catch sight of the lights of their destination at any moment. They had dropped low enough for the trees to have changed into recognizable shape, line upon line. He could make out details on the smaller glacier and the glistening rock face. No sign of flood lighting.

"*Lumière? Voyez-vous?*" The passenger could be useful as lookout.

"*Pas encore.*"

They had plotted the route step by step with Leila at their side. Day after day, evening after evening, when they had finished those exhausting training flights they had poured over the map and plunged along the paper valley with protractors and slide

184

rule. Yahir must take responsibility as well as him. Although they were not actually lost, already Paul wanted to blame him. They could see nothing in the trees. He should have found the target by compass bearing by this time, but the fucking trees covered everything. He did a slow 360. The black wings dipped in a broad sweep across the sky.

"*Voyez-vous?*"

"*Rien . . . rien . . . tournez . . . tournez encore!*"

God, he couldn't go on turning like a corkscrew. Another one cost them a hell of a height loss and any more would bring them perilously close to disaster. He did not fancy going in among those trees in this sort of light. They would be killed for sure. He knew this whole plan was impossible. Had they enough lift to forget the whole thing, to fly on and look for a way out of this killing forest? Forget the rest of it. I've done my best for Maura. The further they flew down the greater the sink rate. Soon they would be caught between the narrowing vortex of the valley and they would sink like a stone.

"*Voilà!*"

Paul caught sight of them on the final leg of the turn. Orange lights, a little square of them cut into the valley wall about a thousand feet below. Six lights that seemed unsupported in the darkness. Behind them was the white torch of the glacier shining under the moon.

He did a fast right turn and the wind hit his face. Which way to land? There was a small crosswind, and with their weight they would come in hideously fast. It would have to be spot on, a full flare out and stall. Like putting on the brake, sharp, sharp. If there was a miscalculation they would be over the side.

They were across the valley and still high above the narrow passage of light. The control bar tightly in, fingers gripping the metal. As always he was conscious of the cold. Turns taking him down steeply. The only sound the fluttering of the sails. They were still too high. He must make a tailwind landing, down and stuff her nose in quick.

He remembered all the times he had practised pinpoint landings. Not an exercise that had appealed to him much, precision, control and finding targets. Missing them had not been a matter of life and death. Now he was undertaking something that was not possible. Miserable luck, having made the flight, so far, to spoil the whole thing now. Losing his grip in holding the wings above his shoulder and falling over the side headlong to the ground. Four storeys. All his powers, all his concentration were fixed on that last turn, coming in from a northerly direction, keeping up flying speed and making for the space between the lights.

The glide angle was right, the speed coming in was horrendous. A few hundred feet makes a hell of a difference. He could see below the lights on the roof smaller lights from windows, the sharp edge of what must have been a wall, and Christ, what was that lurking in the shadows among the lights? A fucking helicopter! Just where he wanted to land. Long tapering antennae of its rotor blades, two small red warning lights. It was strange how his pent-up reflexes allowed a moment for a surge of rage directed at Leila. He'd kill the bitch. She had said there would be no helicopter. She said it would not be there at night time. Of course it was there, just in case the Sheikh wanted a quick getaway.

Just time for a sort of side slip, losing height, losing height. He pushed up and the nose wavered, more speed and a steep push out which sent Yahir's body swinging in its hammock. Then the glider turned back to the lights the opposite way, facing the helicopter, coming in fast. Two men weighing around 23 stone, all the extras, arms and suchlike and no head wind. She was dropping, and it took all his nerve not to raise the nose and stall.

A couple of hundred yards was all that separated him from the line of lights. Still a little height, but now much holding of the bar in his fingers. The mountain slope was close now. The edge of the roof was under them. The lack of wind gave no resistance and they were going down without brakes. There was their shadow in the lights. They were edging towards the blunt nose of the helicopter. He pushed up the bar of the glider with all his strength. Like applying brakes at top speed. Nothing happened except they were coming in with a swoop, and then the higher nose angle and the wind suddenly sluicing off the sails made them approach stalling speed.

They were coming in too high and too fast. Paul thought for a split second of the old days, of the intermediate rogallos which descended in an old-fashioned way while the pilot drifted down pleasantly as if he was on the end of a parachute. The kite that brought them down now was not nearly so forgiving. Tightly-stretched wings, less billow and more batons meant that you had to have it right. And somehow the bulge of the helicopter had to be avoided.

Would they end up like the time he landed with Faisal at Chamonix? One thing was good, he wasn't going to miss, he wasn't going to go over the edge. And there was a cushion of snow, about six inches of it. They were down, and they were alive. Both of them lying in snow, jerked forward, still in their harnesses. There was silence for two seconds while Paul took in how the C et P had swung round and how the frame was bent. It looked a mess. Then two little characteristic sounds, plop, plop, came from beside him and ahead, beside the helicopter, he heard swishing noises and gentle thumps.

Bodies were falling in the snow.

He hadn't seen the guards on the roof. But of course there were guards, just like of course there was a helicopter.

Still strapped in his harness, lying prone, Yahir had aimed his automatic machine gun and got in his shots before they saw clearly what had landed beside them. They were supposed to be at work with the aid of tripod-mounted binoculars, looking around at the mountains. The flanks of Mont Blanc, the glaciers, the Ghio de Freiney and Broullard, the Giaccio del Miage that fell in a great white tail into the valley. During the day they would notice the routes of red-clad mountaineers climbing in single file. Their friends below manning the transmitter could check with patrol cars far away speeding down the highway to Aosta or the customs house at Helbronner or headquarters in faraway Milan.

How long had these guards been on the roof top? A couple of hours? More? The hang glider had come in silent as a bat in the small hours of the morning and the muffled clatter of the landing had attracted their attention too late. Yahir, with his automatic

187

fitted with a silencer, had fired on them instantly. He had been lucky (so had Paul). If they had crept towards them cautiously seeking cover they would have been a lot more difficult to kill.

They had not been inattentive because of chill and exposure. They had come out of the well-lit cabin at the corner of the roof and now lay with their faces in the snow.

No sound disturbed the brightly-lit scene. This was the moment when Paul and his companion had thought they would be acting at speed, tearing off their harnesses. They appeared to have all the time in the world.

Paul unclipped the carabiner and wriggled out of his straps. He had avoided hitting the helicopter by three yards. He had done something great and they were down. He felt nothing for the corpses. They were not his problem. He had done his part.

The main massif of Mont Blanc was over their heads, less clear and overwhelming than it had been before, blotted out by the dazzling lights. The moon that had lit them on their way was hidden by trees. The place where they had stood was the roof of a building that was more or less a large ungainly tower rising out of the snow. Barbed wire enclosed the area round about. The architectural symmetry of the tower was spoiled by a number of ugly little utility buildings around it, barracks, guard rooms, places like that.

The stiffness in his limbs made him rigid. The muscles in his arms which he had used to do the actual gliding felt locked in a way that made him wonder if he would move them again. The cold was in his bones so that he staggered as he took a couple of steps in the fluffy snow. He wanted to urinate. The last thing he wanted to do was something active.

The cold had numbed fear. He thought without a twinge, would someone come up from below? The guards must have had a telephone link with the rest of the building. Had they alerted anyone? Had there been a cry of alarm or amazement over the intercom? The snowy silence continued. In the distance a dog barked. Guard dog? A brief noise, far away near the barbed-wire perimeter. Had the animal heard the sound of subdued shots? Was their activity outside? Nothing here. Except Yahir moving now, very fast.

The illusion of timelessness was over. In fact only a minute had passed since they had landed.

Yahir had been carried along inert, chilled as Paul was, more so. He had no activity to keep him alert, just the fear all along that only Paul beneath him could save him from a crazy death. And he had gone into action like a sheriff entering a saloon. He was moving now, his machine gun at the ready.

Paul followed with terrible reluctance. When he had given any thought to this stage of the proceedings he had developed a vague fantasy about rerigging and taking off on his own. Jumping off the roof, gliding over the trees to freedom. They were ideas that had not seemed much more outrageous than the flight he had just accomplished. (He felt very good about that.) But he knew perfectly well he could never have flown away. He would have had to seek a wind for take-off and expect to be wafted over barbed wire, trees and ice. He couldn't have done it, even if the kite did not happen to be crippled. One of the bars of the A-frame had taken the force of the heavy landing and the inner wing was slightly bent. Nothing you could not repair in a couple of hours, given spares and the right tools.

Yahir was on the move.

He waved his SMG and Paul understood. He had his own weapon at the ready in shaking hands.

Yahir kicked, making sure the men were dead. They had been wearing uniforms. Easy enough to put on a jacket and peaked hat over his flying suit. Little man, big jacket. Harder for Paul, although he wasn't that bulky. Hang gliding pilots were small men on the whole. He knew the purpose of putting on the clothes . . . to buy a few seconds' more time, to fob off the eyes of the TV camera.

In front of the door of the cabin the snow had melted. A telephone inside, binoculars, several pairs, including the one on a stand. A little TV screen showing a slightly blurred room elsewhere. The lookouts could check through four sides of plate-glass windows. But tonight a portion of their view was impeded by the helicopter. The Alouette may have made the landing by hang glider almost impossible, but it had also been in the way of the lookouts' vision. The men sitting and watching didn't even see

189

something flying out of the corner of the eye. After the glider had come in at a speed they had heard a sound. They may have thought a rotor had fallen off the chopper and came out to take a look. Their suspicions weren't aroused because they had not shouted over the intercom first. They had not been attentive to the sweeping hand of the radar whose presence had worried the Almutis for months. (There had been no solution to the problem of radar — they had chosen to ignore it or to believe that it could be overcome by speed.)

The silence, the undisturbed black and white of the television picture, the silent circular movement on the radar screen indicated that no alarm had been raised.

Luck, destiny, was on Yahir's side. Paul's side. It was wrong to think the worst was over. The blast of warm air that greeted them fostered the illusion.

Yahir had changed. It was as if the harness in which he had been carried had been a cocoon containing a chrysallis and something fierce had come out of it. He found the door that led down a narrow staircase. He was going down concrete steps and along a concrete passage.

The eyes of TV cameras looked down on them.

Paul ran behind; he didn't have to kill anyone. The concrete changed to carpeting. There was a corridor with lines of doors on either side. Stiff photographs on the wall in colour that was a little off true showed Mont Blanc, the Matterhorn, the Gran Paradiso Park. A chamois was blown up, large as a cow.

Hardly the royal suite. Paul knew it wasn't. He had pondered the blueprints for hours. It wasn't this floor where your man had his rooms. The rooms were for staff, cooks and suchlike.

Running at top speed down another staircase and into a central lounge. This was a lot smarter with thick beige carpet and pleated beige silk curtains covering bullet-proof windows. The Hilton atmosphere was enlivened by a large Murano chandelier with lights coming from pink and blue lilies. A portrait of the Sheikh showed him wearing a cloak that lapped the floor in front of him in a puddle of ermine. His domed crown was like an old-fashioned German helmet except that it was covered with diamonds.

Paul took in a lot of detail in two seconds. The arrangements of florists' flowers on plinths reflecting the colours of the chandeliers — irises and stephanotis and pink roses that might have been arranged for Mother's Day. The chairs buttoned in brown leather and the glass-topped tables with copies of *The Wall Street Journal* for people to read as they waited to be summoned to the exiled chieftain. The reception desk was in the middle, just like a hotel, and you'd have thought the two men behind it in pinstripe lounge suits at two in the morning were there to scrutinize American Express Cards.

Six guards in the uniform of the old discredited Almuti Royal Guard stood in white puttees, SMG's at the ready. They were alert, like the two men in the lounge suits who had been checking the TV screens in front of them. They knew something was wrong, even if they did not know of the events at roof level. Ten seconds ago they had seen a couple of shadowy figures run past the cameras above the mountainy posters. Alarm bells were going with a noise that made the chandelier tinkle.

They were alert, but it seemed they hadn't time to spring from the stupor of the heated lounge to their full readiness to guard and kill. Yahir, coming in firing, had them in his sights before they aimed at him. One circular sweep and they were down. The last one to fall shot back and a rattle of bullets passed Paul's head. He began shooting too. He shot one of the men in lounge suits in the middle area.

Shouts, noise. Yahir used up five more precious seconds shooting another clip of bullets down at the men on the floor like water from a hose. Then he was running again and he knew where to go. Down the corridor on the right, which was where the Imperial suite was located. More guards, these ones shooting. It looked like all Paul's efforts could have been in vain. But Yahir rattled at them with the confidence of a steeple chaser going over a last fence. He jumped over their bodies and threw open the door of the royal bedroom.

Here was more standard Hilton luxury with similar beige furnishings, sofas covered with oatmeal tweed and a drinks' cabinet. (The question of the Sheikh's drinking habits had played a part in the revolution.) Pictures on the walls showed him inspecting stiff standing soldiers, looking up at fly pasts, wearing chocolate-soldier uniforms, shaking hands with President Ford, President Carter, President Giscard d'Estaing, President Sadat, King Fuad and Shirley Maclaine. A bookshelf contained books bound in blue-tooled leather. A piece of statuary, Almuti and ancient, representing a mounted warrior, lost the horse's head to a couple of bullets.

The Sheikh was already on his feet, a fat man in cream silk pyjamas. In the Emperor-sized bed a blonde girl was sitting up. She shouted something to Yahir who shot her with a couple of bursts. With that machine gun it appeared to be difficult to fire one shot at a time. Before she fell back Paul recognized the girl they had gone to meet at the Bar Belvedere.

The descendant of desert kings behaved with dignity. He knew he was in trouble. Once the guards outside his door were dead, he was doomed. Not all the arms, the guards, the helicopter, the dogs, the radar screen, the television cameras could help him. He was in a hostage situation. He put on his slippers.

The old man managed to remain brave as they began their weird royal procession out of the place. Yahir was grinning; he still wore the hat and jacket he had taken from the dead roof guard. The peaked hat had got pushed to a jaunty angle. He handed Paul the machine gun and held the Sheikh in an arm lock, his automatic at his temple. It would be hard to stop him without the Sheikh dying. They didn't see anyone living as they moved slowly down the corridor picking their way over bodies, and down the carpeted stairs. Paul, also uniformed, hat over balaclava, acted as escort, peering round for people to shoot at, performing the balletic movements of a weapon-carrying warrior on the watch.

He could have remained in the blood-spattered bedroom or tried to find his own way out. He stayed close by Yahir and his moving burden, close enough to offer and receive protection from all the trained gunmen who were watching them.

Outside they broke into a crab-like run as they made their way towards the sentry box and gate. The way across the snowy spaces to the gate was very long. Yahir was shouting as he moved, shouting in Arabic. Paul followed, keeping close, waving the automatic around. Not too close, just in the aura of safety provided by the fact that the Sheikh was alive and would be virtually the same target as his abductors should some watcher care to shoot at them. Paul didn't shoot anyone. Only a dog. The shot and yelp diverted the attention of the two score and more of men who were in that place to ensure the safety of the old man being dragged along shivering in his pyjamas.

No one came to open the gate. Yahir was shouting, I'll kill him if you don't open. Kill him right here. No one came out, but it opened silently by remote control. They must have known it wouldn't make a difference to what happened once the Sheikh was taken outside his fortress. Yahir made him hurry; he was panting now and gasping and his one free arm waved feebly. Off the rough roadway into the forest among the trees that Paul had viewed from above, less than ten minutes ago. There was a bit of fluffy snow on the ground.

The trees muffled the noise as Yahir, without breaking his stride, pulled the trigger of the gun he held to his prisoner's temples. There was a spray of blood and bone fragments as he let his burden slump to the ground. He kicked it before running off into the trees.

Paul flung away the SMG he had been holding and ran after him. What else could he do? He knew that the only way out was to the pickup point on the road two miles away where Leila and transport would be waiting. Once the main difficulties of the mission had been worked out, the rest was simple. The wind and moon had been right and he had flown well. They wouldn't have got anywhere without him.

Yahir paused for breath and waited smiling for him to catch him. The going was slow, weaving in and out of the trees. They had to hurry when they got their breath back. They had not had enough time or momentum to stop communications or shoot the tyres of the heavy-purpose vehicles belonging to the place. They hadn't put the helicopter out of action. They began to run again, this time Paul a little ahead. Yahir shot him in the back.